TOXIC

M. E. Solomon

Chapter 1

Parker Grant was a man. He was a man in size, being six feet two inches in height and two hundred ten pounds in girth. He was a man in age, having reached the chronological position of twenty-nine years with no evidence to the contrary. He was a man in so much that his seed, when partnered with the gift of a woman, could, given nine or so months of deliberation [NOTE: gestation may be a better word choice], produce an offspring whose gender was wholly decided by the temperament of his offering. Parker was a man in these ways. These were the pains and privileges that came with his gender distinction. They were, for the most part, a given of his station. They could not, without considerable legal and medical adjustment, be stripped from his person.

Parker's manhood was not judged by these characteristics alone, however. If it had been, perhaps his life would not be as it was. Perhaps then, he would not feel inadequate and debased; he would have concrete data with which to combat the accusations that had been made against him. Truth be told, those characteristics only served to validate his position on a superficial plane. They held no real bearing on his standings as a man.

There had always existed a baser set of credentials; a collection of unwritten, intangible criteria by which all applicants for the position of manhood, including Parker, had been measured: a stricter, truer test of authenticity served as a foundation for the institution itself. This included, but was not limited to, financial maturity, psychological independence, spiritual wealth, accountability and responsibility, and personal pride. By these measurements, Parker's position was, at its pinnacle, hazy at best.

If the bad check warrant that the two gentlemen from The Peach County Sheriff's Department were attempting to serve was any indication of Parker's standings, he had failed miserably in the category of financial maturity. The fact that Parker refused to answer the door and acknowledge the warrant didn't speak favorably of his standing in the area of accountability or responsibility either. As for his spiritual wealth, he had for the entire length of the gentlemen's visit to his door, (a torturous five minutes), been praying that they would just go away. In this, at least, he was proficient.

Parker was silent. Paranoia told him the officers knew he was home. This was the third time they'd been to his home. Each time he'd pretended no one was home.

They would soon force themselves in and put an end to his shenanigans. He was busted, he thought.

The officers gave the door one last rattle, then their assault ceased. Parker imagined them circling the house. They were probably peeking in windows and trying to jimmy the locks to his car, he thought. He lay perfectly still. If they did find him, it would not be because he gave himself away.

Time moved along with the enthusiasm of rush hour traffic. Minutes seemed like hours. Finally, Parker resolved to look and try to ascertain the whereabouts of his two visitors. He rose from his sofa and crept to a nearby window that had a set of black mini blinds positioned over its panes. Light cut through the blinds in long luminous knives. He crouched there for a moment in indecision. Then with the delicate touch of a spider on a web he slowly, deliberately raised his eyes level with the window.

Parker peeked between the blinds. First light blinded him. He closed his eyes and took a moment to adjust. When he opened them, the sun was still bright but manageable. From his vantage point Parker could see the span of his driveway and the curbsides adjacent to his home. The vacant space in his drive came as a relief. Usually, his Cadillac would have occupied a space there, but for the past week, it had been parked behind his home in a little break between the trees and the house. He called the break the bat cave.

Parker abandoned his watch post and trudged his way back to the sofa. The police had disturbed him but not to the extent of rousing him from his position of pity and self-loathing. Still, he wondered where the officers had gone. He wasn't used to having police knocking on his door, but he knew enough to realize that he was lucky they hadn't known he was inside. The fact that they had come to his home was frightening enough. He had to do something about this, he thought. Maybe he would call Sidney; she was an attorney. She would help him sort through this thing. He knew he owed money. He knew he had to pay, but he just didn't have the means to do that right now.

Parker reached over and picked up his phone. The dial tone told him he had new messages. His voicemail held a plethora of messages; Sidney, Dean, and Sheila had each left several messages. His mother, as well as several editors looking for freelance assignments, had called. All these people had called but no calls were logged from Jessica. Parker listened to the message from his mother and saved the rest.

His mother's message gave no mention at all to their heated argument from earlier in the week. That was her way; it was just another characteristic of his uncanny family.

Parker's family was normal in that their dysfunction was not uncommon. They had the same quirks that other households had, just in higher concentrations. Parker's mother, for example, had an extremely dominant personality. She was what scientists would call the alpha-female. In her family's household, her way was always the right way. This was not an uncommon occurrence in African American households.

***

Sisters often took the lead in matters of domestic happenings. It also wasn't strange to find sisters running entire households in the absence of suitable male companions. The issue with Parker's mother was that she wasn't alone; she had a husband, but still had to assume all the major household responsibilities. Her husband, Parker's father, did little to assist her. He was more the observer than a participator in the family experience. He rarely cut yards or washed cars. His salary was usually split among lottery, liquor and ladies. If house maintenance was to be done, her husband was never available to complete it. As far as bills were concerned, Parker's father paid them at his leisure, if he paid them at all. This left the family in a continual state of financial unrest. Parker's mother found herself constantly having to fix little problems his father had created. This made for a hostile environment--not the best place to grow up in. It also made Parker's mother bitter. She'd spent thirty-one years being disappointed and lied to. She'd had to learn to fend for her children and herself. She had developed the habit of needing to control everything. She controlled her household. She controlled her office. She was in control of her church's finances. When Parker was a high school student, she had been in control of him too; his friends had to be up to her standard. His girlfriends had to be approved by her.

After Parker came back from college, his mother's practice of wanting to pick the women Parker dated had become a heated issue between them. Parker didn't feel the need to have the women he chose to date be paraded around for his mother's approval. He was no longer a child that needed his mother to tell him what was good for him. He felt that if they were making him happy then his mother should be happy for him. His mother didn't see it that way. She would get angry with Parker for his interest in a certain woman and forbid that lady from calling the house. She would make any woman not fortunate enough to have her stamp of approval wait outside when they came by to visit Parker; sometimes she wouldn't answer the door at all. Finally, Parker had just given up and moved to his own place, a small two-bedroom he'd inherited some years ago from his grandfather.

Parker's mother had a way of making people feel like their opinions were wrong and that if they didn't listen to her, the world would end. She was a first-class drama queen. She would yell and scream and curse and shout and threaten and stomp around like she didn't have the wherewithal to hold a conversation. Then, if the person she disagreed with didn't break under the will of her first assault, she would start to cry. This worked particularly well on Parker since no son liked to see his mother cry. Moreover, she would say cruel and vicious things to Parker. She would claim that it was for his own good that she told him these things, but Parker felt like it was more so to hurt him. Parker knew his mother punished him for the mistakes of his father. She didn't see Parker when she was mad at him, she saw Parker's father. This, more than the screaming and the crying and the yelling and the cursing, broke Parker's heart.

Parker thought back on their argument from earlier in the week.

He replayed it in his mind. It was a typical morning at his parent's house. He had been looking through the cabinets in the kitchen for his coffee cup but had been unable to locate it. He'd soon given up looking for his cup in favor of any cup. The conversation that ensued would stay with him for a long time.

"What are you looking for?" his mother had asked.

"A coffee cup," he'd answered as he'd closed the first cabinet and opened the second.

"I think I put them all in the dishwasher," she replied as she rinsed out a dishtowel and hung it over the faucet. She picked up another and began to wring it out. Parker closed the cabinet and turned towards the dishwasher. It was going through its first cycle. Parker could hear the jets spraying down the dishes. He reached down and pulled the lever that would unlock the door and temporarily halt the cycle.

Parker's mother spun around and looked at him accusingly. "What are you doing?" she asked in an indignant voice.

"I'm getting a cup out for coffee," he'd replied as he reached into the washer.

"Don't tear up my dishwasher!" she shouted. With that she'd dropped the towel she'd been wringing, reached over and slammed the washer door shut. Parker barely had time to snatch his hand back.

"What's wrong with you!" Parker exclaimed, checking his hand for missing digits.

"You're not gonna tear up my dishwasher by opening the door!" his mother shouted.

"What? You can't tear up a dishwasher by opening the door! That's why there's a fail-safe lever that shuts it down when you want to open it during the cycle."

***

"You ain't gonna tear up my dishwasher like ya'll tear up everything else!" she replied as if he hadn't said anything at all.

Parker sighed inwardly. He knew what was coming. He hated when his mother went off on one of her tirades. She was paranoid and hormonal and just plain abusive. When Parker was younger, he'd seen his mother go ballistic on his father in much the same manner. She would say the meanest things she could think of to hurt him. As Parker got older, she'd begun to turn those same tirades toward him. For years, he'd been hurt when she'd done this. He'd often broken down into tears as children do when verbally abused by their parents. He'd felt guilty and ashamed of his mother's being displeased with him. His mother had made him feel as if something was wrong with him; that his way was always wrong. After they argued, or more specifically, she attacked and he took the tongue lashing, he always went away upset and psychologically damaged. She would play his deficiencies against him in the most hurtful manner she could devise. She would say things that no one should ever say to a child, let alone their own.

This had gone on for years, starting in Parker's early teens and continuing until just recently; in fact, her tactics had not changed, only Parker's response to them had. Anytime Parker didn't agree with his mother, she would verbally assault him. She was his mother, so he felt very uncomfortable saying cruel things back to her. He had tried, as best he could, to tune her out, but fifteen years of this abuse had taken its toll.

It wasn't until recently that he'd begun to realize that he wasn't wrong all the time and that his mother's assaults were designed to break a person's spirit so that she could have her way. It wasn't done on a conscious level; at least he didn't think it was. Nevertheless, Parker had begun to treat the arguments differently.

His arguments with his mother had begun to go in a new direction. He no longer stood by and allowed his mother to pummel him verbally. Now he fought back.

"Whoa! Whoa," he'd said in his calmest voice. "I'm not tearing up anything. I'm just trying to get my coffee cup."

"That's how y'all do it," his mother had started. "Y'all just tear up shit and then I have to fix it."

Parker's mother's biggest insult was grouping his father and him together by using the pronoun y'all. It was her version of a summary judgment to the conclusion that Parker was just like his father. She knew how Parker felt about that statement. He hated it, but on this day, he would not let it affect him. He knew he wasn't his father.

He also knew that his mother was attempting to cow him, but Parker would not be cowed.

"I'm not tearing anything up. I'm just trying to get a coffee cup," he repeated as his mother squared off with him on the kitchen floor.

"Don't open my damn dishwasher door! That's how y'all always tear shit up; like y'all tore up that icemaker, and I couldn't get anybody to fix it!"

"First of all, the icemaker wasn't broken, it had been accidentally switched off," Parker returned calmly.

"Yeah, accidentally to get at me and drive me crazy," his mother had interjected in her classic paranoid fashion.

Parker had ignored her and went on. "Secondly, the dishwater is not going to tear up just because you interrupt its cycle. That's crazy."

"You're crazy, motherfucker," she'd shouted back! "You leave my shit alone! If you tear it up, you can't help fix it, so just don't fuck with it!"

Parker tried to let the argument go. It wasn't worth the stress that came with it, he thought. "Ok, fine. Let's just let it go," he conceded as he went back to the cabinet to find some other receptacle for his coffee.

But the monster in his mother had been riled up and now there would be no standing down as far as she was concerned.

"You let it go! You can't tell me what to do with my shit! I paid for this," she said, slamming her fist down on the top of the dishwasher. "You ain't got shit, so you don't have to worry about shit. Get some shit and then tell me about what'll tear it up or won't tear it up!"

"Ok," Parker had replied, trying not to get heated. He'd picked out a small mason jar to serve as his substitute coffee cup and began preparing his beverage.

But his mother had gone on. "And don't be talking to me all snide and arrogant like you know something either! Finish school nigga! Then tell me something! You been in school eleven years and still ain't finished!" She'd spit venomously.

***

Parker felt himself getting hot. "Yes, I have, but that's an irrelevant point. That has nothing to do with the dishwasher or a coffee cup!"

"Oh, but it does! Your stupid ass can't even get out of school. How are you gonna tell me anything?!"

"I'm not stupid!" Parker had yelled back finally, turning the argument into a shouting match. "Stupid is thinking that opening a dishwasher door would tear it up!"

"You're not gonna talk to me like that!" Parker's mother had screamed.

"Then don't talk to me like that," Parker retorted.

"I'll talk to you any damn way I want to!"

"Then so will I!"

"No, you won't," she'd said and reached for a nearby saucepan.

Parker had picked up his makeshift coffee cup and retreated to the bar. "If you don't want to be talked to like that, then don't talk to me like that," he returned with a much calmer tone and from a much safer distance.

"You're not gonna talk to me any kind of way. I ain't one of these little bitches who's mind you play with," she fired.

"I don't deal with bitches," Parker returned as he sipped his coffee.

Parker's calm demeanor seemed to infuriate his mother more. She dug deeper into Parker's hurt. "Yeah, I know you don't cause they all left your ass. They know you ain't shit too."

"No, I just don't need all that drama in my life," Parker shot back flustered. "And please stop talking to me like a child! I am not a child!"

"You're my child!"

***

"No, I'm your son."

"You're my child."

"No," he'd reiterated, "I'm your son, an adult son."

"Well as long as you under my roof, I can talk to you anyway I want."

"You're right," Parker replied, as he put down the mason jar and picked up his coat. He didn't have to listen to this tirade and decided at that moment that he would head to his own home.

Parker had started towards the front door. It would take two to argue and he would not be one of them. He had made it about halfway when his mother's last bombardment came.

"Adults don't go around bouncing fucking checks," she'd fired.

Parker spun around to face her. "No adults do. Adults make mistakes, and adults fix them!"

"Oh, I know they do motherfucker! I know they do. You fix'em by hiding in the house when the police come to lock your ass up!"

The blow had hurt him. The sheriff had, just the previous day, come to his home for the first time. The situation had been new to him. The ordeal was, at the time, fresh on his mind. Now, on the sheriff's third trip to his home in as many days, he was not nearly as shaken. Then, though, it was still new. Had he not been accustomed to his mother's ruthless personal attacks; he would have faltered. He was used to them though. He knew what the pain she could inflict felt like and he could no longer be surprised by it. He had taken the brute of the blow and stored it away in a secret place.

"Ok, so I accidentally wrote a bad check…"

"You don't accidentally write a bad check, motherfucker! You don't write a check unless you have the money!"

"I did have the money! They just closed my account before I could deposit the check and I didn't know!"

***

"Yeah," his mother had pounced, "because you're stupid! You're an ignorant motherfucker! You're always talking and don't know shit!"

Her cruelty knew no bounds. She had insulted him on every level and Parker had had enough. "You don't know how to talk to people," he gave. "You're always trying to break someone down instead of discussing things rationally."

"Cause you need breaking down motherfucker!"

Parker ignored her and went on. "You are so intelligent and yet the way that you talk to people is going to be your downfall."

"I know I'm smart nigga! I got my degrees!"

"Yes, you do, that's all for naught if you don't learn to talk to people."

His mother had begun to respond with a hail of insults and accusations, but Parker had heard enough. He'd turned around and headed out the door. His heart had been heavy with hurt; his spirit had been tired, but she had not broken him. For that much, he had been happy.

Parker let the details of that morning slip from his mind and thought of its meaning in grander terms. What did it say about his mother? About his father? How would his father have handled the situation? Probably with indifference, he thought. His father never showed any interest in the family, but that, Parker thought, wasn't his father's biggest problem.

Besides his lack of interest in family happenings, Parker's father also had a problem with truth. Honesty was not a high priority on any of his lists. He didn't tell unsolicited lies or go on marathons of untruthfulness; his dishonestly came when he was faced with the admittance of guilt. If his was confronted, which, thanks to Parker's mother, he often was, about some misstep he'd made in budgeting or life in general, he would lie about having made the misstep or even being involved with it at all. A good deal of the time the missteps were so obvious that denying them only made Parker's father look stupid, but he denied them, nonetheless. This was, Parker thought, due to his father's fear of being wrong. If he were wrong, then he would have to face his wife's wrath without the possibility of truth to protect him. If he admitted guilt, then his wife would be intolerable. She would go on and on about how worthless he was and about how his life was one big fuck up after another. The truth of these statements was not in doubt. His father had made some major mistakes in life. Parker just thought it would be better to not bring them up constantly. If a person is told enough that he lacks any sort of personal worth, then sooner or later he will start to believe it.

    Parker's mother's endless assaults on her husband, albeit valid and correct, created an environment as volatile as the surface of Mercury. Parker's father, having been verbally and often physically assaulted by his wife, would often just leave and stay gone from the family residence for long periods of time. Parker never blamed his father for leaving during these periods of extreme hostilities. He welcomed the calm after the storm. Parker just wished that his father had taken him with him, or at least tried to take him. It wasn't that he wanted to leave his mother; Parker loved his mother. He just wanted his father to love him enough to want Parker with him. But he never did. He never took Parker with him when he left. He never even tried. He would just leave.

As far as Parker's overall relationship with his parents, it was a relationship. His father was his father. His mother was his mother.

Chapter 2

Slowed to an idle as she passed Parker's home. Her initial pass had revealed the presence of two police officers. She stared at the officers for signs of their intent. She observed their demeanor, the alertness of their stances, and the proximity of their hands to their pistols. She frowned.

Sheila began to pull into the driveway but thought better and swerved away at the last second. She righted her car and continued to travel to the end of the street. She hit the steering wheel in anger as she brought the vehicle parallel with the stop sign.

"Can a bitch get a break?" she shouted in frustration. "I just can't get a man without some bullshit attached!"

She pulled out onto the highway and was beginning to accelerate when the reflection of blue lights caught her attention. "What now?" she exclaimed. She pulled her car to the shoulder and rolled down her window.

The patrol car pulled in behind her and activated their bullhorn.

***

"PLEASE TURN YOUR VEHICLE OFF."
Sheila complied with a grumble.

After a moment, the officers exited their vehicle with their hands on their side arms.

"Exit the vehicle please," a stout deputy with a buzz cut called up.

"What's going on?" Sheila shouted as she opened her door. "I haven't done anything. Why are y'all stopping me? What's the problem?" she asked with apprehension.

The stout officer drew his weapon and trained it on Sheila. Another patrol car darted past Sheila's vehicle and came to rest at a diagonal to her car's hood. It was the sheriff's car from Parker's house, and it was blocking Sheila in.

Sheila stood in stunned disbelief.

"Is there anyone else in the vehicle?" the stout officer with the big gun asked.

"Huh?!," Sheila responded confused.

"Is there ANYONE ELSE in the vehicle, ma'am?!" he repeated as he closed the distance between them.

"No. What the hell are y'all doing?" she barked and threw her arms up defensively.

The stout officer grabbed Sheila in an elaborate, but totally unnecessary police hold and forced her, face down, to the ground in front of him. He put his knee in her back to complete his domination of her. Asphalt broke her fall. Her knees took most of the force. Gravel from the roadside pushed through her clothing and assaulted her skin. The delicate flesh of her bosom was poked and prodded by loose gravel and jaunted asphalt.

While Sheila protested, both physically and verbally, the stout officer's partner, a tall lanky officer, slipped around the rear of the car, checked the back seat and then trained his weapon on the trunk. One of the two officers from Parker's home reached in Sheila's vehicle and turned the ignition. He then pushed the remote trunk latch on the dashboard and triggered the hatch.

***

"Get the hell out of my car," Sheila screamed. "You can't do this! I'm not some coked up lunatic! I'm a businesswoman. I'll sue goddamnit! Let me up!"

The officer did not comply with Sheila, but instead pushed down harder with his knee. Sheila screamed and complained and drew quite a crowd of observers, but the officer would not relinquish control.

After what seemed an eternity to Sheila, the officer finally released the pressure on her back and instructed her sit up on her knees and place her hands on her head. He asked her for her name, and she gave it but said nothing else. One of the officers ran her name through their computer system while the other ran her car tag through the DMV. All while this was going on, Sheila was kept on her knees with her hands on her head. The officers not calling in her information kept their guns trained on her chest.

A trail of tears ran steadily down her cheek. Sheila had heard of and even seen the way that the police treated brothers when they were stopped but she never thought that it would happen to her. She was a woman and an educated woman at that. This type of thing didn't happen to her; but it had happened. It was happening now.

The stout officer instructed Sheila to stand. She rose to several drawn guns and a very dangerous looking nightstick. Her eyes darted from officer to officer, flashing with fear and rage. She didn't understand what she had done to warrant being treated like this.

"Why did you pull into that driveway back there?" one of the officers asked. He nodded his head toward the street on which Parker lived.

"What?!," Sheila exclaimed in sudden realization. "You assaulted me because I made a wrong turn?! What in the hell..."

"We didn't assault you ma'am," the stout officer responded as he lowered his firearm.

"You did assault her," an observer from the crowd called. Several other observers murmured in agreement.

"We had reason to think you were harboring a fugitive. Y'all move on," the tall lanky officer ordered the crowd. "This is not a show. Move on."

"Oh, no!" protested Sheila. "You all are my witnesses," she said motioning towards the crowd. "You all wait right there so I can get your names and numbers. This ain't over damnit," she declared as she turned and headed for her car.

The stout officer stepped between Sheila and the door. He took his nightstick in both hands and leveled it at Sheila's chest. "We have some questions for you ma'am. We need to know where Parker Grant is."

"I'm not his keeper. You just left his house. Did you see him? Evidently not 'cause ya'll out here assaulting me! I can't believe this! You just wait," she exclaimed. "I'm gonna sue the hell out of y'all!" Sheila pushed past the officer and opened her car door. A pen and tablet lay on the passenger seat. She picked it up and began scribbling down the officer's names and badge numbers.

"Ma'am, if you see him..." the stout officer began.

"Fuck you! Tell him yourself!" Sheila hopped out of her car and headed towards the growing crowd of observers.

***

Parker pulled himself out of his temporary bunker and began the long trudge to the bathroom. The floor was frigid. Icy needles sent prickly kisses through his nerves. Parker was glad for the distraction. He imagined that he was in Lilliput and that he was Gulliver. The Lilliputians 'swords stabbed at his soles, retreated, and then resumed their attacks with his next step. He lifted the toilet seat and unceremoniously began to make water.

Parker's bathroom was a cross between that of a 70's mobile home and a cheap Daytona motel. A long-term water leak had permanently bowed out the main wall and scarred its Dupont® finish. The baseboards had also fallen victim to the seven-year flood and paid for it with their stability, their beauty and their color. An out-of-date water heater shared a third of the room with an install-it-yourself shower whose vertigo was in danger of failing. Grime and soap stains had long ago given the showers' plastic skin an eggshell tan. The dehydrated carcasses of Dial®, Ivory® and the ethnically commercialized Irish Springs® populated its' floor. Under a second sink that was no longer valuable enough to keep hooked up but too expensive to remove rested a rescued standing ash try; its mango fiberglass hull had been faded by light exposure and misuse. That's where Parker's attention rested. There, in that receptacle, crumbled and torn lay the remnants of his letter to Jessica. He didn't remember throwing it there. He vaguely recalled discarding it during one of his fits, but up until now its location had eluded him. He finished his business and retrieved the letter. Parker reached around to drop the toilet seat and had a sit down.

He'd written the letter when he was drunk.

Jessica, now his ex, had, at the time, been his girlfriend. She'd been acting distant and withdrawn just prior to the writing of the letter and it had been adversely affecting Parker. He'd written the letter in an attempt to reach out to her and rekindle her usually perky spirit but had helped ignited the blaze that would destroy their relationship instead. Parker placed the letter aside and scuttled over to the couch. His mind drifted back to their last conversation. Her piteous tone, her reluctance to deal with the issue, her calm and calculated responses should have all been indicators of the demise of their relationship. He should have read the play and blitzed. All he'd had to do was to say it's not working and walk away. Then he would never have known his fault; that one thing that made him intolerable.

That's what people fear most about being dumped, Parker thought. It wasn't that they were exiting the relationship; they knew the relationship was bad anyway. It was having to listen to someone tell them why they weren't good enough that caused the pain; it was the "leaver's" need to validate their exodus by invalidating the love of the one being left that did the most damage to the ego. That's what hurt.

That's what Parker was battling now. He was fighting the occupation of his life by that fault. If Jessica left, that was fine. Let her go, he thought. She wasn't really that interesting anyway. Parker liked intellectual women and Jessica just didn't fit the bill. Fine, let her go, but don't leave the fault for him to deal with.

Parker was losing. Jessica's words had rung true. Her validations were on the mark. Parker's pulse had quickened at the realization that Jessica had every right to feel the way she felt. She had responsibilities and commitments that could not be neglected. She'd said as much. The words echoed through Parker's mind.

"You're extremely charming and our sex life is spectacular, but I need more than that. I need a man with a real job. I need a man with some sort of responsibility already. I don't know what you're capable of. I've never known you to have a job. You've been living with your parents since I met you. I know you're a writer. The thing is I need stability. I have to be able to take care of Brandon and me. I can't wait on your dream. I'm getting back together with my baby's daddy."

The words had struck Parker like a hammer. Not the leaving part, but the 'why' and the 'who' for. It read "inadequate."

He'd tried to counter with the fact that he had no bills and no children to take care of but by the time it touched his lips the death blow had already reached its mark. They'd each fired off a few more rounds cloaked in civility and the conversation ended. Civilly. Uneventful. Anticlimactic. Not even a fuck you. Nothing had changed except Jessica had left Parker burrowed under the covers.

The fact was, he didn't have a job. He had, in the past year, left his home and taken up residency at his family's home. He was a writer. He was also currently a student. Financially, living with his parents was a sound decision, but truthfully, what grown man lives with his parents?

Parker had moved back home the next day. He'd packed several bags, called the utility company for a quick connect and headed back to his modest lodgings. He'd been there, on the couch, since then. A week had passed. Other than hanging his clothes and putting fresh towels in the bathroom when he arrived, Parker had done little to reacquaint himself with his old home. The phone rang and Parker reached for it.

"Hello."

"Hello? Parker? Is that you?" asked a squeaky female voice.

"Yeah, what's up Sheila?"

"Oh, nothing. Trying to catch up with a brotha' for an early lunch. You interested?"

Parker looked at the clock. Damn, he thought. It's 11 o'clock already. "That would be cool," he replied, "but I've gotta do my laundry today. I'm running outta towels and what not. I'll call you later though, O.K.?"

"You could come over here and wash," Sheila responded, ignoring Parkers decline.

"That way, you can save some money, and I'll finally get a chance to cook for you."

He didn't want to hurt her feelings, but Parker didn't feel like being bothered with Sheila today. Lately, she'd become very attached and that was not the nature of their relationship. "Thanks for the offer beautiful, but I hate waiting on each load to wash, then dry, then waiting all over again. That shit takes all day. All that sitting and waiting would drive me crazy. I like being able to wash in ninety minutes. All the loads go in together; all the loads come out together. I fold them and then I'm done. You feel me?"

But Sheila would not be denied. "Well, how 'bout I pick up some Mickey D's and come help you fold? You know you've got a lot of clothes, and you don't do laundry enough as it is."

This is not working, Parker thought. He tried another angle. "Well, I'm not really ready to leave yet. How about I give you a call when I get ready to leave. That way, by the time you get to the laundry mat, the clothes will already be in the washer."

"Well just make sure you give me enough time to make it down there and stop for food, okay?" Sheila lived in Macon, Middle Georgia's major city, if you could call it a major city. It was a twenty-five-minute drive from Macon to Fort Valley.

Not that it mattered though; Parker didn't plan on calling her until well after he'd left the laundry mat. "Will do," he answered with false privity. He just wasn't in the mood for company right now. He had too much to think about. He had no time to be charming and romantic. His life was stagnant. His mind was contemplating this when Sheila returned to her questioning.

"Chicken with bacon and cheese?"

"Say what?" Parker asked, confused.

"A chicken sandwich with bacon and cheese. From Mickey D's. Remember, the food?"

"Oh, yeah...yeah thanks. Look, I'll call you o.k."

"O.k. sexy man!"

He smiled inwardly. She was definitely determined. "I'll holla at you later," he concluded. "Bye."

Parker tossed the phone on the sofa and went back to separating his clothes. Sheila had been right, he thought. He did have a lot of clothes. He could barely fit his laundry in the four tall trashcans that he used for hampers. He needed to be more attentive to his domestic responsibilities. Parker stuffed his dirty towels on top of his white clothes and carried the basket out to the car. He pushed the first one all the way over to the other side so that the other containers would fit. He carried the remaining baskets to the car and put the detergent in the trunk.

Parker went into the kitchen and began to run dishwater. I've got to get to get it together, he thought. He would start with the dishes. He made sure that it was extremely hot so that the dishes could soak while he left to do laundry. As he was collecting the dishes from around the house, his phone rang again. Parker dried his hands on a dishtowel and reached for his phone. The screen said "Jessica".

Parker froze. Was he ready to talk to her yet? What would he say? All throughout the week he'd desperately hoped that she would call him. He'd looked every time that the phone rang praying that the LCD screen would bare her name. The phone rang again. He thought about answering it and "accidentally" hanging up on her but that would be immature. Maybe he could pretend he was asleep and ask her to call him back.

Finally, Parker decided to just answer the phone and go with the flow, but by that time the voice mail had already picked up. Damn, Parker thought. Now she's gonna think that I'm avoiding her. He was avoiding her, he thought.

Steam from the dishwater hovered over the sink like clouds. Suds from the detergent traveled over the water's surface like islands. Each time Parker lowered a dish in the pool, a small and volatile typhoon appeared. He placed the remaining items in the dishwater and was done.

Finally, he was ready to leave. He turned off the lights and locked the door. As he walked to the car, he remembered his cell phone. Don't want to forget that he thought. He quickly unlocked the door, grabbed the phone from the sofa and headed back out.

I've gotta snap out of it, Parker thought. Sooner or later, everything comes to an end. This thing just ended sooner than I expected.

Parker pulled out of the driveway and headed for the laundry mat.

Parker placed his containers on the floor, then put his detergent on the table and had a seat. The plastic chair was awkward. Its ice cream scoop shape held the body at an unnatural angle. Parker couldn't imagine sitting in them for more than ten minutes at a time. The table where Parker placed his detergent was missing the customary two levels, so it rocked back and forth in an offbeat dance. There was a vending machine with out-of-date candy in it that had been pushed against the front window. A Pac-man machine also resided nearby.

Besides Parker, only one other group of people occupied the laundry mat. An older lady sat at a nearby table smoking Newports® with two brothers.

One of the brothers, obviously the older of the two, had the look of a hustler – trendy sweat suit with a white tee, fresh Reebok® classics, and a color-coordinated cap. Moreover, he busied himself with a deck of cards. He shuffled them and spread them and stacked them back together. He was very handy with a deck. He looked to be in his late twenties.

The second of the two brothers, whose age couldn't have numbered any higher than late teens, dressed the part of the young militant. He wore the Bob Marley/Lion of Judah long sleeve tee shirt with matching red, yellow and green wristbands. His head was locked up and sporadically tipped with cowry shells. His khaki cargo pants held some group of items in each pocket; most likely some special set of items to further the movement. He held the appearance of a hard line black nationalist. The only thing that softened his hard-edge grimace and his no nonsense air was his obviously boyish looks.

The old lady was stoic. Her face held no recognizable expression. She seemed to be looking aimlessly through the television. What little of her hair that wasn't in wisps, was pulled back into a bun. Her flannel shirt retained a crease that only a grandmother could apply. She wore a nametag that read laundry attendant.

Perhaps that's why she seemed comatose, Parker thought. Maybe she's scanning the place for trouble.

Between puffs, two of the three table residents were discussing the social ramifications of Outkast's Album of the Year Grammy® Award. Parker listened quietly while he waited on the washers to stop.

The young militant stepped up to speak. "It's about time that some real artist got mainstream recognition. Outkast has been on their shit for years. Every time they come; they bring the fire. This new album is super tight. They put together two separate albums that, together accurately, represent what Outkast is. And Outkast is Hip-Hop. They also represent that cultural force that is African American Rhythmatic creativity."

"Man, there you go with that crazy mystical shit," interjected the hustler.

"Come on man, why you hating on a bothers' higher-level thinking," the young militant objected.

"Boy, you're 17 years old. What do you know about music anyway," the hustler returned.

The young militant was laying down his music credentials for the hustler when Parker's cell phone rang. The screen read Sidney.

"Yeah. What's up?" Parker began.

"What's up? WHAT'S UP? Why you ain't been answering your phone or coming to your dusty ass door? You hiding from somebody?"

"No. I've just been under the weather." "What, you lovesick over that girl?"

That girl Parker thought but did not say openly. "You know I don't get down like that. She wasn't anything serious."

"Whatever, player. I know you 'loved' that girl. I read the little letter you sent her, all talking sweet and sexy and shit."

"Aw man, you're full of bullshit," the hustler shouted in the background.

Parker ignored him and went on. "Look, I don't want to talk about that shit. Just let it go."

"I know you don't want to talk about it, cause you're hurt. I don't know why you won't stop lying 'bout having feelings. Parker it's ok to be hurt."

"I know that. I wasn't hurt"

"Then why did you write all that love shit in that letter?" "It was game baby girl, all game."

"I know it was, but you still don't like to lose. That shit just gets under your skin, doesn't it? You don't even care that she left do you? You're just mad because she left first."

"Man, stop tripping."

The young militant at the other table lit up the other end of the laundry mat with a fiery accusation "...if you'd stop yelling and listen, I'd get to the point, but every time I start explaining my opinion your ass interrupt me. I can't..."

The outburst caught Sidney's attention. "What's all that noise?"

"Nothing. What's up?"

"So, you're telling me that all that noise in the background is nothing? You having a party over there?"

"No nosy, I'm at the laundry mat. Damn you're nosy."

"I just asked you a question Parker. You don't have to get all indignant."

"I wasn't indignant. You know your ass is nosy Sidney."

"So. I'm grown. I can be nosy if I want to."

"What did you want?"

"Well, I just called to tell you that we're going out tonight."

"Hey, I'mma have to take a rain check. I'm not really feeling up to it."

"Yeah, o.k. I'll be there around 9:30. I'm driving."

"Hey, that's not gonna work for me. I'll have to get up with you another night."

"Oh, that's cool. Make sure you wear some jeans that actually fit your little frail ass. That baggy jean shit is playing out."

Sidney was Parker's best friend. They'd know each other for just over six years. In that time, they had managed to get to know each other better than most friends who had known each other their whole lives. They laughed. They fought. They rode. They smoked. They were road dogs for life. They had dated once but found out that they were not at the same point romantically. That basically added up to Sidney believing in fidelity and Parker not being able to stop himself from fucking other women. Fortunately, Sidney was nosy and full of advice and Parker was insecure and full of problems, so they at least made good friends.

Chapter 3

One of the major projects that Sidney had taken on since the inception of their friendship was altering Parker's style of dress. She was constantly pushing him to move outside of trendy fashion comfort zones. This would have irked Parker severely if it weren't for the fact that she was so damn good at selecting clothes for him.

"I am not wearing nut huggers. I want my balls to be comfortable. That's why I don't wear the tighty-whiteys. I need breathing room."

"You can put on some jeans that don't fall off your butt without them being nut huggers. Grown men don't wear that baggy lil' boy shit. You gotta take it to the next level."

"Your cousin Ralph does and he's forty-six."

'Ralph also lives in a storage unit in my grandmother's back yard. He has an extension cord running out of the bathroom window to power his mini bar and refrigerator. Is that who you want to use as your expert witness?"

She had a point, thought Parker. "Why are we even discussing this; I told you I wasn't going."

"Oh, you're going! Either we go or me and all me little nieces and nephews are coming to your house for a sleep over. So, what's it gonna be?"

"I'll see you at nine."

"Nine-thirty!"

"Yeah, whatever. I'll holla." Parker hung just in time to hear the closing remarks of the young militant and the hustler in their debate on the state of black music.

"Every form of music that we create has its own style; its own rhythm and its own life, but they all have that feel of life in common," the youngster began. "They're real. They have a piece of their practitioners in every note. African American music has life. Outkast gave life to a double disk of that music. I just hope people step up and give them their due."

"Hell no, they're not gonna appreciate it," the hustler fired off. "Black people don't appreciate shit until they take it away from them."

"No. You can't say that."

"Well, it's true," the hustler retorted. "Look at jazz. We never appreciated it as an art form worthy of study until it was validated by Whites. Soul music gets more support and appreciation from the European community than from the African American community. James Brown can sell out an amphitheater in Germany but can't get his own people to come to a free concert. It's sad. They straight took Rock- and-Roll. They took it from us, and we didn't even flinch. How did we let that happen? Now they're doing the same thing with Hip-Hop. Eminem..."

"Don't start that."

"No. No. No. This has to be said. Eminem is a good lyricist. He has a lot of talent. But his success is as detrimental to Hip-Hop as the creation of Elvis was to

Rock-and-Roll. His is the acceptable medium for the art form. You see as long as African Americans were the practitioners of the Hip-Hop culture, American society rejected it as a valid art form. It was not a skilled literary media. But as soon as they get a white practitioner, they hail it as an art form worthy of an Oscar®. How is that? Why now? Why not some of the African American practitioners before him? They were just as good, if not better. Why? Because African American's are not acceptable mediums for art in this country. We can't present anything for artistic evaluation. We have to get a surrogate white performer to cosign us. We have to have a white champion. Remember all the jazz greats? Those African American brothers from Harlem that sacrificed everything for their craft? Who do they acknowledge and support? Kenny G! Kenny fucking G! How do you explain that? Now Outkast has taken to another level, but these 'Bama's' won't appreciate it. They'll pigeonhole them and alienate them. How sad is that."

The young militant was about to retort when he got the strangest look on his face. The hustler seemed to follow his eyes and then inherited the same strange look. Parker was just about to turn around so he could discover the cause of the distraction when the culprit confessed.

"Hey Parker," Sheila said with an innocent smile.

"Hi," said Parker as he left his seat to greet her.

"I thought you were waiting until I called you," Parker asked with slight annoyance.

"I was," Sheila replied, "but I thought about the fact that if I'd waited on you to call then by the time I got here and got our food, you'd be done. And I didn't want you to be up here all lonely and what not. So, I decided to just head for Fort Valley and hope that you called by the time I got here. So why didn't you call me?"

Parker lowered his voice to a whisper. He didn't want to be the center of entertainment for the laundry mat. "I didn't think that it was fair to have you come all the way down here to help me wash my clothes. I'm not that lazy."

"Here, have a seat," Parker offered as guided Sheila to his table. He really didn't want to be bothered with Sheila, but he didn't want to hurt her feelings, so he conceded to himself that he would have to make this luncheon date.

"I've got our sandwiches and fries and I stopped and got you a bottle of orange juice," Sheila rattled off as she spread the food neatly out on the table.

Parker pulled up another chair and sat it opposite to his. "So, what's going on Sheila?" he asked in his most inquisitive voice. "What have you been doing to keep yourself busy?"

"Nothing, besides looking for you," Sheila replied as she sat in the chair Parker offered. "You just dropped off the face of the earth. You can't just be doing that to a sister: taking advantage of her and then not calling."

"Now, why you tripping? You know it's not like that. I've just been busy sweetheart."

"I know. I was just messing with you. You could have picked up the phone and called me though. I just wanted to talk to you. You know, see how a brother was doing."

"Well, I appreciate it," Parker returned with sincerity. I feel better knowing that somebody cares about me."

"Come on now superman! I know your phone stays on ring. Your player card is black. A sister just wants to hang out with you every now and then."

"I know. I don't know why a brother's so damn hard to get in touch with. I need to do better." Parker munched on his fries and silently pondered his predicament. If he didn't come up with something quickly, Sheila would work her way back to his house and he wasn't ready for that. His house was still a mess; there were dishes in the kitchen sink and books and paper lying all around. On the other hand, maybe some female company is what he needed. He needed to pull out of the funk that he'd been in over the last couple of days. Sheila would be down for that.

No, he thought. He just wasn't ready for Sheila yet. "When I leave, I think I'm gonna go see my mother. If I don't, she'll come by my house, and I can't have that."

"I feel you," Sheila said, sounding a little disappointed. "So maybe I can see you later?"

"What, you're getting ready to leave me already?" Parker pushed with mock disappointment.

"No, I'm not leaving yet," Sheila replied with the perkiness returning to her voice. "I'm going to enjoy you while I can," she said with a smile.

"As will I," Parker said with a smile. "As will I." He picked up his juice and began the cumbersome task of entertaining Sheila.

Parker Grant was the finest brother Sheila had ever seen. No, seen wasn't quite the right word; Parker was the finest brother she had ever experienced because Parker was an experience. At 6'2", 210, and finer than a motherfucker, he was her dream man. He was intelligent, witty and charismatic. These qualities made the man so damn sexy.

Unfortunately, none of these qualities were in the forefront of Sheila's mind as she watched Parker getting his chitchat on with his little laundry buddies. This motherfucker is tripping, she thought. He's got me bringing him food and shit because he's so busy, but he's got time to try to captivate a couple of weedheads.

Sheila put on her 'I'm so pissed at you, but you don't really have a clue' smile and climbed back in her ride. "That nigga is self-absorbed," she mouthed to herself.

This shit needs to pop off soon. I need something showing me what this nigga is thinking, Sheila thought. What does he really want? He's talking in riddles. No relationship but he wants me to act like there is. No dating other people, but I need to understand that he's got this issue he's dealing with and it's not good for him to avoid his emotions.

Sheila repeated the last statement aloud. If that ain't some bullshit, she thought. This shit is crazy! Hell, I must be crazy.

She pulled her ride into traffic and headed for the interstate. Sheila's thoughts of heading home were interrupted by the ring of her phone.

"Hello," she spoke into her flip screen Motorola.

"What's up, chick," Dean chimed in from the other side.

"Oh, nothing," Sheila returned as she straightened up and began looking for a place to turn around.

"You want to burn?" Dean offered.

"I'm already on my way," Sheila returned as she whipped around in the carwash parking lot.

"What you just decided to just pop up at my house without calling?"

"No, I turned around when I saw it was you calling."

"So, you just assumed I was going to invite you to smoke?"

"When else do you call me?"

"Fuck you Sheila," Dean yelped sarcastically.

"Fuck you Dean. Is my girl there? Tell her I said what's up.

I'll be there in a minute."

Sheila pulled into Dean's driveway about twenty minutes later. She brought her car to a stop next to Dean's '95 candy-apple-red Saturn.

Dean and his family lived in a modest one-story home about nine miles east of Parker's place. His neighborhood was customarily quiet. With the exception of a few local boys who'd occasionally walk down the street and antagonize whatever dogs they could find fenced in or tied up, nothing ever really happened there. Dean's home sat in a small valley amidst a grove of pecan trees. The location was great for its aesthetic value, but the pecan trees made it especially vulnerable to tornados. The roots of the pecan trees didn't go very deep into the soil, rather they crept along it, continually diving into the dirt with only the rounds of their spines breaking the surface and exposing their existence. If a tornado-strength wind ever tested them, they would most assuredly fail and send them toppling over atop one another and by proxy into Dean's living room. Despite this unlikely but very real possibility, Dean's home was a model suburban domicile. It was a three-bedroom, two-bath Tudor-style ranch with a stained-glass front door and a storm door at the rear.

The turn from the street into his driveway broke into a sharp decline and leveled out at a smooth stretch of pavement. The area was large enough to hold two vehicles comfortably or three if everyone crawled out on one side. Four stepping-stones with butterflies and frogs engraved in their surfaces led from the driveway to the rear porch: One was split down the middle; the three remaining stones were intact. A large, rounded awning held upright by two auxiliary columns planted in a four-foot concrete riser comprised the rear porch. It was more of a covered door. It held enough room for two people to stand unassaulted, while a third unlocked the door, should they have the occasion to need to escape the rain. It was a small white house with a spacious backyard. The windows were decorated with custom-colored mini blinds that accented the décor in whatever room they hung in. The yard was neat and well-kept. The drive was swept and maintained. A pole stuck up from the ground in the far-right corner of the back yard. Chained to it was a large white pit bull who lay quietly fanning his tail. A lawn table with matching chairs sat under a large pecan tree. Underneath the table was cooler and atop the cooler sat a half-emptied bottle of Corona. Dean was leaning over the table performing an organ transplant for a Garcia Vega Cigar, which, it appeared, had been gutted from tip to toe. Dean was a master surgeon and his work reflected it.

After much ado, Sheila exited her car and joined Dean in his makeshift operating room. "I can see you've been at it a while already," Sheila said as she pulled up a chair next to the surgeon.

"All day long," Dean replied with a smirk. "What's up girl?"

"Oh, it ain't nothing. Same ole shit. How's my girl doing?" Sheila replied.

"She's in the house." import and picked up a plate that most assuredly was munching food. "So, what's my ole trifling ass cousin up to?" Dean asked as he gnawed on a hot wing.

"Shit, why're you asking me?" Sheila shot back with indifference.

"Don't act crazy. You know you see that nigga every day."

Sheila managed to fire off a "Fuck you Dean," before she burst into laughter. "I'm not around Parker that much.

You know how he is. If he doesn't want to be bothered, he won't even answer the door."

"Yeah, you right," agreed Dean between giggles and bites. "But you still be with that nigga all the time. Hell, you probably just came from over there." Sheila answered the question with silence. "Well, you know the nigga," Dean replied, careful not to mention the unspoken answer. "I'm just asking how he's doing? Is the nigga alive? Is he working? You know, just general shit."

"Stop lying," Paula interjected as she exited the house. "You want to know every damn thang cause you're nosy." She handed Dean the bottle of ranch dressing.

"You just stay out of it," Dean said with a chuckle and a swipe at his soul mate's behind. "I didn't ask for your opinion."

"Well, I gave it," Paula answered with a fake attitude that barely hid her real smile.

"Anyway, he's doing fine," Sheila finished as she pulled a camel from her cigarette case. "And like I said, I don't be around Parker that much, it's just that when I am around him, this is one of the few places that we go out to. You know he doesn't like to go anywhere." An awkward silence followed. "Anyway, I just stopped by to see him and he's fine. He's doing his laundry."

"That motherfucker needs to. He's got too many gawd-damn clothes! Vain motherfucker! And then he got you up there watching him while he washes his clothes! I'm telling you," Dean proclaimed between licking the wing sauce from his fingers, "my cousin is crazy, and your ass is crazy for fucking with him. I love that nigga, but he is slap crazy."

"Yeah, but that nigga is so cool. He's cool with his shit." "Till he get caught up."

"Yeah, then his ass be so shook."

"Hell yeah," Dean said with a laugh. "That nigga be so blown he can't even sit still," Dean screamed over the two women's laughter. "I feel so bad for him but at the same time that shit be funny as hell. That nigga crazy Sheila, he crazy."

"Yeah, but I love that crazy mutha fucka' though," Sheila admitted.

"I do too, but I still know that nigga ain't no good for you. If you think he is then your ass is the one that's crazy," Dean retorted. "I'm serious girl. You treat that nigga way too good to put up with that kind of shit and I'll tell that nigga the same thing. He know that shit."

Paula and Sheila nodded in agreement. Dean lit the import and commiserated with Sheila.

The Cenacle was owned and operated by Theodore Barnes, a portly gentleman in his late thirties with a penchant for great music and food. Theodore was the color of cocoa butter with hazel eyes. He stood a respectable five feet eleven inches tall and wore his hair in style of most balding African American men in denial. He was an educated man, though not formally, having opted instead for a more hands-on approach to the acquisition of knowledge. He was originally from Chicago but had moved to the area for financial promise early on in life.

He'd made good on that promise through the bail bonds business, though his demeanor spoke nothing of those stereotypically assigned to his profession. He wore a suit of clothing not unlike a banker; his shirt was crisp and his tie modest in design. Dark slacks and hard-soled leather shoes completed his general daily wardrobe. He conducted his business in a courteous and thoughtful manner. He was punctual and prompt. His word was, in essence, his bond.

Theodore operated both his bail bond business and The Cenacle out of a centralized location. His offices consisted of two rooms, one small, one large, located in the rear of an auto body repair shop. The smaller of the offices was set up for receiving clients and other manner of clerical duties. It held a wooden desk of modest proportions, a high- backed black leather chair for the receptionist, who was currently absent, two brown folding chairs to house visitors, a small bookshelf in desperate need of expansion, and three gray file cabinets.

The larger of the rooms was more of an all-purpose utility area. There was a large wooden desk at which Theodore Barnes did the majority of his business. A recliner rested in a corner; a stack of folding tables leaned against a rarely used alternative exit. Stacks of boxes were lined up along the walls. A smaller table with a hotplate and a microwave sat by the entryway that separated the smaller room from the larger.

A long picnic-style table in the rear of the larger room served as the base of operations for The Cenacle,

Theodore's literary contribution to the African American cultural community. The Cenacle was, at its base, a magazine that covered African- American Culture and Society on an academic level. It discussed politics and fashion, history and current events, technology and demographics in terms of their scholastic significance. In addition to the regular offerings of most ethnic-based periodicals, however, The Cenacle also reviewed the offerings of hip-hop practitioners from a literary point of view. It dissected and critiqued the lyrics of songs for originality, composition, alliteration as well as a number of other literary qualities. This niche made The Cenacle a successful up and coming magazine on many college campuses and urban epicenters. It wasn't on the level of a Source or an Ebony, but it was growing, and Parker had been able to get in on the ground level.

***

Because of the magazine's relative newness and its inconsistent budget, no one that contributed to its pages was actually paid for their work. Theodore had been upfront about this and had promised that if and when the magazine became profitable, he would compensate all his writers generously. As a show of his dedication to his team of writers, he too went without salary. He made the magazine's financial records accessible to anyone who questioned his declaration. No one ever looked at them, however. They all knew that it wasn't money that drove Theodore. It was his love of African American culture and hip- hop. It was Theodore's desire to contribute something to society. It was his way of declaring hip-hop, an original and infectious phenomenon, as an art form. That was what drove Theodore.

Parker and Theodore had been working together for over a year. They had become good friends. Parker wrote for The Cenacle because Theodore was his friend; and because he believed in what Theodore was doing. He also wrote for the magazine because it offered him exposure and experience. Now most other magazines wouldn't hire a writer with no prior experience in journalism. But Theodore had hired Parker after reading a rough draft of one of Parker's stories. Perhaps it had been out of need that he'd been hired, but whatever the cause, the relationship had been a success. Parker got exposure and Theodore got good articles for his magazine. It was a good relationship they both appreciated.

It had been almost three weeks since Parker had been into see Theodore, well beyond the usual amount of time that elapsed between meetings. Theodore made light of this fact when Parker stepped through the office doors.

"So, the dead have arisen," Theodore said, as he rose to shake Parker's hand. "I thought you'd fallen off the face of the earth. Where you been boy?"

"Had some issues to deal with," Parker responded as he shook Theodore's hand. "I've got that article for you." Parker handed over the single folder he'd brought with him and sat in one of the brown folding chairs.

Theodore placed it on the desk and gave Parker a solemn look. "What's up Parker? What's going on man?"

"I'm straight Theodore," Parker replied. "I'm just stressed is all."

"Okay. I'll accept that. Just keep your eyes on the prize partner. Don't let troubles get you down. When it gets tough, work it out. Don't get bogged down. It's not good for you, man."

"I gotcha," Parker answered. Theodore's comments made him nervous. He respected him. He was real.

"You live day-to-day, Parker," Theodore said in a serious tone. "You'll sell enough ads for your rent then stop. You'll cover your gas, and then quit. That's not mature partner. That's not the way the real world is. You need some stability. Whatever you're gonna do, do it. Just don't half ass man. You're too talented for that. I've got a new assignment for you. Hold on while I grab the file." Theodore disappeared into the larger office and left Parker to his own devices.

Parker sat contemplating the sobering advice of his friend and boss. Theodore's concerns were valid. He was living in the now, Parker admitted to himself. He had no steady job; he had no long-term plans of note. He was a writer, but what was the significance of that? What was he doing with his talent? What was his life plan?

Theodore returned to the room and brought Parker out of his introspective mood. He tossed another folder on the desk and reseated himself before he began to speak.

"I've set up an open-ended interview with DeSha Dunkin down at the Bibb County Sheriff's Department.

She's doing an identity theft seminar the month after next, and I want you to do an article on it."

Parker's heart skipped a beat. The idea of being in such close proximity with the law scared him. His warrants were out there. Any law enforcement officer that decided to check his record would be able to see them and that would make his life so much more difficult. He'd have to figure out how to do it without anyone wanting to investigate his own criminal history. Hopefully, it would just be a small article. "A feature article or just a blip?" Parker asked as he flipped through the folder.

"I'm thinking a full spread. I want pictures, interviews, schedules, the whole shebang."

There went that hope, Parker thought. "So, you want me to go to the seminar and do interviews."

"No, no," Theodore corrected. "I want this story to run prior to the workshop." Theodore leaned over the desk and looked Parker directly in the eyes. "Interview Officer Duncan and everyone who'll be working with her on this project. Find out if she can give you the names of individuals who've been hit with identity theft. See if they'll talk to you about it. Get in-depth with her. Make her involvement the emphasis of the article. Concentrate on her work with this particular type of crime. Find out what's her motivation. This identity theft thing is big now. Let's try to be ahead of the ball on this one."

Parker closed the folder and placed it on the desk. "When's my interview set up for?"

"It's open-ended, so you can pretty much go whenever you're wanting to, but don't wait till the last minute, Parker. This one's kind of big," Theodore admitted with a conviction. "Do several interviews with each person so you get a well- rounded story."

"I've gotcha, man," Parker said reassuringly. "I'll get on it this week."

"Good," Theodore answered as he rose from his seat. "Now get the hell outta my office. My wife is coming by for lunch."

Parker grabbed the Dunkin file and stood to leave. "What are you all gonna do for lunch?"

"Didn't you hear me, player?" Theodore said with a mischievous smile, "I'm having my wife for lunch!"

"Play on player, play on," Parker shouted. The two men shook hands and parted ways.

Chapter 4

Sidney showed up at Parker's place around nine-thirty p.m. The muffled sounds of her Alpines bumping Sleepy Brown announced her arrival. Parker pulled on his turtleneck and went to meet her at the front door. Before he could make it there however Sidney began knocking and shouting for him to let her in.

"Open this damn door! You can't stay boxed up in there like a hermit! Open up!" Sidney shouted with almost comical authority.

"O.k. I'm coming," returned Parker as he unlocked the dead bolt. The door swung open and revealed Sidney in all her goddess-like splendor.

"Hello there gorgeous," she exclaimed. How do I look?"

Sidney looked divine. Her fashion ensemble began with a fitted camel-colored turtleneck that divided at her belly button and draped down the sides. An Indigo stone washed jean with a muddy tint gripped Sidney's hips and thighs like their loosening up would mean their death. She accented her ensemble with the right combination of earth-toned bracelets and necklaces. The outfit was finished off with a natural snake- skinned trench coat with matching pumps. Super models wished they were that hot.

"You're, a'ight," answered Parker with mock nonchalance.

"Humph! I know I look good! I ain't never gotta pump gas!"

They both laughed. The inside joke was that if a woman was too fine, her man would constantly fill her car up with gas just to keep from having her bend over in public.

Parker headed into his closet to pick out some shoes.

"So why are you in such a good mood?" Parker asked while inspecting a pair of Oxfords.

"Remember that possession case I was working on?"

"Yeah."

"It got dismissed and the client paid me today. Too dressy," Sidney said referring to the Oxfords.

***

"Parker retrieved a pair of Lugz® casuals. "So, you're buying dinner, right?"

"No, but I've got the appetizer!" With that Sidney reached in her purse and pulled out a gallon sized zip lock bag stuffed with Jamaica's finest.

"Where did you get that?" Parker asked, dropping the Lugz®.

"When it came time to make payment, my client only had 9 of the ten thousand dollars that he owed me. So, I cut him a break. Later, when I went home, he'd left me a thank-you card and a package on my porch. I opened it up and this was in it." Sidney held up the package again for inspection. "I called my home girl and she said that ole boy shit is extreme! It's straight from the shores of Montego. Those are some extremely gangsta' type movements. Like in the Godfather when the Don did the favor for the dude, but the dude didn't have a way to repay him. The Godfather gave him a pass. Then the dude went home and sent him back some cheese or something. This is my cheese! Those are too casual."

Parker took the bag from Sidney and inspected it. He broke the seal and was instantly rewarded with one of the most potent fragrances he'd smelled in a while. "How you gonna be accepting green from your clients. You're an attorney. You so wild!"

"Hey, I just defend the law! I'm a burner alright? That's me. I'm not going to turn down a payment of any type," Sidney returned with a whimsical smile.

Parker shook his head and put the Lugz® back. "Grab a Vega and get to rolling."

"You roll and I'll pick you some respectable shoes." Sidney tossed Parker a Garcia Vega and squeezed past him into the closet.

"Cool, but be assured, I'm getting some of this for my private stock." Parker placed the bag down and prepared the cigar. Sidney grabbed his Durango's and went to the kitchen to grab a mason jar.

"What made you pick that shirt?" she asked as she returned with the small mason jar.

"I don't have on a shirt. I have on a sweater."

***

"I know. That's why I asked you what made you choose that shirt."

"Oh, you trying to be funny? What do you think I should wear?"

"I hung a shirt on the doorknob."

"Smart ass," Parker snapped as he glanced at the hanging shirt. "Where are we going tonight?"

"I figured we'd do Taboo; you know in Fulton County."

"That's straight. We can smoke this on the way."

"Light it now. I got one in the car for the road." Sidney filled the mason jar with the fragrant import and sealed the lid. "Let's ride."

"Cool," responded Parker. "Just give me a second."

"For what?"

"I gotta change my shirt."

Parker and Sidney arrived at Taboo at 10:30 p.m. Tables were set out with red velvet tablecloths and rice paper running down their centers. Rose petals were tossed across the rice paper in an orchestrated randomness with a single votive as the centerpiece. The chairs were arranged so that the two occupants faced each other not the band. Lighting was low. Besides the votives on the table, the only sources of light were three low-voltage soft-tube lights that ran the length of the stage wall. The back wall held the door and the bar. Portraits of jazz greats were spread out all over the remaining walls. There were portraits of Monk, Davis, Gillespie, Parker and Kirkland organized in a diamond configuration on the wall closest to the door.

The opposite wall held enlarged snap shots of Ella, and Holiday and Vaughn and Lansing spread out evenly.

***

Parker and Sidney sat at a table near that wall. They lounged between the hypnotic Sara Vaughn and the sensual Apple Lansing. Parker thought that their seating was particularly special since it would be Apple Lansing who would perform tonight; Apple was the only songstress from the portraits on the wall still living. Parker had heard her story around the jazz circuit. She was supposedly the daughter of a New York nightclub songstress and a delta blues singer. She had grown up in smoky nightclubs and backwoods juke joints. At the age of thirteen she stepped onto her first stage; it was the Chicken Shack, a chitterling circuit hot spot for new artists. She'd gone up to perform because her "Uncle" Fishhead, the bartender at the club, had promised her a rib plate and a Pepsi Cola if she'd sing his favorite song. When she sang, her voice, even so young, stirred the soul of the entire club. Apple felt the lure of the stage and played into it. She sang the song with the suave and sway of her mother; her movements coincided with the rhythms of her father's band. When she finished the song and walked off stage the entire audience was in an uproar. They said that Apple had an intoxicated look on her face. They said that she even admitted to feeling lightheaded. She was infatuated with the idea of being a performer. Her mother, being several decades in the business, had pulled her aside and told her about the woes of being an African American artist in America. She told her daughter about the sadness and disappointment that came with the joy and the excitement. Her father, who played in the band that gigged at the Chicken Shack came up and added in the severely strained financial situations that musicians are often in. But Apple had heard the roar of the crowd. She had learned what it felt like to be the center of attention. She would not back away from it now. She never looked back. From that point on she'd developed as an artist. She had had many problems over the years. Everything from bad managers to bad marriages, but she'd finally gotten adjusted and become the dynamic songstress that everyone had known she would be. She would be performing tonight. Apple Lansing would share her soul with Parker. They would commiserate their pain together.

The band had already begun warming up, but the songstress had not yet taken the stage. Sidney and Parker ordered drinks – a margarita and a Crown and Coke respectively. From their table they had an excellent view of the stage. The tables in their section rested on a two-foot riser. The added height allowed them to look over the entire club. Well-dressed couples occupied the majority of the seating area. Groups of single women and men were migrating between the bar and the reception area. On the wall opposite Sidney and Parker the club owners had positioned several leather chairs; some were couches some were recliners. A huge spiral-designed oriental rug covered the floor under the leather chairs. It looked like an area in a comfortable living room.

The drinks arrived and Sidney asked the waitress when the show would be starting.

"It usually starts at around eleven," the waitress replied.

Parker checked his watch it was two minutes till eleven. "Thanks," he replied and handed her a tip.

"It sure is thick in here," Sidney commented. "I didn't know this many people appreciated Apple Lansing."

"Yeah, well evidently, they do. This place is packed," Parker said. "If we were in MGA this place would be empty."

"That's because people in our neck of the woods don't appreciate anything that's not associated with bootie shake." "Pitiful isn't it."

"I'm just glad I could get us in here. And these seats are great. I can't believe that we got such great seats."

"These are great seats. Who'd you have to fuck to get them?" Parker said jokingly.

"Whatever negro! This pussy is not for sale!"

"Now, now! Be a lady! We're in a nice place," Parker mused.

Sidney was about to tear into Parker when the stage lights dimmed. A change in the rhythm announced the coming of the songstress.

The room went dark. Except for the flicker of the votives, no light penetrated the void. The room was quiet. Then, from out of the darkness, a tiny light began to glow. And with it a voice, though barely a whisper, grew also.

"You are.........the light.........that ....shines in me......." she sang. "You are ......the bright.....ness...and I can't see........anything.....anything......as heavenly........as you.......as we........Heavenly, heavenly.......heavenly heavenly...you're so..."

With each note the lights beamed brighter and brighter. By the time Apple reached her second verse, a warm golden glow radiated from the stage and her voice boomed throughout the room. Apple, a beautiful brown-skinned goddess, stood in the center of that glow and she was radiant. Her skin shimmered. She wore a simple strapless black evening dress. A split ran up the right side of it, stopping at mid-thigh. The hem of her dress tapered down into a point on the left side. Her shoes were gorgeous; they too were black but with silver accents on the heel and toe. All these things added to her elegance.

Apple sang of pain and neglect. She sang of love lost and gained. Apple cooked up a spiritual mix of vocals and scatting and then spread her soul over the top of it. The band partook of the feast and fed Apple in turn.

It was a miraculous show. Apple had sung like Parker was the only person in the building. Her stage show was amazing. Each and every note she sang exuded love. Parker realized that he had never known love that was as good as Apple sang about, but he knew pain as bad as what she wailed of. So, they shared in that pain. Apple sang of her pain. Parker applauded in recognition of his.

After leaving Taboo, Parker and Sidney decided to go to The Classic's Club, a popular Atlanta strip joint, for drinks and conversation. Parker picked a table by the bar so that they would have easy access to the waitresses and, by proxy, the drinks as well as a clear view of the entrance. When visiting businesses that operated in the gray area of the law, Sidney always kept her back to the wall and her eye on the door. She was, after all, a member of the Georgia Bar Association. Still, she didn't shy away from the criminal atmosphere of the cities flesh district. Most women had a problem going in strip clubs, but Sidney was cool about it. Sidney said she saw it as an advantage to see men in an atmosphere where they felt comfortable being themselves. Plus, at high- end strip clubs, women usually drank for free. Parker appreciated her for her open-mindedness and admired her for her financial shrewdness. Besides the insight and free drinks, the strip club was about the only place they could go and socialize with good music and great drinks at two in the morning. It was one of their impromptu after-hours places. Not too crowded and not too formal. Sidney had invited two of her friends she'd run into at Taboo to meet she and parker at The Classic's Club.

They were just finishing their first round of drinks when Sidney's friends arrived. She waved them over and signaled for the waitress to come and take another drink order. Parker watched as they approached.

The taller of the two, Toni, Parker thought he'd heard Sidney called her, was a top-heavy red bone with short curly hair. Her walk said that she was a little uncomfortable in her surroundings but didn't want it to show. Despite that, she carried it well.

The other sister, who happened to arrive at the table first, had an ass that you could sit a tray on. Her skin was the color of Hershey's chocolate. She seemed perfectly comfortable in her surroundings. She didn't act as if this was her first time in a strip club. She may have spent some time on the stage herself, Parker thought.

"What's up girlfriends," Sidney greeted as two women approached. "You all remember my good friend Parker, don't you?"

"Yes," replied the brown-skinned sister with the big ass. "I'm Sugar, Parker," she commented as she offered her hand. "Do you remember me from Sidney's housewarming party?"

Hmm, sounds like a stripper name to me, Parker thought. "Yes," Parker lied as he accepted her hand gently. "Nice to see you again."

"This is our friend Antoinette. We call her Toni though." Parker and Toni shook hands silently.

The waitress arrived and took drink orders. Parker had a Coke because he'd taken over the responsibility of driving. Sidney ordered a Long Island Iced Tea. The two sisters ordered Apple Martini's.

"I don't see how women can work in here," Toni whispered after the waitress left. "I have more respect for myself than that."

"Hold up now," Sidney interjected. "Why you gotta be hating on the sisters in magic city shaking titties just to pay the rent...."

"LORD TRYING TO HUSTLE MUST BE SOMETHING THAT WAS HEAVEN SENT!!!" they all finished.

"Ya'll heard the 'Kast," Sidney continued. "This is just a job. Sometimes you have to do what you have to do to get by. Plus, that's their choice. They decide to do this."

***

"Well, I think it's cool," Sugar added. "They're using what they have to get what they want. That's the American way!"

"I knew your ole freaky ass would say some mess like that, Sugar. That's why I didn't even bring it up to you," Toni said with a smirk. She turned to Parker and in her most alluring voice asked, "What do you think Parker? Could you date a woman who stripped for a living?"

"Would I, could I, or have I?" Parker asked.

"All of them," replied Toni.

"Well," Parker said, sipping his drink, "I would date a stripper. It would be hypocritical of me to patronize a strip club but not respect the people who worked in it. As for the 'could I' question, theoretically I could date a stripper. I mean I'm a decent looking guy wouldn't you think Sugar?" Sugar blushed. "As for the 'have I', well yes, I have dated strippers before."

"What?!," exclaimed Toni "You dated a stripper?"

"No. I have dated several strippers. And the majority of them prefer the term dancer."

"That's nasty! How could you do that?"

"Do what?"

"Date someone that's been around all those men, pawing on them and touching their private parts?!" Toni spat with mock disgust.

"Well, most women have been around a lot of men. The majority of Sidney's clientele are men. Does that make her a bad person?"

"But that's not the..."

"Does that make her a bad person?" Parker repeated. Sidney gave Toni a sideways glance.

"No," Toni answered.

***

"And just to be sure we're correct," Parker signaled for one of the huge security men that was standing near their table. The man walked over and asked what he could do for them.

Parker asked, "Sir, could you explain to these ladies what would happen if some unruly gentleman got out of hand and placed his hands on one of the young ladies working here?"

The security guard complied, giving the ladies a graphic and detailed account of what would happen to the unlucky gentleman who chose to place his hands on any woman who was working in or visiting The Classic's Club. When he was finished, he excused himself and went back to his post.

"So, you see," continued Parker, "there isn't a lot of touching going on in reputable establishments. Some clubs don't have the strict codes of conduct this one does but the industry standard is 'no touching'."

"I just couldn't do it. I don't want a bunch of strange men looking at my naked body all the time," Toni admitted. I might see them on the street, and they'll want to try me or something. That ain't cool with me. It just ain't."

"Well, that's why you're not a stripper," Sidney answered with a roll of her eyes. "Hey! Look at the way she's making her ass cheeks clap like a cymbal! That's not normal!"

They all turned and stared at the dancer on the stage. She was holding on to the ceiling bar and bouncing her body in a way that made her ass cheeks slap together. Her buttocks sounded off thunderously. A small group of men gathered at the edge of the stage to offer her financial support and verbal encouragement. The deejay, seeing an opportunity to capitalize on the popularity of the dancers' anal applause techniques, switched to the Busta Rhymes song "Make 'em Clap". The song had the desired effect. Several other dancers joined their coworker on stage in what was most definitely the most bizarre 'standing ovation' Parker had ever heard or seen.

"You work it girls! Do the damn thang!" Sugar shouted.

"You freak," Toni exclaimed as she downed her drink and signaled for the waitress to bring her another one.

***

"You drunk," Sugar replied with a laugh and a not so lady like hand gesture. "I'm me. I like me. Freak or no freak, Sugar gon' be Sugar!"

"Amen to that," Sidney concurred.

"Why'd you call her a freak?" Parker asked.

"Because she's over there looking at that girl shake her ass and shit. Sugar's a freak," Toni declared. "She's always talking about some freaky shit she's done or wanting to do."

"So, you don't like doing erotic things?" Parker posed.

"Yeah, sometimes, but I'm not into all that weird stuff."

"I don't do weird shit" Sugar shot back. "I do things that I like to do. It's my body. I know what I like. That's what I do!"

"As is your right," Parker interjected. "I think that a woman who is mature enough to explore her erotic side is extremely attractive. Toni is just sexually repressed."

"What?! Me, sexually repressed. Oh no, player. I gets mine. I gets mine on a regular basis. Just because a sister don't do summersaults and back flips doesn't mean that I don't get down for mine."

"So, what if your man wants you to..."

"That bitch ain't got no man," Sidney and Sugar fired off in unison.

The table burst into laughter. Toni laughed so hard that she spilled her drink and had to order another.

"No, I don't have a man," admitted Toni with a smirk. "But like I said, I get down for mine!"

"Let's say you did have a man," Parker continued. "If he wanted to do something that you considered 'freaky', would you do it? To please your man, I mean."

"It depends on what it is," Toni replied.

***

"That's why your ass ain't got no man" Sugar fired again with bulging eyes and a comical smirk. "If you don't do it for him, these bitches in the streets will! You gotta take care of your man's needs or someone else will!"

"Well, it's just certain things I won't do."

Sidney spoke sympathetically. "No one's saying you should go hump a cow or anything Toni, you've just gotta be open to different things is all. Just remember to be open and enjoy yourself and all that sexually inhibited behavior will disappear."

The waitress arrived with Toni's drink and asked if everyone was doing okay.

"We're fine thanks," Parker replied. "Hey, can you do me a favor?"

"Sure," the waitress replied. "What is it?"

"Can you ask that young lady over there to come dance for my

friend?" Parker requested. "Which one?"

"That young lady," Parker replied, pointing to a petite dancer with ample breast and generous backside.

"Ok, and who is the dance for?" the waitress questioned.

"Oh, my friend Toni here of course," he said laying a hand on Toni's shoulder.

"What! Oh, no. A sister don't get down like that," Toni responded. "What's your problem Parker? You been watching too many Lil' John videos. You done lost your mind!"

"Come on sweetheart. Live a little," Parker cooed. "We're in a strip club. It's ok for you to get a dance here."

"I don't think so. That just ain't me. I ain't never done anything like that before. I'm not gay," Toni declared as she held out money for the drink.

***

Parker pushed her money away and paid for the drink himself. "I didn't say that you were. I just want you to experience something outside of your usual comfort zone. It's just an experience, not a lifestyle change. If you like it, then you've expanded your horizons. If you don't then you wouldn't have lost anything because I'm paying."

"What if she thinks I'm gay?"

"Just chill out, Toni. Have some fun! Let loose. You're among friends. Enjoy yourself! Go get the dancer," Parker commanded the waitress in a voice laced with mock authority. "You sit down and enjoy the experience," he ordered Toni. "This is my gift to you."

Toni looked nervous but said nothing. Instead, she downed her martini and signaled a nearby waitress for another.

"Yeah baby," Sugar exclaimed. "We gonna bring that freak outta ya! That up tight ass is gonna loosen up tonight!"

"Ah hoe, shut up! I don't see you getting a lap dance," Toni shot back with mock defensiveness. "Put up or shut up!"

"You know you're right," interjected Parker. He signaled to a dancer nearby to come and talk to him. She arrived just as the other dancer sent over by waitress arrived.

"Which one of us do you want to dance first?" the taller dancer asked as they waited for the next song to begin.

"Actually, I want you both to dance at the same time. I want one of you to dance for my friend Toni," Toni smiled and dropped her head shyly. "And the other one to dance for my friend Sugar."

"Well alright!" Sugar exclaimed. "That's what I'm talking 'bout. Shake a little ass and titties!"

Everyone laughed. Sugar's wisecrack had quailed the nervousness that permeated from Toni. The song changed and the dancers began to disrobe. The song, "Splash Waterfalls", by Ludacris, was a favorite of Parkers. This was sure to be a good show, he thought.

Sugar's dancer was tall and slightly muscular. Her name, she said, was Sunshine. Her breasts, nice firm C cups, worked well with her physique. She had a tattoo of the sun just over her left nipple.

***

Sunshine's legs were long and shapely; her hair was cut close-cropped to frame her face. She seemed reserved and quiet.

The other dancer, Hotcakes she called herself, was shorter than the first, but seemed to be full of energy and zeal. She wore several ankle bracelets and a 'Thug Misses' tattoo on her ankle. Her posterior wiggled independently of her body's natural stride. Parker thought of it as having a life of his own.

"You're so wild," Sidney said to Parker as the dancers began their sensual assault on her two friends. "Do you always have to play the Hugh Heffner?"

"Hey, it's what I do," he replied.

Parker watched as Hotcakes seduced Toni.

While they were there, one of the dancers had gotten a little too out of control and bitten Parker on his thigh. She'd offered to give him a couple of extra dances to make it up to him, but he'd declined.

Chapter 5

The dawn met Parker working on a short story for an anime periodical. He'd only lain down about two hours before he'd risen to chronicle the epic tale that had crept into his mind while he slept. A calico blanket, taken from Parker's resting place in the sitting room, draped his shoulders and gave him the appearance of a demented monk rocking incessantly during his prayers. The Common Sense 'Resurrection' album conversed casually with Parker, occasionally giving him inspiration. His fingers defiantly struck the keys of the laptop, daring them to accept the challenge of keeping up with his mind. He was in his creative zone. Mornings, his favorite time of the day, gave him the solitude that he needed to work. The previous night had been very enjoyable, but he'd still not been able to keep his mind off the Jessica situation. This had left him feeling gloomy and depressed. Under normal circumstances, being depressed would be a bad thing, but for Parker, or at least for Parker's writing, depression was the stimulus for a creative extravaganza. The morning had been very productive for him.

Ideas for literary pieces moved through Parker's mind endlessly. No matter where he was or what he was doing, his mind was never far away from his writing. Life was too stressful to think about all the time, he often said. Sidney said that he lived in a fantasy world. She teased him about having the characteristics of one of those Dungeons & Dragons® guys who locked themselves in a room for days at a time with some role-playing game. Parker defended himself by saying that he was an artist and by proxy prone to do strange things. She was right, however. He understood why the Dungeons and Dragons types locked themselves away from the world. He knew how disappointing life could be. Those guys used games to escape. Parker couldn't do that, but he could sneak away to a corner of his own mind and hide there. He could create his own fantasy world. His writing was the ticket into that world.

Parker's fascination with fantasy was not entirely based on his love of literature. As a child, his mother, being the overprotective parent she was, had not allowed Parker to venture outside of his front yard often. Since he was the only kid of his age in the neighborhood, he had been forced to find some other way of spending time, especially because he was too young to appreciate sleep or just resting. So, Parker initially gravitated toward the ancient art of tinkering.

After being punished several times for his efforts to do unneeded repair work on the household's appliances and electronics, however, he abandoned the idea of being a tinkerer and turned instead to books. More precisely, he had turned to reading. He'd read everything he could get his hands on. Books, magazines, pamphlets and newspapers were all fair game to him. He'd read romance novels and Good Housekeeping© magazines and Jehovah's Witness pamphlets and Harper's almanacs. Parker had perused the encyclopedia and traversed the dictionary. He was, for all intents and purposes, a closet bookworm. He loved reading because reading took him places. He could go to the far reaches of the Third World with National Geographic©, or to the exclusive and extravagant social halls of London with Travel© magazine. He could be a hit man in San Diego or a cop in New York. He could shed the stressful and depressing cloak of his home life and try on a coat that was a bit nicer. It was his escape.

As time went on, Parker discovered fantasy and its ability to take the reader completely away from the pitfalls of modern human existence. He could go where the world was beautiful and where people were still noble. In the worlds of fantasy, evil was tangible and obvious. Not hidden in the recesses of the human mind. And everything didn't have the taint of neglect and misuse by mankind that the real world had. Pollution was nonexistent. Starvation was unknown. The lands were as mysterious and alluring as anything he had ever imagined. Parker could explore these worlds and their people. He could become them. He could leave behind Parker, the shy kid with the skinny legs, whose mother wouldn't let him leave the yard. He could have the girl that everyone wanted. He could know just what it took to make everything right.

When he'd realized that his lot in life was to write, fantasy had been his natural genre selection. He wrote in several different areas now.

He did realistic fiction and poetry and spoken word as well as occasional articles for the news magazines and the periodicals. None of these drew him in and transported him away from his worldly distress like fantasy, however. It allowed Parker to be away in a place all of his own creation. He could go where his problems could not reach him.

Parker was in that place now. He was away on a distant planet trekking through a luminous cavern. The cavern was cut some three miles beneath the surface. The natives of this planet, Parker contended, lived in these caverns to protect against the unrelenting blaze of the planet's three suns. The rock – if you could call it rock – that lined the cavern's walls and formed its ceilings was semitransparent, Parker typed, so the fiery glow of the planets' suns penetrated well past the cavern where Parker's character traveled. Because of the translucence of the caverns and brilliance of the suns' light, the cavern surfaces had a living feel to them. The constant variations in illuminations gave them the impression of breathing. The cavern floor was covered with sparkling sand that transported the light from one cavern, through the rock-like surfaces, into the next. The sand had a spongy texture, as did the walls and ceiling. Parker imagined them being the celestial version of a honeycomb, only with a lot more strength and bounce. His character, a fugitive from a nearby city, contemplated his options as he walked down the labyrinth of light. Parker explained how his only hope at survival was to leave his tyranisque home city and start a village of his own.

A horn blew outside and brought Parker back to this world. Dean had arrived sooner than he had expected. Parker grabbed his boots and hurriedly pulled them on. Dean knocked at the door as he was saving his work and shutting down his notebook. Parker walked over to the door and let him in.

"You ain't ready yet? That's cool. Where Sidney at?" he asked, walking back toward the bedroom.

"In the bedroom knocked out," Parker commented as he pulled on his sweater.

"Sidney?"

"Yeah Dean. What's up," Sidney called from the other room.

"I brought your charger from the house."

"Thanks Dean," Sidney said as she entered the small sitting room. "Where ya'll going?"

***

"I gotta drop Parker off at home," Dean said as he grabbed the trash bag. "I'mma go ahead and take this trash out for you Sidney."

Dean grabbed the bags and headed for the door. Parker retrieved two bags that Sidney had placed in the pantry for later disposal and followed Dean outside.

Parker noticed that Dean had changed significantly since the time when they were roommates. He was now a courteous and considerate person. True enough, he and Parker still argued but that was the nature of their relationship. They were able to function in their volatile and veracious friendship. It worked for them. They enjoyed it. Parker had seen the subtle variations in Dean's personality. He seemed to be more focused. He hadn't always been that way.

Earlier in his life Dean had shared the same lifestyle as Parker now lived. He'd done everything for the moment. Women were just accomplishments for him. Like Parker, Dean had been a whore of considerable proportions. In their younger years they'd not been very committed to anything outside of themselves. Now, Dean talked very enthusiastically about his family. He had a kind and endearing attitude towards his wife. His respect for women had grown considerably. He and Parker had often spent their evenings comparing player cards; now Dean had elevated his player card to the family plan. He had found someone to make him believe in love. Moreover, he had learned to believe in it so much that he was now participating in its most sacred institution: marriage.

Parker felt a new kind of respect for Dean. His cousin had come to adulthood. They reached the dumpster and began their return journey.

"So, what you trying to do today?" Dean asked as he fished out his Benson and Hedges.

"Nothing really. I've got an article to write for a journal, but other than that, I'm bumming it today."

"How 'bout we go see Casper?" Dean offered casually. "Word?" questioned Parker?

"Word," answered Dean.

Parker's mood perked up. Casper was, hands down, Middle Georgia's most reputable cannabis supplier. His product maintained a constant level of quality that was unmatched by any other grassroots distributor in the area. His product was packaged by measured weight as opposed to visual confirmation; this gave Casper a professional image in the eye of his customers and also allowed him to accurately track the efficiency of his purchasing and packaging strategies. He never gave out of product. He never was inaccessible to his customer base. He was the hustler's version of Sam Walden, the Wal-Mart® guru. Dean had introduced Parker to Casper several months back. Casper had impressed Parker with his business-minded approach and his salesmanship. Nothing gave him more satisfaction than seeing a black entrepreneur successfully navigating the road to business, even if it was an illegal one. Casper had the green that'll reverse a cataract.

Like Parker, Casper was into politics. On occasion, they had spent long hours smoking and discussing the political state of America and its effect on the smaller community. Casper shared Parker's idea of the double-edged sword. They believed that America had an obligation to make right the transgressions committed against the African American people. Their contention was that America had never really accepted responsibility for the state that African American communities were currently in. America had not given an honest look at the dehumanizing, demoralizing and destructive psychological patterns that being bought and sold, then beaten and hanged, then treated as second-class citizens had had on the African American psyche. No one had looked into the levels of self-loathing that had been bred into the subconscious of African Americans, or how this self-loathing had been passed on from generation to generation. They believed that America should address the issue. That was the first edge of the double-edged sword.

The second edge, which Parker thought was the most important, involved African Americans and their refusal to step beyond the now. Parker had stated repeatedly that, as a people, African Americans were too quick to accept their 'place' in the world. Everyone, including the African American community, knew that America treated African Americans as second-class citizens. Parker's argument was that as a people, African Americans needed to rise above that and come into their own.

Casper agreed that a reinvestment in communities needed take place. African Americans needed to turn their attention back towards building strong communities; that, as a people, the patronage of African American businesses should become a priority. The preparation of an African American political agenda needed to begin. The search for new dedicated community leaders needed to begin. In short, African Americans needed some do for self-knowledge. This was the second edge of the double-edged sword.

These points were the basis for most of their discussions. Casper and Parker would go back and forth, with Sidney providing legal insight and Dean lending comic relief. A trip to Casper's would be very welcomed, Parker thought.

Dean and Parker reached the door just as Sidney was returning to the sitting room.

"Y'all could have told me you were hanging out today. I "We just decided that we were," defended Parker.

"So how did he know to pick you up," Sidney countered.

"I called him this morning so I could go home, conduct some personal hygiene, and change clothes. Besides, you're a big-time attorney. You gotta take your ass to work," Parker fired off with a grin.

"Yeah, you can't hang out with the riffraff anymore," Dean added. "You might get seen with us or something."

They all laughed and sat down. "Y'all wait while I freshen up and put on some clothes."

"We'll wait while you wash your ass," Parker requested. "Don't forget all that sweating your ass did in the club last night."

"I know. Wasn't it hot," Sidney exclaimed. "They went overboard with the heat! I know they want their patrons to be comfortable and all but DAMN!" They all laughed. "I'll be a minute. I just need to take a shower and change into some clothes," Sidney shouted as she disappeared into the bathroom. "Don't leave me!" she screamed from behind the door. Dean and Parker sat down to wait.

They arrived at Casper's one hour and forty-five minutes later. The trip there had only taken about twenty minutes plus a twenty-minute pit stop for Parker to conduct personal hygiene. Sidney had usurped the other hour and ten minutes getting ready.

Casper lived in a rural region between Fort Valley and Warner Robins. The drive was three miles long, all unpaved Georgia red clay. His home, set on a grassy acre between two sparse grooves of trees, was isolated by miles of uninhabited flat lands. The house was a western-style split-level with a wraparound porch. His lawn was conservative, opting for expanses of beautiful grass and an assortment of small shrubs rather than the elaborate mix of flowerbeds, southern ferns and azaleas that usually came with the style of house. A small shelter stood behind and a little to the right of the house. It was a simple shelter, consisting of six eight-foot two-by-fours planted in the ground to support a piece of eight-by-twelve plywood that served as the shelter's roof. It had the appearance of a fancy lean-to; under it were six bowls. These belonged to Casper's babies, six Great Danes that shared the property with him. The smallest of these canines stood just under four feet from head to toe. All the dogs had massive shoulders and heads. They were trained to protect the homestead. No one approached the property without their being aware.

As they traversed the hazards of the red clay driveway, two of the Danes sounded their alarms and intercepted them. The dogs trotted alongside the car. The others, Parker thought to himself, were somewhere watching. When they finally reached the front yard Casper was on the porch waiting. He gave a command to the Danes, and they silently disappeared.

"What it is," Casper said as he walked out to meet his guests.

Sidney was the first person to exit the car. "Hey Casper," she said with a smile and a hug.

"What up Dean, Parker," Casper greeted in turn. They all exchanged pounds and walked into the house.

Sidney had called from the car to alert Casper of their imminent arrival. In anticipation, Casper had rolled a two-finger blunt. He handed it to her.

"Ladies first," Casper spoke as he transferred possession of the blunt.

"Such a gentlemen," Sidney remarked as she put fire to the import.

Everyone sat down around the living room table.

"So, what brings my most excellent friends to my neck of the woods?" Casper asked.

"Nothing. Just fucking off really. I don't have to work today, Sidney called in on some bullshit and you know Parker ain't got no real job," Dean answered.

"Fuck you Dean," Parker answered sarcastically. "We decided to take a day off. What's going on with you?"

"Oh, I've been watching the CNN news report on this gay marriage stuff. This shit is ridiculous. America is getting ridiculous."

Parker knew Casper's patterns. He was trying to bait Parker into a debate. Parker decided to stretch it out. "Oh really?"

"Yeah," Casper confirmed.

"Yeah," Sidney co-signed. "Are ya'll gonna go back and forth with this 'who's gonna start the debate' shit or are you'll gonna start the debate? You all play so much. Dean," she called as she offered the import. "I believe this is yours."

Parker could only smile. Casper burst into laughter.

"Well, what do you think about gays marrying?" Casper asked,

attempting to curtail his laughter."

"About gay marriage or the right for gays to marry?" Parker shot back.

"The right to marry," Casper clarified.

"Oh, I have no doubt that they have the right to marry. They're guaranteed those rights under the constitution."

"What provision of the constitution is that?" asked Sidney, the resident legal advisor. She took out her sack and began to role a second blunt.

"The part that guarantees equal rights. What's good for the goose is good for the gander," Parker commented.

"So, you don't think gays getting married is wrong?" Casper continued.

"I didn't say that."

"You said you were for them getting married."

"I said I was in agreement of their having the right to marry. Whether I agree with them getting married is irrelevant. The issue is whether gay marriage is constitutionally protected. I think it is. They are discriminating based on sexual orientation. In Utah you can marry more than one woman. That's an alteration of the conventional man and woman definition, yet that stands. Why not gays?" Parker asked assertively."

"So, you don't care if they get married?" Casper persisted."

"Why does it matter if I care?"

"Because you're a citizen of this country. You have an obligation to protect the rights of its citizens. That means taking a stand on things that you believe in."

"Listen to this shit, Dean," Sidney interjected. "The dope man and the serial polygamist talking about citizen's rights!" Dean chuckled and took another toke.

Parker ignored them and went on. "The issue isn't about what we believe in. It's about what the law allows for and what it doesn't. Where's the confusion in that? The law doesn't say that homosexuals are bad or dirty and should therefore be treated differently. The law says that 'all men are created equal' partner. That means the rights and services that are offered to one citizen must also be offered to the other. If the government has seen fit to offer a governmental contract system called marriage for the union of two citizens that happen to be a woman and man, then they must also provide those same services for two citizens that happen to be a woman and another woman. Both sets of individuals are citizens are they not?"

Casper nodded his head in agreement.

"And the government's role in business is to make sure that everyone is playing on a level playing field, right?"

"Right," Casper admitted. He accepted the blunt from Dean and took a toke. The potent import clawed at his chest, but Casper refused to release it. Casper closed his eyes and began to speak. "What about the moral obligation?"

"You can't dictate morality," Parker countered. "It's just not possible. All we can do is make sure that the laws that we enforce are fair to all citizens, be they heterosexual or homosexual. The law provides that nothing shall be denied to the minority that is accessible to the majority."

"Spoken like a real chief justice," Sidney said as she finished rolling the second blunt. "Unfortunately, public opinion often dictates the way the law is interpreted. This is one of those cases where right and wrong will take a back seat to the fears of the people. As long as these old folks are afraid of catching "gayness," homosexual Americans will continue to be discriminated against." Sidney pulled out her lighter and put fire to the import. "The right wing is strong. It'll take the entire country to bring their backwards thinking under control."

"What about people who aren't a part of the right wing but have religious issues with homosexuality,"

Casper asked as he passed Parker the import. "Don't they have the right to vote with their consciences? They aren't discriminating against anybody."

"We can't debate religious motivations in a court of law," Sidney offered.

"So, the real issue isn't whether it's morally right, it's if it's constitutionally guaranteed," Casper added.

"And that's been my point all along. It doesn't matter what I think of gays getting married. I could think that it's the nastiest thing in the world and it wouldn't matter a hill of beans. It's a constitutional issue." Parker took a deep toke of the import and leaned back.

"How's school?" Casper asked Parker.

"Oh, it's straight," he replied. "I've got a project to finish for tomorrow. Everything else is just about coasting along." "How much longer you got?"

"That negro isn't ever gonna graduate," Sidney shot off. "He's just gonna keep on going to school until he's dead."

Everyone laughed, including Parker. "Man, I graduate at the end of the semester. Y'all some crabs in the bucket man, some crabs in a bucket. A brother took his time getting his degree. It ain't about how long it takes you. I got it damn it! It's mine!"

"Hit dog will holler," Dean interjected. The entire room burst into laughter.

He had been in school for quite a while, Parker thought. Until last summer he'd been taking only two classes a semester; that was all that his work schedule would allow.

He'd suddenly grown tired of school however and switched his plan from two classes and a full-time job to a full load and sporadic writing assignments. He'd locked up everything at his home and moved back in with his parents to cut down on the financial burdens that might have interfered with his school obligations.

He wanted to finish school. He wanted to have something in his life that was finished and was good. This was it. It was the beginning of a new era in his life. When he graduated, he'd be able to get a job as a professor. He would move away from here. He would leave behind all the disappointments in his life. He would miss Sidney. He would miss his parents, but Parker needed to escape. He needed to get away. The world was growing small again. And he was claustrophobic.

As he exited Interstate 75, Parker thought of how well his day had gone so far. The visit to Casper's had left Parker in a positive state of mind. His friends were dear to him. Just being in their company, along with the import, made any morning grand. So, after an excellent morning in their company, he decided to be productive and get started on his article for The Cenacle. Parker sat at the traffic light at the Byron exit and flipped through the information Theodore had given him on Deputy DeSha Dunkin. A cursory glance of the Dunkin file had given him some idea of where to start. The file had detailed information on specific identity theft victims as well as background on Deputy Dunkin but not much on the crime of identity theft itself, he thought. He would go over it once he reached his home but before the day was over, he needed to contact Deputy Dunkin for an interview. He could wait until he reached home and call her, but his propensity for procrastination might prevent him from doing so. The import had the habit of bringing on paranoia. He didn't need to worry about the folks tracking his phone signal and arresting him. It sounded ludicrous as he thought it, but such was the effect of the import. He decided to do it immediately before his nerve left him. He grabbed his cell and called the Bibb County Sheriff's Department as he pulled from the traffic light.

"Good afternoon, Bibb County Sheriff's Department, how may I direct your call," the voice on the line chimed.

"Good afternoon could I speak to Deputy Dunkin, please," Parker replied coolly.

"Do you mean Deputy Dunkin, sir?" the voice corrected.

"Yes, yes. Detective D. Dunkin, please."

"One moment please," the voice cracked before being replaced by chamber music.

Be cool. Parker thought. I do not want to sound like I'm hiding something. It was several seconds before Deputy Dunkin came on the line. Parker used that time to curse himself for not taking a pseudonym. At least then it would have been easier to mask his identity.

"Deputy Dunkin," came a bubbly voice through the silence.

"Yes. Good morning," Parker answered in his most official voice. "My name is Grant. I'm a reporter for The Cenacle. My editor, Theodore Barnes, said he'd already spoken with you about an article."

"Oh yes, yes," the Detective replied. "You're that cute writer with his picture by his advice column. I'm DeSha."

"Nice to meet you, DeSha," Parker put out coolly. He sensed a vibe coming from the lady detective. Perhaps it would work to his advantage. "I hope I didn't disturb you."

"Not at all, Grant," DeSha said in a sultry voice. "You're helping me do my job. I'm also responsible for informing the public of any potential criminal threats. Mr. Barnes told me you were very capable of helping me get this issue out in the public's eye."

"I'm glad you feel that way. It's good to work with someone who's passionate about their work."

"Well, I'm a very passionate person," the detective responded suggestively.

Parker hesitated. He knew the message behind her comment. He'd heard it before. This could be a way for him to get his personal issues straightened out. Then again, he'd probably end up fucking her over and making the situation worse. He decided to play it neutral. "When can we meet to discuss the situation?"

"How about later this afternoon," she offered.

Parker made his counteroffer. "I'm actually having a research meeting this afternoon. Can we make it tomorrow morning?"

"I've got a meeting with the mayor tomorrow morning. How about around one?"

"That works for me. Where shall we meet?" Parker asked.

"How about Desserts First on Vineville," Deputy Dunkin suggested. "They have great cherry shakes. Have you had one, Grant? A cherry one?"

"Not in a while, DeSha. Perhaps I'll have one tomorrow." "Great then. I'll see you then."

"Alright," Parker closed. "Enjoy the rest of your day." Parker tossed his phone on the passenger seat and headed for his home.

Chapter 6

By three p.m., Parker had made his way back home. With his day of hanging with his folks finally over, it was time to get down to business. His plan for the afternoon was to research his article on identity theft, wash his ride and then finish his cleanup project. He checked his messages and found several from Sheila, one from Tamena but none from Jessica. Why would he, he thought? They were over. What would she want to talk to him about? Still, he felt shitty.

Parker grabbed his CD case and looked for something to change his mood. As he flipped through the pages, he thought of the Jessica situation. What was so different about it? Why was it any different from the other women he'd broken things off with? Was it as Sidney said? Was it because she had broken up with him instead of him doing the breaking? Don't think about it, Parker told himself. This was not the time to ponder such depressing situations.

Do I want to listen to rhythm and blues or some Hip-Hop, Parker thought? He needed cheering up. Hip-Hop it would be. Parker flipped to the section of the portfolio that held his Hip-Hop collection. What will it be, he thought? The Gza/Genius CD caught his attention. It was an excellent work. The Gza was a phenomenal lyricist and a stand- alone type artist who wasn't afraid to reach beyond the status quo. But no, thought Parker. The Gza is a bit too melancholy. He flipped to the next page. The page held several CDs from the collection of UGK. UGK, The Under Ground Kings were among Parker's favorite Southern artists. As a unit they tackled the Southern black struggle like few other artists had been able to. Their affinity for the dope boys and hustlers made them a big hit among would-be thugs and shot callers. At the moment however, they were a bit too abrasive for Parker's tastes. On the opposite page were Parker's Mobb Deep CD's. Too violent for today. Parker went through the sections one by one. Eightball and MJG, Jigga, Nas, Goodie Mob, Kayne West, all were good works, but not befitting his mood. Finally, he came to a set of discs that were more representative of his current attitude. Parker had stopped on the pages with his Outkast collection in its' entirety. Yes, thought Parker. That's what I need to hear. He pulled out the discs, all nine, including two special order discs with the soundtrack songs on them. He unloaded the Sade discs that had dominated his airwaves for the last week and placed them back in the portfolio. One by one, he loaded in the discs: SouthernPlayerlisticCadillacMuzic, ATLiens, Aquemini, Stankonia, The Greatest Hits Album, The Love Below, then Speakerboxx and finally the two soundtrack discs. Now, he thought, I can get down to business.

Parker put the player on random and went to the closet to retrieve his project materials. On the coffee table, he placed two pencils, a top-loaded spiral notebook and a stack of articles on identity theft that he'd downloaded from the internet. He went into the kitchen and prepared a bowl of Honey Bunches of Oats®, then fixed himself a mug of apple juice to go with it. He placed these items on the other end of the coffee table and sat down.

For the next twenty minutes Parker reviewed the articles he'd downloaded. He organized them in three categories: biographical data, tabloid-type articles and album reviews. The tabloid-type articles made up the majority of the information he had. There were several pages of album reviews but only two pages of biographical data. Parker took notes on all of the album reviews and copied down the biographical data. He transferred his information to note cards and then evaluated what he had. The tabloid-type articles would add spice to his presentation but would not be very informative, he thought. He could probably have gotten by with just using the online information he'd gathered if he'd gotten some sort of sample of the artist's actual music. Oh well, he thought, I'll just have to go to the library and listen on the website. Maybe there's a video at Yahoo Launch® or something, he thought optimistically.

Parker gathered the articles he'd reviewed and placed them in a manila folder. He stacked his note cards in a neat pile and slipped them in his jacket pocket. Time for a trip to the library, he thought. What about riding music? What would he bump on the way? He thought of the CD's he'd seen while looking for some studying music. What had he seen that he could ride out to? Parker grabbed his CD portfolio and turned again to the Hip-Hop section. He flipped through the pages until he came to the area with the Southern artists. He took out the T.I. CD and placed it in a plastic cover for its trip to the car. Good riding music, he thought, good music indeed. Parker put his cell phone in his pocket and headed out the door.

In the driveway sat his 1982 Cadillac Sedan Deville. The Cadillac represented the closest he had ever come to loving anything. Parker had gone to great lengths to restore the car to its classic form. Its body was a beautiful pearl white with a burgundy leather interior. Real mahogany paneling garnished the doors and dashboards; the woodwork came compliments of his uncle's carpentry shop, as did the custom-made door handles and lock mechanisms; each of which was a tiny replica of the 1970's black power fist. These were also carved from mahogany. All of the original chrome had been restored to its elegant luster. Goodyear classic tread white walls gripped custom Cadillac one-hundred-spoke rims. The only modification to the body was the removal of the standing Cadillac hood ornament. In lieu of that, a flat Cadillac emblem had been applied to the surface of the hood. Inside, Parker had a customized eight- track that worked as a trigger device for a 6-disc CD changer he had mounted in the trunk. The sound system was not loud or gaudy, but it was professional. The speakers were hidden beneath the interior. The amplifiers were housed in the trunk with the disc changer; and when Parker ran his sound system, there was no rattling.

Parker hopped in his Cadillac and started her up. It had been over twenty-four hours sine he'd last crank her up; still, she started up like she'd been running all day. The engine ran quietly and smoothly. It was a Cadillac, Parker often said, it was supposed to run smoothly. After adjusting the stereo and idling the engine, Parker shifted into reverse. He slowly backed the Cadillac out of the driveway and onto the street. Once he'd cleared the driveway, he shifted into drive and was on his way. Next stop, Macon, he thought.

Parker looked at his fuel gauge. It read a quarter of a tank. I can't make it to Macon and back on that, he decided. A Cadillac burned gas. The cheapest gas prices were at a filling station on Vineville. Parker headed there.

***

Sheila reached Parker's residence just before the first rain began to fall. Thick dark clouds hung low on the horizon. Flashes of light periodically appeared and then disappeared across the sky. Lightening shimmered through the clouds like a sequin dress. This was lovemaking weather, Sheila thought.

The loose gravel of the unfinished driveway made crunching sounds beneath the car's tires. Sheila brought her vehicle to a stop in the space where Parker's car was usually kept. His Cadillac was nowhere to be seen. Anyone else wanting to visit Parker would have taken the car's absence as a sure sign that he was not a t home. Sheila knew better, however. She knew that Parker often drove his car behind his house and left it there to avoid unwanted guests. It had probably been there on the day the asshole police officers were looking for him, and there was a good chance it was there now.

This was an unexpected trip. She hadn't called to let Parker know she was coming, nor had he, during their previous encounters, given her any indication that it was ok to just stop by. But Sheila felt that Parker didn't really need to say it was ok. He needed her. He was alone. If it weren't for her, he'd be quite pitiful. Truly, he would be in serious trouble without her. She was the helpmate he needed; he'd never openly admitted it, but she still knew this. He was a grown man living alone. He didn't have a wife or an official girlfriend. He didn't have anyone to look out for him. He needed her to be there for him. That made it okay for her to just stop by Sheila rationalized. She was doing him a favor. She removed the keys from the ignition and placed them in her purse. Think positive, she thought. If you want this man, you're going to have to go out there and get him.

Damn, Sheila thought as she grabbed her purse and exited her vehicle. I sure hope I haven't made this trip in vain. This is a long way to come for nothing.

A light rain began to fall as she made her way to the front door of Parker's home. A quaint metal awning hung over the door and protected her from the majority of the precipitation; she huddled close to the door to avoid the rest.

"Parker!" Sheila called as she knocked on the rickety screen door. "Parker, it's Sheila. Let me in! It's raining out here!"

Sheila stood silent and waited for a response, but Parker did not answer. She knocked again and listened more closely. She became aware of the rain tapping incessantly on the awning overhead. It reminded her of a steel drum. Behind her, cars splashed through newly formed puddles of water. She heard leaves rustling around in invisible funnels. Still, no response came from inside the little house.

Damn! I should have called first, Sheila thought, as she rummaged through her purse for her cell phone. This is seriously fucked up! Every time I try to do something nice for this brother, I end up getting the shaft and not in a good way! Damn, damn, damn, Sheila thought as she shielded her cell phone from a sudden burst of rain. The wind began to blow harder, and Sheila was forced to return to her car.

Parker was just about to turn onto Vineville Avenue, when his cell phone rang. He looked at the screen. It was Sheila. Damn, thought Parker. I'm stressing over a woman that doesn't want me when I have one right here who can't get enough of me.

Parker answered. "Yeah, what's up?"

"Hello," came a drowning voice from within a flood of sound.

"Turn down the music. You sound like you're in a car," Parker shouted.

"I am in my car," Sheila replied as she adjusted the volume on her radio.

"What are you doing off work?" Parker asked as he pulled into the service station.

"My boss is all upset over that Passion of Christ movie again. She was running around complaining and whining and shit. I had to get out of there!"

Sheila worked as a nurse practitioner at the Middle Georgia Medical Center. Parker had met her there three months ago while he was doing an article on HMO's. She had provided him with valuable information and priceless insight into the medical industry's thinking on insurance and the patient. He'd taken her to dinner in appreciation and had ended up sleeping with her. Neither of them was ready for a real relationship so they agreed to enjoy each other's company when possible and not complain when it wasn't possible. It had worked out well for a while, but lately Sheila had been acting like she wanted to elevate the status of their relationship. Parker was trying to ignore her attempts at bringing up the subject, but she was becoming more and more persistent. Parker prepared himself for her latest attempt.

"What's wrong with the movie?" Parker asked.

"Nothing. That bitch is upset because she's Jewish and the movie brings up the fact that the Jews killed Jesus."

"Why is she mad at that? It's true," Parker commented as he unlocked the gas cap and began to fill up his tank.

"She's mad because she feels that the movie's another form of anti-Semitism. She says it's anti-Semitic because it shows the Jews in a negative light. She says that it's gonna bring bad blood between the Jews and the Christians."

"She's talking like they bloods and crips!"

"Yeah, she says that that's the problem but that's bullshit. From what I see, the movie is biblically correct. And the Jews did kill Christ. That's a fact."

"Yeah, well I don't think the Jews want to hear that. They've worked very hard to build this image of humbleness and philanthropy," Parker said. He returned the gas pump to its resting place and went on. "They probably see this movie as very damaging to that image. But it's true. It's so true. They strung Christ up on a cross. There's no way around that."

"What do they want people to do? Just forget about what was done?"

"I guess so. They want us to be sensitive to the feelings of Jesus' crucifiers. You know it's not politically correct to point out peoples' shortcomings; even if they did kill Jesus," Parker said sarcastically.

"They didn't say anything about the way the Germans were portrayed in Schindler's List," Sheila brought up. "That joint made you hate the Germans. I didn't hear the Jews standing up and protesting about that," Sheila spat.

"That's because in that movie it showed how hard the Jews had it."

"Well, Jesus didn't have it easy. Every time people talk about the crucifixion, they make it sound all holy and sanitized. That's not the way it happened! They kicked Jesus' ass! They beat the shit out of him. They whipped him...no! No! They flogged him and then made him carry that heavy ass cross! Then they took big ass metal spikes and nailed them through his hands and feet and hung him up to die! How can you not make that shit sound gruesome?"

She had a point, he thought. Parker went into the store and paid the cashier for his gas and a pack of M & M's.

Sheila went on, "Anyway, I decided that I'd take the day off and see what all the hoopla was about. You up for a twilight show?"

There it was, Parker thought as he put on his seat belt and pulled out of the station. "I would love to but a brother has a research project that has to get done today. Gotta keep the dream going you know."

"Oh, I feel you. What about later on this evening?"

"That could be a winner. Why don't you call me after six and I'll let you know."

"Ok, but you're not going to continue to put a sister off," Sheila replied. "I'm gonna stop asking you to do things."

"I know, I know. I'm just busy right now, you know. We'll get up soon. I promise."

"You better be glad I like you, Parker Grant. Otherwise, I'd shoot your ass!"

Parker laughed. "Thanks for your pass. I'll talk to you later, alright."

"Bye," Sheila answered.

Parker hung up the phone and headed for the interstate.

Chapter 7

Houston Avenue had the look of a good neighborhood gone wrong. Victorian-style homes with missing shutters and rotting columns crowded together on patchy lawns. Porches had become resting places for misused furniture and appliances in disrepair. Broken-down automobiles peeked out from behind dilapidated garages and from under makeshift tarps. Many of them had not known life for some time.

A liquor store, a beauty salon, or some hopeful entrepreneur opening the detail shop of the month had claimed every other corner. They were housed in the remnants of once quaint mom and pop grocers but had not been kept up. Now they looked neglected and in ill repair. The best of these were only in need of paint or new lettering for a sign. The worst were constantly being considered for demolition. Most were somewhere in between.

Several men indigenous to the area waved at Parker from their shade tree checker game. He returned the greeting with the customary head nod and drove on. People were out today, thought Parker. Two women in nursing uniforms were haggling with an older gentleman over the price of various gift baskets that he had stockpiled in the back of his station wagon. At the stoplight, Parker was treated to an unexpected show; one of the stylists from Travone's House of Styles was having a loud and quite graphic altercation with her boyfriend. The stylist was deep into a full-blown neck-rolling-finger-pointing conniption. Her boyfriend was trying to quiet her, trying to calm her down but to no avail. Parker turned up his music to give them some measure of privacy. He turned the car west on Rocky Creek Road and headed towards the Bloomfield area.

Bloomfield, Macon's largest African American blue-collar neighborhood, started just beyond the Eisenhower/Rocky Creek intersection and continued around the fringes of the city. Ranch-style homes shared the horizon with clusters of trees and church steeples. Bloomfield. The home of Dab's, Macon's number 1 black sports bar. Parker had spent several pleasant evenings at Dab's. He wasn't the type to enjoy large social settings, but Dab's comfortable atmosphere made them bearable. Plus, Ms. Dab treated her customers, primarily the African American community, with the respect and acceptance they couldn't get at other bars. Seating there was decent. Thanks to a supermarket that shared the property with Dab's, parking wasn't an issue either. Interstate 75 was less than a quarter of a mile away. Dab's location made it a popular spot for the Middle Georgia social circles. On his last trip there, he'd run into Charmaine, one of his many ex- girlfriends. That night she'd had her hair up in a ball, with several dozen spiral curls spilling from its center. Her makeup, what little of it there was, looked flawless. For the evening, she'd worn hazel contacts, but honestly, Charmaine was just as sensual in her wire-rimmed glasses. A modest caramel shell top had draped her bosom and stopped just above the most perfect hips that God ever sculpted. Her posterior set out in a manner that rendered most off-the-rack jeans useless. Hip-huggers were more accommodating but exposed more panty than Charmaine was comfortable with. Her boots were 4-inch heels. Spiked. Laced in the back. Leather.

Yes, thought Parker. He'd dated many women from the Bloomfield area, but Charmaine was definitely the most memorable. Charmaine, a mother of three, lived in an apartment complex just across from the Post Office. They had dated just prior to Parker getting hired at City International Insurance. Charmaine was a holy roller with a weakness for sex. She loved it and hated herself for it. Parker thought back to the intense conversations they'd had about premarital sex and the sinfulness of it in God's eyes. He would often agree with her just to get out of what he saw as a totally pointless discussion. He knew she'd break down and eventually give in to the yearning. It wasn't that he'd wanted to lead her into temptation or anything; it was that she was going to give in to temptation anyway. He was just along for the ride. She had her own mind. He wasn't into making moral decisions for other people. She had to decide what was wrong or right for herself. As long as her principles hadn't interfered with his needs, he had been happy. Had she ever presented him with a situation that conflicted her principles with his, or lack thereof, he would have dissolved the relationship rather than bend to anyone else's will. On top of that, he and Charmaine had had an incredible sex life. For such a religious woman, she was well versed in the arts of lovemaking and fucking. She knew just the things to say to get a man's juices flowing.

Parker slowed down as he past Charmaine's old apartment complex. He silently honored the memories they'd shared. A part of him missed her. He'd spent many wonderful nights in her bed. And on her floor. And on her couch. Parker laughed to himself and rode on.

He and Charmaine hadn't worked out because, at that time, Parker couldn't commit to any woman, much less one with three kids. He thought back on how expensive it had been just to feed them burgers and fries. He'd seen Charmaine drop outrageous amounts of money on doctor visits and school clothes and holidays. The expenses involved with child rearing were phenomenal.

Parker also recalled his fear of being labeled a sucker for taking care of some other man's children. He'd had big issues with that. At the time, he hadn't understood the important role that stepfathers play in helping to heal the family. Hell, even if he'd understood at the time, he probably would have still been afraid. He was stressed thinking about it now. Not the issue specifically, but the pattern it represented in his life. A pattern that had come out of the corner swinging.

Parker slowed to a crawl behind a wrecker pulling a Box Chevy.

"Charmaine," muttered Parker. "Sweet, Sexy, Sensible Charmaine."

Charmaine had helped him get himself together during his early days at City International. She'd fixed him lunches and done his laundry and ironed his suits for work. When he didn't have money for gas, she'd come up with it. Charmaine had been an excellent woman for Parker. She had been a supportive friend, an excellent lover and had shown the ability for being a great mother to the children they had talked about bearing. Parker should have jumped at the chance to settle down with her. Instead, he had abandoned Charmaine as soon as he'd gotten on his feet. He simply stopped calling her. He hadn't meant to end things like that. He hadn't called her one night when he had promised her, he would. The next night and the next, he'd found reasons not to call her. Before Parker had realized it, it had been two weeks. When he finally did call her, she wouldn't even talk to him. He hadn't blamed her. He had been wrong. He knew it then; he knew it now. If he'd talked to Charmaine about his fears and concerns, maybe he would have reconsidered or at least given her some insight into the situation and closure of a more mature nature. But he had sabotaged the relationship with his immaturity. He'd acted like a punk instead of a man.

Parker frowned as he navigated the Rocky Creek/Bloomfield curve. That was Jessica's problem, he thought. She hadn't been able to see manhood in his actions. She couldn't see him making those important decisions that distinguished childhood from adulthood. Back when he was with Charmaine, he'd acted childishly too. He'd run from the responsibility that came with the adult situation he had been in. Now Jessica was, in essence, accusing him of the same thing. Almost six years later, she was charging Parker with the same crime: Perpetrating a man.

"Fuck her," Parker spat out, but it wasn't out of anger. It was frustration that had him worked up so. Had he grown so little psychologically in six years? Was he really that pitiful?

Parker hit his left signal and pulled into the quickie-mart. He needed a smoke. Having decided to leave the engine running, Parker opened the car door, then thought better, turned the ignition off and pocketed his keys. The hood is still the hood, he thought.

He routinely scanned the parking lot as he headed towards the convenience store entrance. The quickie mart, which up until 6 months ago, had been the only commercial commodity on the block, now shared its lot with a chain dollar store. The corner plot of land now seemed crowded and cramped.

Parker thought back to Charmaine. On a deeper level the fact that he didn't call her and break things off properly represented a more serious problem. It showed that he had no faith in who he was, and what was right for him. If he no longer was interested in the relationship, he should have just told her. It was normal for people to break up. Why had he been afraid then? Why had her opinion of him been so scary for him to face? He shouldn't need some woman to validate him. That he did said something bad; it said that what other people thought of him was more important than what made him happy. Parker frowned as he entered the store. I couldn't leave her because I couldn't bear to have her blame me, Parker admitted silently. I didn't want her thinking I wasn't the man she thought I was. Her image of me defined who I was. I needed her to believe my hype, Parker realized. He needed a Black-and-Mild®.

The counter where the cashier worked was surrounded by 3-inch fiberglass. Cases of various products were stacked and double stacked in every available corner and on every end cap. There were two people already in line. Parker took a place behind them. What makes me need constant validation, he asked himself?

The customer in front of Parker bought a box of Kools, the brand his father smoked. Parker thought of his father and smiled.

Lately, he'd come to believe that he'd grown up being very hard on his father. His opinion of his father was shaped by the numerous shortcomings that he'd been a victim of during his tenure in his father's house. He'd seen and heard his mother argue and then plead with his father to do better. He'd been there through it all. He'd consoled his mother often. It had a negative effect on the relationship he and his father shared. Parker had lost respect for him. He didn't want to be anything like him. They hadn't spoken more than fifty words, total, to each other over a period of eleven years. He had been too angry, Parker thought. Parker paid the attendant and headed back to the car.

Since his last run in with Jessica, Parker had begun to analyze his own actions in the same strict standards that he applied to his father. He looked at his life in parallel to his father's. Parker lit his black and started the car. His own problems, though unique to his life, followed the same patterns as his father's. He looked at the situations his father had been in and how he had always, once given the details of the situation, been able to intuitively know whether his father was actually telling a lie or telling the truth. Parker sighed as he pulled into traffic on a side street.

It was because he knew him, Parker thought. He knew his father's patterns of living. He knew his intuitive thought patterns. He knew, on a fundamental level, what feelings and emotions motivated his father's actions. He knew because they shared those feelings. Parker had come to realize that he was a newer version of his father. The realization was frightening.

Parker pulled into the library parking lot at 5:15. An attractive administrator Parker had been seeing on and off waved from the window of her corner office. Parker waved back and signaled her to call him. Women, Parker thought. The weakness that he had inherited from his father.

Parker's infamous liaisons with women were second only to his father's. The constant problems Parker's mother had with his father's infidelity were the same problem his past girlfriends had had with him, Parker thought. This was a point Parker had previously rationalized by telling himself that there were different sets rules for marriage and single life. He'd always said his defiance of monogamy would end the day he got married. He'd convinced himself that marriage was some magical place where everything just suddenly changed for the better. He thought that that's when he would change. Parker had come to realize that his thinking was flawed.

Parker reclined his seat and inhaled deeply on the black.

Every time he got involved with a woman, subconsciously, he was trying to correct the cycle that his father had perpetuated. He thought he'd been doing what was romantic for the sake of romance, and to a certain extent he was. But the problem was that he'd learned romance from books and television. He never saw real romance. His father was a player. He was never romantic to Parker's mother. The only guide Parker had was watching what his father didn't do and then doing it. He had always been looking for a woman who could make him a better man than his father had been. He wanted to be different than his father. He wanted to be a good husband and a good father.

The smoke was as thick as mist. Parker lowered the window and vented the compartment. He turned off his cell phone and put it in the glove compartment.

Somehow, Parker pondered, I went wrong. Instead of becoming a good man, he had become his father. He had become the womanizer. He had become the careless, unappreciative destroyer of lives. He was his father, only worse. His father had only ruined one set of lives, Parker thought. He had destroyed dozens.

Parker put the black out and resigned not to think about it anymore. He wasn't his father, he thought. He was his mother's son. He was a good man. He just needed a woman, a good woman to bring it out of him.

He navigated the library stairs and entered with a mission.

Chapter 8

Sheila turned up the car stereo and lost herself in the music. The rhythms corralling through the compartment rushed into her spirit and temporarily washed away her disappointment. She forgot about her soaked clothing. She pushed away the dampness of her ruined Manolo Blanc shoes. She released the fact that she had failed to secure some quality time with Parker. She focused instead on the Apple Lansing song playing in the system:

'You gon' wake up one morning Negro, and find your sweetness gone', you gon' wait too late cool Negro, and I'll be moving on!"

Sheila hit the repeat button and allowed Apple to empathize with her for two more rotations before she finally conceded to reality, turned down the stereo, and dealt with the situation at hand. She was soaked. Parker was gone. She was pissed.

I knew I should have called, she thought. Why didn't I just call? Then I would have known that he wasn't at home, and I wouldn't be sitting her looking like a wet rag doll. Well, I'm not wasting these tickets, Sheila decided as she checked her purse for the movie passes. But I can't go wet.

Sheila thought of her options. She wasn't in the habit of keeping clothing stockpiled in her car, so pickings would be slim. There were a couple items she'd picked up from the laundry: her work uniforms and a formal dress she'd had taken up in the waist; hardly proper movie attire. Her gym bag was in the trunk. Perhaps it held something more suitable. She knew there were socks, a clean tee shirt, and tennis shoes in the bag. Did she pack her gym shorts or her sweatpants? If it turned out to be the sweatpants, she'd be set. They were nylon with a matching zippered hoodie. It was her favorite workout gear; the outfit was both pretty and practical. Plus, rain wouldn't soak into them like it had her Dolce & Gabbana jumper. Dry clean only, she fussed as she rung out one of her sleeves.

"Well, time's a wasting," Sheila declared as she shifted around and began to maneuver her way into the rear of her car. She pulled a handle and lay her seat as far back as it would go. Please let it be sweatpants, she prayed as she climbed into the back seat. A cloth latch was stitched to a panel in the center cushion to allow access into the trunk from the back seat. Sheila pulled it down and began her search for her gym bag. The trunk was pitch black without its lid up. Sheila was forced to feel around in the dark. She located a tire iron, a half empty oilcan, a pile of dirty rags and a thermos before she was able to find the gym bag.

"Sweatpants!", she exclaimed, once she'd fished out the bag and examined its contents. Finally, something in my favor. Now to get out of these wet clothes and into this sweat suit without killing myself. Sheila unfastened the clasps along her shoulders and attempted to extract herself from the soaked jumper, but the expensive fabrics clung to her body like a second skin. Dolce & Gabbana was not meant to be taken off in the back seat of a compact.

Where can I change? she thought. There was the Dairy Queen up the street, but it had filthy bathrooms; those at the convenience store on the corner were smaller than her back seat.

"Damn, Parker," she shouted. "If you were here, I'd be able to change! Hell, if you were here, I wouldn't need to change!"

Sheila thought of and discarded several ideas before she remembered seeing Parker's bathroom window raised. She could fit through the window with very little effort. But that would be breaking into Parker's home. She would be willfully violating his space. That was wrong. But his window was up, she reasoned. His bathroom floor was getting wet. His rugs were probably already soaked. Sheila imagined the puddle that must already be forming there amongst the rugs and other toiletries.

I'll just go in, change and shut the window, she decided. That'll only take a minute. I'm already here.

Sheila thought for another moment before gathering her things in the gym bag, jumping out of her car and rushing toward the open window.

A small silver SUV turned into the driveway just as Sheila was pulling Parker's front door shut. Shit, she thought. Just what I need, a witness to my B & E charge.

Be cool. If I don't act suspicious, they'll be none the wiser, she hoped.

The Ford Escape came to rest right behind Sheila's car. The engine idled down but did not shut off. Sheila imagined the driver dialing the police and informing them of a well-dressed burglar leaving the scene of the crime. The occupant paused and then stepped out of the idling vehicle. In terms of complexion, the driver was what most people would refer to as high yellow. She wore a burgundy velour Baby Phat jacket with matching pants. Her nail polish flashed an accent color that was mirrored on her lips. Her shoes were white Phat Farm classics.

Sheila recognized her from the pictures Parker kept in his bedside drawer. It was Jessica, Parker's ex-girlfriend.

She was the color of chocolate milk. Parker drank her in with a schoolboy's enthusiasm. He had spotted her as soon as he'd come in. Her body was spectacular. She had Beyonce' ass, with a body like Pam from that Martin Lawrence sitcom, and facial structures of Nina Long. She walked like one of 'dem gurls' who, through no fault of her own, didn't realize she was one of 'dem gurls.' She wore very happy jeans. At least Parker thought that he would have been happy as those jeans. She was helping another patron, so Parker had taken a seat nearby and waited patiently. He placed his research on the table and drank her in.

Her aura read like the music of Billie Holiday; both beautiful and tragic. Her skin spoke of a restrained youthful enthusiasm; her eyes hinted at the captor. Her movements were liquid. No clumsiness existed in her demeanor. She smiled and gave birth to one thousand sunshines. Parker watched the goddess, eager for an opportunity to approach her. She finished with her patron and started to walk in the opposite direction of Parker's table. As she did, something happened that Parker hadn't anticipated.

She turned around and stared defiantly back at him. Parker blushed and she smiled. She chuckled softly and shook her head. With this inconsequential, but reassuring sign of faith as a motivator, Parker got up from his chair and significantly reduced the distance between them.

"I could feel you watching me," she said as he approached.

"You're right," he admitted casually.

"Do you normally stalk patrons at the library?"

"I wasn't stalking, I was staring, and you're not a patron, you're an attendant."

"Still, you can't just be staring at people." "I apologize. Did I offend you?"

"No."

"Do you accept my apology?"

"Yes."

"Good then we can start this relationship off right."

"Hold up slim, this isn't a relationship. I don't even know you."

"You're right. Again, I apologize. I'm Parker; you are?"

"Alfreda," she said and chuckled. "You're crazy! Do I need to call security?"

"Well, I'm sorry, but you're pretty. I don't see women as pretty as you that often. I got carried away."

"Oh. So, what are you doing in the library?"

"I told you that I'm here looking at a pretty lady."

"Staring at a lady."

"Pardon me, staring."

"Good, now what were you doing here before you became the 'Library Lee Malvoy." Parker scoffed and pretended to be insulted. "For real, now! What are you here for?"

"I'm doing an article on identity theft." "ID theft?"

"Yep."

"Why would you want to pick some obscure topic like identity theft to report on? Why not pick some musician like Hendricks or John Lennon or Marley?"

"See, there you go assuming that I had something to do with the selection of my own topic. That would make too much sense. I would have picked someone that I was interested in and actually enjoyed researching. But no, my editor gives me some obscure, albeit brilliant, subculture topic to research. I would rather be doing it on Marley."

"You into Marley?" Alfreda asked with a suspicious grin "Love 'em to death," Parker replied.

"No, but are you into Marley?" Alfreda questioned more so with tone than grammar.

"Are you referring to his harmonics or his herbatical habits?" Parker asked with a whimsical Freudian intensity.

"Both," Alfreda replied with a coolness that Parker thought was sexy. "More so the latter."

"Yes, I burn! You burn? How you gone be a burner working in the library?" Parker whispered with mock ferocity. "Librarians can't burn!"

"Library Attendant," Alfreda corrected. "And stop loud talking me! I'm at work!"

"I'm not loud talking you! I'm whispering as it is!"

"But this is my job fool! Don't ask me nothing like that at work!"

Alfreda folded her arms and turned away to mask her amusement but wasn't quite quick enough to hide her smile. Parker saw it and went in for the big one.

"You right. Again, I'm sorry. Give me your number and we can talk later. Here, write it on the top of my research paper."

"Hold up, I can't give you my number. I have a boyfriend." Under normal circumstances Parker would back off, but it was crunch time. He would not be discouraged.

"I should hope so," he responded sarcastically. "You're definitely not going to get a man once I tell everybody about your lack of good communication skills."

They both burst into laughter, then remembered where they were and reduced it to a hearty chuckle. "For real though, I just think you're cool. I respect the fact that you have a man. I just think that you'd make an interesting friend."

"You can tell that I'd be a good friend just by looking at me?"

"I didn't say a good friend, just an interesting one. Every woman needs a few friends of the opposite sex. If for no other reason, it keeps her man on his toes because he's always afraid that that friend might replace him." She laughed. Parker went on. "Just consider me that friend that your man always thinks wants to take his place if the chance ever presented itself."

"Oh, that's how you see yourself?" Alfreda asked.

Parker just smiled and handed her a pen.

Sheila and her best friend Rasha exited the theater after the main wave of moviegoers had already left. They'd stayed behind to read the credits, specifically the soundtrack credits. There had been a song during one of the love scenes that Sheila had thought was one particular artist and Rasha had thought was another. Rasha had been right, but it had taken a lengthy discussion after the credits to get Sheila to admit to defeat. It wasn't so much that she hated to be wrong, as it was that she hated to quit talking. Luckily, Rasha was birthed of the same breed of talkative people. Having stretched the artistic credit question as far as it would go, the ladies transferred their energies toward another topic: Sheila's recent trip to Parker's.

"So, I'm out there looking all cute and shit, thinking I'm about to get some, and this mutha fucka ain't even home. Then it's raining, hard! I mean, I'm under the eave and I'm still getting wet! The wind is blowing so damn hard that rain is falling sideways just to make sure it hits me." Rasha giggled. "Girl I was wet from head to toe. My new Dolce & Gabbana jumper was drenched. My Manolo Blanc shoes, girl? Soaked. I was pissed!"

The automatic exit doors of the theater floated open, and the two divas stepped out into the afternoon sun. "Well, I had won these movie passes, and I wasn't about to miss out on my movie and some ass too, so I just crawled my ass right through his window and changed in his bedroom!"

"What bitch?" Rasha asked in surprise.

"You heard me. I crawled through an open window and changed my clothes.'

"So, you done broke in this man's house and changed your clothes while he wasn't there?"

"Yeah girl! And look what I got." Sheila reached in her purse and pulled out a stack of folded papers. She unfolded the stack and handed it to Rasha.

"What the hell!?" Rasha stared in disbelief. "You stole the man's phone bill? What kind of psycho shit are you on, girl? What the hell are you gonna do with a phone bill?"

"I don't know," Sheila admitted as she grabbed the stack of papers from her girlfriend. "I wasn't planning some great heist. I just took them. It was impulse."

"So, you just impulsively break in a mutha fucka's house and steal his -- his phone bill?" Rasha paused as a car passed by then proceeded to make her way across the street. "What are you gonna do with a phone bill? That's got that man's personal information on it. You're not about to tell me you're doing that identity theft shit are you," Rasha said, clutching her purse to her breast in mock fear.

Sheila shoved her best friend playfully. "Hell naw! I told you I didn't plan to take it, I just did. That's crazy ain't it?"

"Yes, bitch! That's crazy," Rasha declared as she reached her truck. "What the fuck was on your mind? You don't plan on paying it do you?" Sheila looked down at her feet and fumbled with her keys. "Hell naw, bitch! Don't be paying that mutha fucka's bills. That ain't the nature of yawl's relationship. He ain't your name. You can't call that mutha fucka when your shit is short. Don't do that shit. That's crazy. You need to just throw that shit away and when he goes to talking about it, act like you don't know shit!"

They both burst into laughter, partly because of the comedy of the statement and partly because of its truth. Sheila knew that it might not be the best thing to do. She knew that it wasn't something she and Parker had discussed. Rasha's comment had been on point. Sheila was breaking protocol. "Hell, you right, girl," she said as she stuffed the papers back down in her purse.

"Does it have detailing billing?" Rasha asked in a mischievous voice.

"Naw girl, just some shit that lets him access his account online."

"So, you on some psycho shit and can't even snatch the right shit. You're pitiful, bitch, extremely pitiful."

"I guess I was just doing something."

"You were just doing something alright. Or something was doing you! You're sprung bitch." Rasha fished out her keys and activated the keyless entry. "You're so in love that you run around committing larceny in order to be with this man and he didn't even ask you to. THAT DICK MUST BE MAGNIFICENT!" Rasha shouted a little too loudly.

"It damn sure is," Sheila exclaimed with a high five to her home girl. "It damn sure is" Sheila's car was parked two spaces to the left of Rasha's Explorer. Sheila made her way to it. "I'll call you later girl, ok?"

"Ok. Just make sure it's not from central booking. Throw that shit away," Rasha advised in a serious tone.

"I will girlfriend. Take care." With that Sheila hopped in her car and headed home.

A light rain fell outside. Watery storm troopers raced down the eaves and off the roof's edge, then landed on the asphalt with a splat. Those who survived banded together and now congregated in the cracks and recesses of the sidewalks and the driveways. Clouds, eager to assist in the aquatic assault, blocked out the sun to hamper surveillance. A film of gray now covered the sky and everything under it. Rivers of soldiers marched down each side of the street, and then disappeared down storm drains, where the fight would continue. Some watery battalions carried spoils from their campaigns: sticks, branches, even various foodstuffs pilfered from some conquered stronghold.

Chapter 9

Parker stood under the eve of the library plotting a safe path to his car. He had not anticipated the rain. Two-and-a-half hours ago, he had entered the library on a sunny afternoon. He'd spent his time in the library online researching his identity theft article and conversing with one Alfreda, the library attendant. Clouds had blown in while he'd been researching and blanketed the area with precipitation. Now his beautiful day had become a rainy evening. So much for washing the car, he thought. Oh well, it was getting late in the day anyway. Better to save automobile maintenance for Saturday mornings. Parker tucked his research finds under his shirt and dashed across the courtyard to the car. He leapt over several small rivers, skirted a half a dozen lakes and splashed his way through a messy delta before finally arriving at his vehicle. He located the right key immediately and was soon inside his dry and comfortable car.

What would he do now? The rain had ruined his plans to wash his car. Not that he would have wanted to wash it this late in the day anyway. The library expedition had taken longer than he'd expected. Between the obscure topic of his research and Parker's frequent breaks to chit-chat with Alfreda, he had been off track more times than he could count. Now, he had an evening with no leisure activities. He could go home and finish up his cleaning project but where was the fun in that? He wasn't Alice; he found no excitement in cleaning. Besides, his house was depressing these days. It was filled with memories that he wasn't comfortable addressing just yet. It was the location of his commiseration of the Jessica situation. He didn't want to be anywhere that would bring those memories back to the surface. Unfortunately, his home brought up those memories. He needed to spend some more time away from it, he decided.

Parker started the car and let it idle. What could he do? He could go hang out at Sidney's, but she'd told them on the way home that she had a date this evening. Off of GP, it just wouldn't be cool to step up in her crib like that. It was hard enough for people to see them as friends as it was. He wasn't going to hate on some guy by barging in on his Mack time. Hell, he wasn't gonna prevent Sidney from getting her groove on. Friends didn't do things like that. As for Dean, there was no doubt that he would be busy. He knew that if he called Dean and told him that he was bored or without anything to do that Dean would tell him to come over. That, however, would be inappropriate. These days Dean had his family to consider. There was a certain amount of time and energy that Parker imagined it took to be married. There was also, Parker assumed, a sort of unwritten law of inclusiveness that had to be honored when visiting a married couple's house. You had to visit the couple, not just your homeboy. Parker couldn't just go over and hang out with Dean. He had to hang out with

Paula also. That always made him depressed. He always felt like a third wheel when he did this. When it was just Dean and him, they were two homeboys hanging out, but with Paula there, it was changed to Dean and his wife hanging out with his lonely friend. It was like Dean and his wife Paula were members of an exclusive club that Parker wasn't a member of. He could visit it occasionally, but only as an outsider. This was the way of marriage, Parker thought. It was better to visit Dean's home when he had a date with him or when Sidney could come along. Then he didn't feel so obviously lonely.

He put the Caddy in drive and pulled off. Was that the problem? Was he feeling alone? Parker pulled up to a green light and waited for it to change.

He could call Alfreda he thought. She seemed to be pretty good company. Hell, she was the reason he spent so much time in the library. They had some great conversation. As long as he didn't approach the idea of them hooking up, she'd probably go for dinner or drinks. She was actually a pretty safe date. She had a man already and was not looking to jeopardize their relationship with infidelity. As far as she was concerned, Parker wasn't even dating material. He could have a good time with her without the burden of expectations. The problem was, Parker thought, he might want to call on Alfreda again. He might really want to be around her. She had a way about her that was at once likable. Plus, she was extremely attractive. Could he be around a woman like that without wanting to get involved with her? He'd better not chance it, he thought.

The light changed and Parker headed towards the mall. Might as well do a little shopping, he thought. That way, if I can find something to do, I'll have something to wear.

Parker slowed down and then brought the vehicle to a stop in the traffic line behind an F-150 at the next red light. He reached over and retrieved his phone from the glove box. As soon as he turned the phone on, the familiar 'you've got messages' tone went off. An invitation for the evening perhaps, he thought. Parker pushed the necessary codes and listened to his messages.

"You have one new message, and two saved messages," the automated operator churned. "First message, received at 7:15 p.m."

"Hello again Parker," came a voice that he recognized as Sheila's. "Look here, I'm about to hop in the shower, so if you try to call me back, I probably won't answer. I was just gonna invite you over for some pizza and movies. If you're interested, come on over. I'll order extra. Hopefully, I'll see you later sexy man." The message ended.

"First saved message," the operator began. Parker hung up the phone. There was something to do, he thought. Sheila was interested in sharing time with Parker. She never kept it a secret. She'd been trying to spend some QT with Parker for the last several days. Maybe he'd break down and take her up on the offer, he thought optimistically.

And what about her offer? She had another offer on the table that Parker had yet to address. What of Sheila's love? What about it? Could she be the romantic situation that he desired? Could she be the best woman for him? After all, she did show a desire to please him. She gave his thoughts and opinions honest considerations. She was beautiful. She was the kind of woman who'd always be beside her man; no matter what the situation is. That's the one mama told me to find, Parker thought. His mother told him to find someone who was in love with him, not someone that he loved. That made life a lot easier for you, she'd declared.

Sheila was these things. Sheila was the chronic. She gave womanhood, a glossy shine. Parker could have the lover he actually

wanted. The light changed and traffic began to creep along. On the

eastbound shoulder of the parkway, a construction crew was busy fabricating an additional lane. Traffic bottlenecked at the beginning of the site and then cannonballed at its ending. Parker was just passing it when his phone rang. The screen read Smoke, Dean's nickname.

Parker answered the phone. "What up, partner?"

"What's up, asshole."

"Ain't nothing, shit face," Parker replied. "What's going on at the Dean?"

"Shit. How 'bout at your mama's house," Dean replied jokingly.

"Fuck you. I don't live with my mama anymore, goat neck."

Dean chuckled. "What you doing for it tonight?"

"Ah, I got some shit to do."

"I know what that means. I won't see your ass for another two days!"

"Naw man, it ain't like that. I just gotta little something I gotta do."

"Whatever. Look Paula cooked some chili. You can come and get some if you want to."

"Hey, I appreciate it."

"Yeah man, alright. I'm out here."

"Hey man."

"Yeah,"

"Hey look, you know why I date so many women?"

"Cause you a ho."

"Naw man, for real. Do you know?"

"Naw! Gone tell me."

"Cause I can't find everything I want in one woman. find one sweet, elegant, classic, sophisticated, intelligent, sexy, and freaky down ass gangster bitch."

"Damn!" Dean laughed hysterically. "That heifer gonna be schizophrenic."

"I know dawg. I want that chick that keeps it as real as I do. I want one that does it like I do it, feel me?"

"That's what we all want, partner. Everybody got things that would attract them; you know what I'm saying?

I got a Miss Perfect, you feel me. I got a shawty in my head that encompasses everything that I want. She's the muthafuckin' one. She's it! For me, that's Paula. She's what I want. I sat down one day and thought about what made me happy. I mean truly happy. I wrote 'em down."

"You can't write, bitch," Parker interjected.

"Fuck you," Dean replied, and moved on. "I realized that the qualities that I appreciate in a mate, the things that gave me the most happiness were all in Paula. We can hang out and do nothing, know what I'm saying? None of that 'let's talk' all the time shit that most people need to be around each other."

"Oh, so we don't talk?!" Paula exclaimed from the couch behind Dean.

"I mean we do talk but we don't have to be doing something to be around each other all the time," Dean quickly corrected.

"Good save, slick!" Paula yelled from the rear.

Dean continued. "We don't have to be doing nothing to enjoy being around each other; feel me? We're just happier around each other. You gotta recognize that person. You gotta call a spade a spade and stop trying to over-rationalize your situation. You ain't gotta have nothing but what makes you happy, you know what I'm saying? You ain't gotta make your momma happy. You ain't gotta please your daddy. Hell, you ain't gotta please me. Just do you bro."

"True. True," Parker said introspectively. "I feel you, man. I just got to get my shit together man. Hey man, I'll holler at your ass later."

"Yeah, I'll holler fuck boy."

"Alright bitch ass. Later," Parker said as he hung up the phone.

Parker altered his course and headed for Sheila's home. If she wanted to see him, then he'd oblige.

He was cute, Alfreda thought as she organized the periodicals. She paused on a particular magazine by Oprah. Now there's a sister that's got it together, she thought. I wish I could have half of her luck. Alfreda placed the magazine on its respective pile and moved to the next.

Parker seems to be a really nice guy, she thought. She really enjoyed their conversation. She'd seen him out before and was always attracted to him. She had secretly contemplated approaching him on several occasions but never really had the opportunity. She felt a tingle throughout her body when he looked at her. The way his body just flowed when he walked was so damn sexy. His spirit seemed to excite the air around him wherever he went. When he entered a room, she was instantly drawn to him. His voice was both calm and chaotic.

Alfreda picked up a House Beautiful magazine and put in its correct place. I wonder what kind of house Parker wants, she thought. I hope he doesn't like ranches. I hate ranches, she contemplated. Is he into family? I wonder what his mother's like?

"What you over here smiling at," Bumble asked as she bumped the book cart into her best friends' ass.

"What?" Alfreda asked coming out of her stupor. "Girl, you scared the hell out of me! You need to watch what you're doing," Alfreda whispered savagely. She attempted to put up a show of mock anger. She quickly gave up the ruse however and chose instead a fit of uncontrollable laughter. "Girl you're crazy! I almost died," she exclaimed. Alfreda laughed with her best girl, Bumble.

Alfreda and Bumble had been friends for the last three years. They'd met through a mutual male friend who for reasons unknown to either of them had committed suicide on September 23rd, his birthday. They'd consoled each other at the funeral, gone and gotten the date tattooed over their hearts and been the closest of friends ever since. When Alfreda lost her job Bumble had gone to her manager an asked if Alfreda could work at the library. She'd even offered to give up some of her hours to cover her shifts. They were real friends. They partied together. They cried together. They even lied together. They were a pair if ever a pair there were.

Alfreda was the Chad Hugo to Bumble's Pharrell Williams. She was out there in the open. Always blatant with life. Never apologizing for who or what she was. She was Bumble, the daughter of a sometimes mama and a no-account daddy. Alfreda was somewhat more reserved, at least in proclamation if not in actions. She saw different colors when she looked at her life as compared to

Bumble's, but it was really the same scene. Nevertheless, they were friends.

"What you over here daydreaming about?" Bumble asked innocently. "You had a look on your face that should never be seen in public."

"What kind of look?" Alfreda asked in feigned ignorance.

"A 'I'm going to fuck him' look," Bumble replied with an air of knowledge.

"Fuck who?"

"I saw you talking to ole boy,"

"True! True! I was getting my chat on," Alfreda admitted with a smile. She put the periodicals a side and pulled Bumble close. "His name is Parker Grant. He's a writer and a poet. Bumble you remember him from the festival thing."

"You talking 'bout the "honey pot" guy?' Bumble asked in a lusty voice.

Alfreda's first real experience with Parker had been during a concert at a festival last summer. He'd done a series of poetic pieces with the last piece being one called The Honey Pot. It had been very erotic and had a profound effect on most of the women in the audience, including Alfreda. She had talked about that piece and its deliverer for a whole month afterward. He was her eye candy. "Oh yes girl. That's him!"

"Oh, hell yeah! That's one sexy mutherfucka."

"I know girl. He asked me for my number!"

'He did!" Bumble exclaimed. "What did you do?" she continued gripping Alfreda's hand in schoolgirl anticipation.

"I gave it to him!" Alfreda cheered.

"What?" Bumble shouted as she slung loose from Alfreda's hand. "Bitch, you live with a man! A whole nother man and you giving muthafuckas your phone number! Bitch, you crazy!"

"What!" Alfreda answered defensively. "He's just a friend."

"He's just a friend until you fuck him," Bumble replied with a chuckle. "You like drama. Why else would you do that?" Bumble loaded the sorted periodicals onto the cart. And then started sorting the hard backs from a nearby stack.

"I'm not going to let something like that happen. I love my man. Ricardo is a nice guy. He's been very good to me."

"Yeah, but you want to fuck this Parker guy. You want him. You don't feel that way about Ricardo," Bumble pointed out. "Plus, you know that smooth-ass bald-headed motherfucker is probably crawling in pussy. Don't set yourself up for failure. You'll be crying in six months. I ain't trying to deal with your ass then. Stick with the tired ass motherfucker you got. That way you know how to deal with him. Your shit ain't perfect but it works for you. He's cool with your child."

"Because he's a child too," Alfreda interjected.

"Well, that makes you a child molester cause you're fucking him!"

"That's not what I mean by child and I'm not really fucking him."

"Well, he's fucking you. Now whether you get anything out of it is your business. Either way he looks like a man and walks like a man, so I call him a man," Bumble surmised.

"Yeah, but Parker's a lot cuter than Ricardo," Alfreda admitted as much to herself as to her coworker. He was a fine brother. He had ambition too she decided silently. "Plus, I genuinely enjoyed his company. He makes me laugh."

"And which one of those is going to stop Ricardo from putting a foot in your ass?"

"And see, that's another thing: Parker didn't seem to be the type to beat on a woman. I'm digging that about him." Ricardo sometimes grabbed her and shook her violently. He'd thrown her into a cabinet once and bruised her back. She hadn't told Bumble about it, but it was obvious that she'd known.

"Girl," Bumble shot as she stacked the National Geographic®, "You're playing with fire. Keep fooling 'round. It's gonna be ugly. Real ugly."

Alfreda pretended to be angry but there was no use. She was enamored of Parker. He fascinated her. He was fine. He was intelligent. And he was available, even if she wasn't. And he was an artist. A damn good poet. She'd seen him at that show that one time back before she'd moved in with Ricardo. He was hot. But beyond that, he made her smile. In just the brief time they'd talked, she'd felt excited and beautiful and appreciated. It had been a while since she'd felt that way. She decided that she wanted to feel that way again.

"I know what I'm doing bitch," Alfreda threw at Bumble. "I'm grown," she assured her friend. "You just worry about straightening out your trifling ass life."

"Fuck you too bitch," Bumble said with a laugh. "He is fine," she admitted. "And I heard he can fuck."

"For real girl?"

"Hell yeah!"

Chapter 10

Sheila lived in The Parks, an affluent singles condominium community in North Macon. In Sheila's community the streets were cobblestone. Hand-laid red brick sidewalks lined both sides of the roads and the pathways leading to the lobby entrances. An antiquated electric lantern stood sentry every 15 feet or so, giving the community a warm tangerine glow. Manicured lawns with military corners stretched up and down the dainty little streets. Oak trees watched over each neighborhood in groupings of fours and fives; they too soaked up the shine of the lamps and took on an orange tint to complement their emerald hues. There were three pools on the property: two outdoor and one indoor, as well as a fully equipped fitness center. Tennis courts and a rugby field occupied the back five acres. The Parks were substantial in size and exclusive in membership. The '82 Cadillac Sedan Deville fit in quite nicely with the Mercedes and Porsches parked in most of the driveways. There were dozens of antique vehicles in The Parks. There were certainly dozens of Cadillacs to be sure, but none like Parker's. His was a classic. It was the vehicle of a collector. He sat in it, gathering his thoughts.

Parker sat in his car and contemplated what he was about to do. He could very well be walking into one of those situations that would change the nature of one of his relationships. What was he willing to sacrifice for the chance at happiness? Was it worth the stress and denial that commitment represented? She wanted more. He knew that. He knew that she was no longer satisfied with the status quo. She wanted a title. She wanted standing dates and personal drawers. She wanted spare keys and monogamy.

Monogamy. Monogamy was not the issue. Parker was one hundred percent, without a doubt, irrevocably for monogamous relationships. In fact, at any given moment, he could be discovered to be involved in at least three. He found the love and commitment and indestructible vulnerability of monogamy to be intoxicating. To have a person's entire purpose in life be your happiness is a powerful feeling. Truth be told, Parker's greatest dream was to have the perfect relationship. All of his wants and desires satisfied by one magnificent, immaculate, incredible, woman. He often times found extraordinary manifestations of one or more of these characteristics in his women. They were for a time, his fantasy come true. But reality had a nasty way of tainting the purity of Parker's fantasy world and reality often brought that world crashing down on him. Parker had been unable to accept the shortcomings of these women on a long-term basis.

They were after all, only human. They had been shaped by their own life experiences. What was important to Parker was not always as important to them. As he thought, Parker realized the role that his mother played in this. He wondered how much of an impact his mother's approval played into his relationship matters. Was he, on a subconscious level, attempting to placate her objections? How often had he found women who made him truly happy only to abandon them over some petty altercation or insignificant happening? Then he would find the next Miss Not-So-Perfect and fall in love with the idea of her. He was a serial monogamist.

No, monogamy was not the issue. He just didn't want to be pushed into anything. He needed time to discover. It's unfair to look at it that way, he thought. I'm just going for the movie and pizza. No stress. Just food and fun. I've gotta stop overanalyzing shit, he thought. It's for the now.

A large butterscotch-colored leather saddlebag lounged in the Cadillac's passenger seat. The bag was Parker's regular social event escort; it followed him around and doubled his security blanket as well. It also served in the capacity of Parker's little entertainment collection; an assortment of items was stored here for the purposes of fun and entertainment. Playing cards, a regulated amount of Casper's import and Dominos were among the staples. The handcuffs were special guests. Other items: poetry, writing utensils, dictionary, condoms, were likely, though not guaranteed to reside in the bag on any given day. Parker grabbed his leather socialite and headed in the direction of Sheila's condo.

The entrance to Sheila's condo was arranged in the manner of a lobby. There was a breezeway that gave residents and guests access to any one of eight condos.

The lobby itself consisted of two levels, each holding the general entrances for condos A through D and E through H respectively. A set of standard carpet-covered precut stairs transported guest between the two levels. Nondescript striped wallpaper adorned all surfaces not covered with carpet, ceiling or door seal.

Parker took the stairs to condo F. The door had a spring wreath attached at its center. It was a bit gaudy, but not in a bad way. In the midst of the floral bonanza was the peephole. Parker watched it as he knocked on the door. He waited. No answer. He knocked again and waited. Again, no answer. Had he misunderstood the message? He knocked a final time and then dialed Sheila's number. It rang but no answer came.

Fucked up, Parker thought. I guess no one wants to hang with ole Parker. He put his phone in his pocket and headed back down the stairway. As he reached the bottom, his phone rang. The screen read Sheila.

"Hello," he answered.

"Hey, did you just come knock on the door?" she asked.

"Yeah, that was me," Parker said as he reversed his course.

"Sorry about that. I just got out of the shower. I knew I was gonna miss you coming! Look, I'm gonna throw something on. The door is open. Why don't you come in? I'll be out in a minute."

"Ok, cool." Parker heard the phone disconnect as he again reached condo F. He turned the knob and went in.

He entered a semi-lit living room. Several small, varied-output lamps lent strength to the dozens of candles that battled the darkness. The only major component in the room was a sofa. It was an overstuffed cashmere love seat; it held court on an imperial floor rug. In the corner was a carving of a river flowing in a constant circle. It represented the circle of life. Another corner held a large, unorganized pile of pillows. Each one was a different color and design. The colors all fell within the hue of earth tones though. Parker imagined that to be the reading area that Sheila spoke of so often. On the wall, in front of the sofa, stood a slender oak and glass entertainment unit. Its shelves were bare except for the television, a Bose sound theater and a handful of what-nots placed sporadically about. The television, a high-density thirty-two-inch Magnavox, sat on a shelf in the center of the unit. The Bose sound theater sat just to its right. The Magnavox was on a break, but the Bose system was on the job; the last offering from the jazz acolyte George Benson was playing.

"The remote is on the table and the movie is in the player," Sheila called from her bedroom. "Make yourself at home. I'll be out in a minute."

Parker picked up the remote and sat down on the couch. It was one of the universal models that could control all of the user's electronics. A few pushed buttons brought the television up and put the stereo on break. Parker cruised through the menu until he found the correct channel for DVD play. When the screen came up, it displayed the main menu for one of Parker's favorite modern movies: "Oh Brother Where Art Thou."

"Nice pick," Parker called back to Sheila.

"Thanks," she replied as she came up the hall. "Welcome back, Blackman," she greeted. Sheila was dressed in a pair of clingy black gym shorts and a gray tank top. Her legs, smooth and shapely, glistened in the warm candlelight. Her crimson afro had been pulled back and restrained by a thick black ribbon. Drops of water clung to her hair. It sparkled.

"Are you gonna be ok while I get us some popcorn?" she asked. "Yeah, I'm straight. Take your time."

"Good," she replied and disappeared into the kitchen.

While Sheila made popcorn, Parker browsed through the special features of the DVD. He chose the actor interviews and pressed select. "When's the pizza get here?" he asked as he listened to George Clooney.

"In about an hour; I just called them," She called back from the other room. "I got two because I know that your ass can eat." Sheila walked back into the living room with a bowl of fresh Orville Redenbacher® popcorn. "So, what you got in your little goodie bag?" she asked, referring to Parker's saddlebag.

"The usual; a little of this and a little of that. Why, is there something you're needing me to get out?" Parker teased.

"Stop tripping," Sheila retorted. He remembered the last time she'd seen that bag. They had been here, in her condo, discussing her role as a nurse in the overpricing of medical care. Somehow, they had gotten on the subject of imports for medicinal purposes and Sheila had admitted an idle curiosity with the herb. She'd confessed to having never tried it because of the conflicting reports on its effects on the user. She did eventually try it though. She'd tried and liked it. She'd only partaken of the import on that particular occasion but had expressed an interest in trying it again. Now would be her opportunity, Parker thought.

Sheila handed Parker the popcorn and plopped down on the couch. "So, what are we watching first?" she asked in her usual bubbly voice.

"You got more than one movie?" Parker inquired with surprise.

"Yeah, I rented that one from the video store," Sheila replied pointing towards the movie case. "The other ones, I bought. There in the bag on the nightstand."

Parker picked up the bag and examined its contents, "The Usual Suspects," another favorite of Parker's, "Driving Miss Daisy," his guilty pleasure, and a DJ Wiz mixed CD. Baby girl had done her homework Parker thought. "What's on the CD?" Parker asked holding up the case.

"Oh, that's that good, good," Sheila returned as she took the CD from Parker. "You ain't grown enough to hear that yet, but keep at it young buck!"

"Yeah, whatever" Parker said with a smile. He reached down grabbed the remote and selected the play mode from that menu screen.

Sheila settled down on the couch and nestled in next to Parker. He looked at her strangely, as if to question her motives. Sheila, reading his eyes, but having no true understanding of their meaning, offered him popcorn.

The popcorn ran out halfway through the movie and since Parker needed to take a restroom break, they both agreed to press pause for the cause. "I'll grab the popcorn," Sheila said as she stood up from her nesting place under Parker's arm. "Use the bathroom down the hall because my other bathroom is messed up."

Parker watched her as she floated into the kitchen. She moved like one of the girls in a Sean Paul video. His arm felt strangely empty without Sheila there. He thought of the things he liked about her and found the number to be quite plentiful. "Sheila, oh Sheila," he sang quietly as he left the couch and headed for her bedroom.

Her bedroom, like her living room, was sparsely populated. A king-sized sleigh bed dominated the far-right corner. Towards the center of the left wall a golden recliner with a well-cushioned ottoman set up residence atop an ornamental throw rug. The room's only source of light came from a slender standing lamp with an oversized umbrella shade: the light it emitted was subdued. The entry to the bathroom was midway down the wall opposite the light source; the corridor just beyond the entrance served as a boudoir/vanity chest. As he passed through, Parker noted with approval how organized Sheila was. Her clothing hung in color-coordinated sections. Each section was then separated by length of shirt or trouser. Her shoes, also color-coordinated, ran from front to back: flats, mules, heels, stilettos, and boots, respectively. I wonder if this is just for me or if she's always like this, he thought. Parker wanted to know.

He peeked into the chest of drawers, and found her personals organized and divided in much the same manner as her other items; he was impressed. Parker quietly closed the drawer and entered the bathroom to do his business. When he finished washing his hands, he returned to the living room. He opened his bag and retrieved his import. Its fragrance permeated through the jar. Potent, thought Parker, potent indeed. Sheila had not yet returned from the kitchen. Parker decided to surprise her with a sampling of the import. He carefully removed two 1.5 leaves and proceeded to construct two plump offerings to the import deities.

Just as he was finishing the second leaf, Sheila returned from the kitchen.

"Hey, let me get that," Sheila commanded as she discarded the popcorn and reached for the import.

"No, my sister," Parker replied. "You must get your own." With that he produced the second of the two leaves that he'd rolled. Sheila took it with appreciation. She sat beside Parker and lit her import up. She inhaled deeply and smiled. Parker had no idea what he was in for.

Parker inhaled deeply. His respiratory system tried to expel the smoke, but the import clung to his lungs. Parker spoke between tokes, "This is nice."

"So, you plan on getting me fucked up, then taking advantage of me?" Sheila asked as she dumped her ashes.

"That's ridiculous," Parker said calmly. "Why would I have to get you fucked to do that?"

"Oh, so you're calling me a whore now? "No, I just got it like that."

"Oh, you do?"

"Don't I?" Parker asked with a smirk.

Sheila rolled her eyes at Parker and hit the import to hide her smile. "This is a funny ass movie," she said, changing the subject. "I should have rented this a long time ago."

"Yeah, I told you that, but you don't like to listen."

"Whatever. You're always running your mouth. Hey, what the hell," Sheila shouted as she turned her attention to the television. On the screen, George Clooney was singing an old folk song. The angle that the scene was shot from exaggerated his facial features. He looked almost cartoonish.

"Yeah!" shouted Parker. "I.... am a maaan of constant sorrows....I seen trouble all my days....." he sang with George.

"You know this shit," Sheila asked in astonishment.

"Yep! That song is off the yanker! Listen to them boys singing! They for real girl! That's tight!"

Sheila burst into laughter. Smoke went down the wrong pipe and she began choking. Parker started to laugh at her choking and soon he was choking too. For almost ten minutes they laughed and choked together. It wasn't until they were almost over their bout with the giggles that Parker realized that they were under the effect of the import.

"I think we've got a good buzz going," Parker said as he reached over to retrieve the DJ Whiz CD. "This is some damn good product!"

"It damn sure is," Sheila affirmed. "Here, let me see that," she asked as she reached for the CD. Parker held it out, but Sheila missed his hand and fell onto the couch. "Better than I expected," she said as she righted herself.

Parker laughed. "Obviously it is. Why don't you let me put it in," he asked, holding up the CD.

"You can do that," she said coyly.

"Yeah."

"Put it in I mean," she said with a devilish grin.

"You so wild!" Parker exclaimed with a smirk. He ignored her comment and went on. "Is this system hooked up?" he asked, referring to the Bose.

"No, the CD player is broken on that one," she said as she turned off the television. "Look on the shelf outside my bathroom. There's a player in the corner. Plug it up by the bed."

Parker went to the shelf and found the CD player. He plugged it in and placed the disc in the operating compartment. "Just start it anywhere?" Parker called back out to Sheila.

"Yeah," she replied as she came up the hall.

Parker pushed play. Several seconds passed; finally, the music started. It was the winter jam by Avant, I Can

Read Your Mind. "I love this song," Parker declared. "This song is hot!"

"You know," she replied. "You can groove to it," Sheila said as she entered the room. She started to dance. Sheila got into the song and began to dance to it. Slow, seductive dancing. She was dancing, Parker realized, for him. Parker's eyes danced over Sheila's thick thighs as the melody flooded her with sexual energy. Her hips waded seductively through it, riding the rhythms and embracing the cadence. Her eyes rested as the music guided her from one movement to another. Parker unconsciously moved forward. The swaying of Sheila's body was drawing him in.

"...I can read your mind baby..." Avant whispered. Sheila's breast did a silent serenade of their own.

"...I know what you're thinking". Sheila drew down a button, Parker drew in a breath.

".... it's alright...it's ok...." Sheila sashayed her way towards Parker with a mischievous smile. The closer she moved, the more intoxicating her movements became. Her advance slowed to a torturous pace; the music seemed to slow with her. Her moves were neither rushed nor choreographed. Instead, they were deliberate and hypnotic, impromptu and reactionary.

When Sheila was finally close enough for Parker to touch, she surprised him by playfully pushing him down onto the ottoman. She did a slow dip and drew his head to her breast as she rose. Slowly, suggestively, Sheila rubbed her body against Parker's. The melody's bass line followed her gyrations. Her hips moved in a way that communicated their desire to be caressed and held.

Parker's head pressed gently against Sheila's stomach. Her skin was warm and soft. The scent of strawberry preserves drifted from her pores. Her breast, heavy with desire, pressed anxiously against him. His hands found her back and explored its form. He traced her spine with feather touches; his fingertips danced on the small of her back.

Parker tilted his head and found Sheila's bellybutton pressed against his lips; he ran his tongue around its rim, discovering its texture and its taste. Parker bit and then kissed the miniature cavern until Sheila's back arched. He realized that she was pulling him closer, inviting his exploration.

Parker pushed forward. His hands found the hem of her shirt and dove under it, flesh now meeting flesh. Fingertips chased sensations down the length of her back, corralling them in her desire.

Sheila sighed. Parker could feel her pulse quicken. With each beat, her heart threatened to leap from her chest and join him in his. Her commitment to the moment was unquestionable.

He rose, wanting more than an intimate embrace. Parker drew Sheila to him, and their eyes met. Her eyes were beautiful, he thought. They were jewels in the sand, emeralds in ice, enthralled sunlight. He ran his hand through her crimson hair. It was soft, and fine, and kinky at the same time. Parker gave it a gentle tug. Sheila closed her eyes and let her head drift back willingly. In the candlelight, her cheekbones became more pronounced. They mirrored strength and stability. Sheila was a natural beauty, he thought silently. Parker traced her cheekbone with his index finger, beginning just below her temple and gliding down to her cheek; he traveled across her face until he came to her lips. They were full and enticing. Her lips were ripe tangerines, delicate fruit to be savored and appreciated. Parker's fingers found the entrance to Sheila's mouth, and it yielded to him. His fingertips danced on its surface. He yearned for the pleasure of her kiss. Sheila, as if she had read his mind, brought her eyes even with his in submission. Parker lowered his lips to hers. The world around him died away and an electric universe was born. Soft met with soft. Wet met with wet. This was the long pressed- against-her preamble to the glory of the near future. They were expressing emotions now, not just reacting to physical need.

Parker let his hands drop to Sheila's waist, then below her waist. He felt the soft ample flesh of her posterior. His hands kneaded it gently; Sheila moaned in approval. He gently guided her back until the bed pressed against her knees. Without comment, Sheila surrendered to gravity; Parker went with her. The bed embraced them. Their bodies melted together; the end of Sheila's body and the beginning of Parker's were indistinguishable.

He explored her body, nibbling on her neck and kissing her shoulders. With little effort, Parker removed Sheila's shirt. Underneath she wore a burgundy silk brassiere with small butterflies embroidered on its trim. Heavy breathing caused her breasts to swell each time she inhaled; the elasticity of the fabric held them captive. Parker ran his finger underneath the brassiere's edge. Sheila's flesh was warm to his touch. He slowly, deliberately unfastened the bra's clasps. Sheila's breasts rejoiced at their newfound freedom. She vocalized as much. The delicate muscles of her neck strained with need. Parker teased her shoulders with feather kisses then traveled down to her breasts. Sheila's ebony peaks stood out against her smooth butterscotch skin. Parker climbed her sweet soft summit with his tongue. The way was slow and long. When he finally arrived at its peak, he celebrated by dancing a tango with her nipple. Sheila moaned involuntarily. Parker indulged for an eternity then reluctantly descended the peak only to retrace his steps on its twin.

After a time, Parker made his way back to Sheila's lips. They kissed the passionate kiss of old lovers, wholly and completely engrossed in each other. Sheila wrapped her arms around Parker and attempted to switch their positions, but Parker denied her. He was not yet ready to relinquish control. Instead, he lifted her arms above her head and signaled for her to let them stay there. Parker broke their kiss and traveled down the valley between Sheila's breasts; he stopped briefly on the smooth flat lands of her stomach. He flooded the exposed flesh with kisses while his fingers playfully brushed at her sides.

Sheila gripped his head and urged him towards his destination.

Parker took his cue from Sheila but purposely missed his target, choosing instead to migrate to her thighs. He alternated between kisses and nips on her inner thighs.

Sheila's approval was evident by the regularity of her moans.

Moving at a snail's pace, Parker thoroughly covered all the spaces leading to his destination with butterfly kisses. Then, when there were no other places that hadn't been kissed, and other corners that hadn't been nibbled, Parker reached his destination and Sheila reached the stars.

Chapter 11

It was a great morning to wash a car. Parker had arrived back home from Sheila's at around six a.m. He'd decided to go ahead and get a jump on detailing his car before the day got away from him again. He hadn't even sat down to eat breakfast. He'd put his cell phone on the charger, his saddle bag in the closet, changed clothes and went to work on his Caddy. Parker started with the chassis; he washed his car in warm water with Dawn® detergent as the soaping agent. Then he moved to the tires and scrubbed them clean. Next, he vacuumed the interior and the trunk; he had an old shop vac that he'd rescued and nursed back to life. He then washed and oiled his dashboard and door panels. Parker cleaned all the crevices and corners thoroughly. He took his time to detail the carpet and brush down the seats. Time could not keep up with Parker. He'd been at it for two straight hours. If he hadn't needed to go inside and get his keys so that he could go to the store for a new air freshener, he'd have never known that he'd missed Sidney's call.

Parker put his keys down and picked up his phone. The cell phone's screen listed that she had called at six-thirty a.m. It was strange to have received a phone call from Sidney so early in the morning, he thought. Parker was the only person in his social circle who woke up before ten o'clock. Usually, it was him who would wake people up at the crack of dawn. Yet, Sidney had tried to contact him at six-thirty a.m. Was everything all right? he thought. Parker picked up his cell phone and checked his messages. Sidney had left a message asking him to call her. She sounded calm on the message, so Parker felt a little bit better. Still, he called her to make sure everything was all right. He dialed her home number but got no answer. Parker sat down and then dialed her cell. Sidney answered the phone on the second ring.

"Hello," Sidney answered in her normal voice.

"What's up? What had you calling me at six thirty in the morning?"

"I gotta be at a workshop at nine a.m. and it's in the A. I was trying to see if you wanted to ride along. It's too late now. I'm in McDonough."

"That's cool. I didn't feel like going to the A anyway," Parker lied. "How was your date last night?"

Sidney let out a sigh. "Man, I ended up humping my hand," she admitted in a sad voice.

"I told you about fucking with them weak ass cats that you deal with. If you can't bring him around your peoples, then he ain't worth it," Parker barked. He was not at all happy with the way Sidney hid her boyfriends from him.

"Whatever, look traffic up here is bad. I'mma have to get back with you later, alright?"

"Yeah, ok, I'll holla."

"Me too. Bye."

Parker disconnected the call and was about to put his cell phone down when it rang again. Parker didn't recognize the number but was in a pretty good mood, so he answered it anyway.

"Hello," came a strange women's voice. "Hello, is this Parker?"

"Who's calling?" he answered avoiding her question.

"Ah, this is Alfreda Redwind. I was calling for Parker," she replied respectfully.

"Oh, hey little miss, this is me," Parker replied, relieved. "I thought you were a bill collector or something! What's going on?"

Alfreda laughed. "I got a bit of an emergency," she said through her giggles. "I need to take my car to the shop, and I don't have a ride back to work. My cousin was gonna take me but she's MIA. I can't find anyone else to take me. Do you think that you could hook me up with a ride?"

This was unbelievable, Parker thought. He'd never thought that Alfreda would call him. He'd enjoyed their conversation but had thought that their contact would never go farther than that.

"Sure," Parker said, trying not to sound too anxious. "It's gonna cost you lunch though."

"That's cool. I can buy you lunch," Alfreda agreed.

"No, not buy me lunch, go to lunch with me," Parker corrected.

Alfreda was quiet for a moment.

"You know I have a boyfriend, Parker."

"And? I don't want to go on a date; I just want to eat some lunch. You think much too highly of yourself," Parker said in his funniest sarcastic voice. "Let's just see if I can bear to eat around you first and then we'll go from there, ok?"

Alfreda laughed. Ok, I'll go to lunch with you. Just don't try to get me to cheat on my man, ok?" she asked sincerely.

"Ok. Deal. We won't even have to talk about your relationship or any kind of relationship for that matter. Let's just get something to eat. What time shall I meet you? Wait a minute, you look sneaky. We better go to lunch first, and then I'll take you."

"You're so crazy," Alfreda said. "Ok, we can go to lunch first, but you better not stand me up! I'll meet you in the new park by the bridge on Spring Street at eleven."

"What time do you have to drop the car off?"

"At 3:30," she replied.

"That's a bet," Parker confirmed. "I'll see you then.

Parker ended his call. The day was going great, he thought. He went back in to get the wax for his car.

The day was a beautiful one. The warmth of the sun had settled in upon the earth and a nice cool breeze had stopped by to visit. Nature sang a melody; an orchestra of birds presented the high end of an original sonata while the Ocmulgee's rushing waves and crashing currents provided the tenor. A choir of crickets, beetles and other insects added accompaniment. Autos passing in the distance took notice of the outdoor concert and honked and screeched and revved their engines in lieu of applause. It was a day worthy of the appreciation by all who were in the mind to appreciate such things. Parker happened to be among those who did appreciate nature's magnificence. The day was perfect for a picnic and the hidden alcove was the perfect location.

The alcove was a spot that Parker liked to go to when he wanted to enjoy nature without having to actually go to the country. It was quiet, close to an interstate, and just downright beautiful. Parker had only been waiting for about three minutes when Alfreda arrived.

She pulled up in a white Toyota Camry with smoke gray tint. Her car was sensible; standard alloy rims and a modest ex package. She hesitated for a moment then whipped into the parking space on Parker's right. Alfreda sat there for a moment, Parker supposed, fixing her makeup or working out her last-minute jitters. He sought to make her more comfortable, so he exited the Cadillac and went around to her driver's side door. When she noticed him there, she smiled and rolled down her window.

"Hey," she said in her quaint southern drawl. "Sorry about that. I was just finishing up a call to my mother."

"No problem. You always want to let somebody know where you are just in case your date turns out to be a psycho," Parker offered leisurely.

"You're a fool," Alfreda replied with a grin. "But you're right! I was telling my mama where to find me so that if you try to abduct me or something she'll know where to come looking."

"Child, I don't need anybody else to be taking care of," Parker said as leaned against his car. "It's hard enough feeding me. Kidnappers have to feed and clothe their hostages. Your ass would be hungry and naked!"

Alfreda laughed and started to get out of her car. Parker opened her door, and she stepped out. She was dressed in classic outdoors wear. She wore khaki slacks with a white button-down blouse. The slacks fit snug to her waist and her well-shaped posterior, then flared out towards the bottom. The blouse had three-quarter length sleeves and mock cuffs. Black patent leather boots adorned her feet. Alfreda grabbed her purse and then addressed Parker.

"Don't be trying to get my bootie, now Parker. I told you I have a man, ok?"

"First of all, I couldn't get all your bootie in one trip if I tried," he said staring at Alfreda's generous backside. "Secondly, I'm a gentleman, and unless forced to, I try never to bring up any subject that may make my lady friend uncomfortable. It's rude."

Alfreda laughed hysterically. "Why are you so crazy! You just be saying things! Does your mama know about you?"

"Yes, and she's very happy with the way I turned out," Parker said as he lifted the picnic basket from the back seat.

"What's that," Alfreda asked in a curious voice.

"Oh, that," Parker said, referring to the contents of the basket, "is our lunch."

"Uh! We're going on a picnic!"

"Yep. Just like Miss Daisy and Huk in Driving Miss Daisy," he answered in his best southern accent.

Alfreda continued to laugh. "Where are we gonna eat?" she asked.

"I figured we'd walk until we found a spot that suited our taste. Is that alright with you?"

"That's fine with me."

"Well let's get to walking then," Parker said as he closed his car door and started towards the trail. "And don't you be trying to get my bootie while I'm out here either," Parker warned. "I'm saving myself."

"For what," she asked.

"For Christmas, baby, for Christmas."

They walked and talked for an hour. No specific topic dominated the conversation. They didn't seem to need one. Their discussions were natural. They lead into each other. They spoke of politics and religion, of literature and music; they spoke a little on everything. They shared the soapbox. Parker and Alfreda were getting along nicely. When they finally decided to stop and have their lunch, Alfreda made a confession.

***

"I've never been on a picnic before. This is my first one."

"Well, I'm happy to oblige," Parker said in his cheeriest voice. "Here let me lay out this blanket and we can have a seat." Parker spread the blanket out before them and placed the picnic basket in its center. "Have a sit, my lady," he said with a sweeping gesture.

"Thank you. You're such a gentleman."

"Well, I try." Parker handed Alfreda a sandwich and started looking for the mayonnaise packets. "I have water and Sprite. Some people are on the healthy kick stuff you know."

"Oh, I'm not one of them. I like my soda and my chicken!"

"Good cause that's what I've got!"

They laughed and divided up the eateries. Parker had packed an eight piece from Churches Chicken with a family-sized mash potato and corn, two apples, a box of raisins, two honey buns, two bottles of water, a pitcher of Lemonade, a king-sized Almond Joy and a mason jar filled with a nice blend of Bohemian import. Sheila was overjoyed. They ate silently. Around them the birds carried on conversations among themselves. The breeze brought in tidbits of sound from a nearby family. Cars periodically zoomed down an adjacent street. While they finished eating, Parker pulled out an import and offered it to Alfreda. She smiled and accepted it graciously. They toked in silence, each riding the euphoria to their own personal paradise. Periodically their worlds would converge, and they would catch themselves staring at each other.

They had chemistry. They both felt it, but that subject was taboo. Parker had agreed not to talk about a romantic relationship. Their interaction was to remain strictly platonic, much to the disappointment of them both.

Parker sat back and looked across the sky. "So why are you mad with your boyfriend?"

"It's not that I'm mad at him, it's just that I'm not happy," Alfreda said as she lay down on the blanket next to Parker.

"Explain," Parker requested.

"Well, he and I aren't matched well; you know what I'm saying? We've been together for a long time, I mean since high school, but when I went away to college we seem to grow in different directions. I started liking different things, wanting to go different places, but he wanted to do the same stuff that we'd always been doing. That kind of redundancy grows old fast. I just feel like I've outgrown him, you know? I mean, I love him. He's always been good to me, but is that enough? Is it enough that somebody's good to you?"

"Well, that depends on what you want. If all you're looking for is someone to help pay the bills and take care of you then maybe that is enough. What about romance? Is he romantic?"

"Hell naw! I get the same tired ass box of candy every Valentine's Day. If we go out, we go to Red Lobster. Don't get me wrong, I like Red Lobster, but sometimes I want something different, you know?" Parker nodded his head in agreement and Alfreda went on. "Like this picnic; I've never been on a picnic before. Why doesn't he do things like this? It's not expensive. We probably spent more on drinks at Red Lobster than you spent on this entire meal."

"Oh yeah, call me the cheap skate," Parker spoke sarcastically.

"That's not what I mean," Alfreda corrected. "I'm not calling you cheap. I love what you've done here. It's just that I wish I could get my boyfriend to do stuff like this."

"So, I'm good for inspiration but not relations? I see how it goes down now," Parker joked.

Alfreda laughed gingerly. "You're so silly! Can't you be serious for just a minute?" she asked.

"OK," Parker said in a sober tone. "Seriously, I think you're a very attractive young woman. Your intelligence amazes me. Your beauty astounds me. If I had it my way, you would be my woman. You'd have surprise picnics in the park and flowers for no reason and kisses for every reason and 'I love you's' for all reasons. I don't have my way though, so instead let me tell you what I would do. I would ask myself how upset I would be if this person left me. I would ask myself why I would be upset. If your answer to the first question is not very and your answer to the second question has nothing to do with love, then I would leave. You're only wasting your time and his if you stay."

Alfreda was quiet. She looked across the field at a passing vehicle. Parker imagined that she was thinking of a nice way to tell him to go to hell. She had a right to, he thought. He had broached the forbidden subject. He had mentioned something other than a platonic relationship between them. She had pushed the issue, however. She had insisted on hearing his opinion, and he had given it to her.

"I like you too," Alfreda said quietly. "I do. I've got a man though, and I need you to respect that."

"I do," Parker replied.

"Good. Then I can say what I need to say. I like you. I think you're a nice guy. I would like nothing better than to learn about you, to get to know who you are. I have a man though. I'm not happy with him but he's still my man. That means there's a certain amount of respect that he deserves and I'm going to make sure that I give it to him. That's why I don't want to talk about relationships. That way, when he and I are over, it's because it's over, not because of the idea of you and me. I know how attracted I am to you. I know how much I enjoy being around you. I can only justify being around you if it's understood that we're just friends."

They sat quietly. Parker thought about what she had said. He thought of her troubled relationship and the possibility of a future for him and her. He also thought of Sheila and her desire to be with him. She'd made it known, in no uncertain terms, that she wanted him in her life on a more permanent basis.

But what of Alfreda's declaration? She liked him also. Her words hinted at the possibility of a future for them. What should he do about that?

"I have a son you know."

Parker's heart stopped. She has a child. What now?

Alfreda read his expression and responded. "Oh, so you have issues with a woman with kids?" she asked cautiously

"No," Parker lied. "I didn't imagine you with kids. It's not so much an issue as it is a new bit of information."

"Does that make you less likely to date me?" she asked tentatively.

"I couldn't date you anyway."

***

"Why not?"

"Because you won't date me."

"But if it I would?"

"Would what?"

"Would date you?"

"Then what?"

"What if I would date you, how would you feel about me having a child then?"

Parker thought hard. It had always been taboo for him to think of serious relationships with a woman who already had kids. It was a type of situation he had always been wary of.

It wasn't that he didn't like kids. It was that he didn't like sharing. He was never really comfortable around kids. Probably a hungover phobia from high school; his face was ice. No movement, no emotion, just pure control.

"I'm not really sure what you're used to in a man, but I guess that it's fitting me. I'm not into the whole hating on parents thing. You have responsibilities that were present before I met you. I can respect that. Yours just happened to come in the form of a child. Some men have a problem with that. I can respect that, but, as for me, I don't limit myself like that. I see it like this: either I can appreciate your motherhood status as another beautiful thing about you, or I can squander the opportunity to create something beautiful with the most magnificent creature in existence."

Parker saw Alfreda blush and registered this crisis in the "W" column. He had dated women with children before. They were some of the most faithful and giving, but he had never, ever considered them for life-long mates. It would tie him to an obligation that he had not deserved. Parker didn't have a problem with the obligations of mothers; he just had a problem sharing that obligation.

His issue, he felt, made him somewhat less of a man. It made him obviously shallow, and he hated himself for it. His flaw was in this knowledge: once it was time to commit, he would exit. It was as predictable as the rising of the sun. Parker would not put that kind of pressure on himself. It simply wasn't a level of responsibility he was willing to accept. He watched Alfreda's response to his statement, and he smiled inwardly.

"That was beautiful," she responded.

"It was the truth," he replied.

"Oh, I know it was," she affirmed with a twinkle of sarcasms. "No really, its how I feel."

"Oh," she responded disappointed.

"What," he asked.

"You know what Parker," she asked rhetorically. "Men say that to a sister thinking she'll believe it, when they don't even believe it themselves. And they think that we don't see it. If you believed that, then you really would have a chance at something beautiful. Most men haven't gleaned that knowledge. They're still thinking that it's about the responsibility. It's not. It's about the privilege of shaping the destiny of a young life. It's about believing in yourself so much that you can promise God that you'll succeed. It's about sharing those unique experiences with someone new. And seeing all that love reflected back at you."

Parker was sick to his stomach. The thought of that type commitment terrified him. He closed his mind to the idea and collected himself before his feelings registered on his face. He flashed back a smile to diffuse the situation and redirected the conversation.

"I have an idea," he presented.

"And what's that?" Alfreda asked carefully.

"How about we be friends?" Parker asked. "That way, we can still enjoy each other's company without all the nasty stigmas of infidelity and "responsiphobia?"

"You're so crazy," Alfreda shouted in laughter.

"Yeah, but you like it," Parker said with a smirk.

Alfreda attacked him with a honey bun.

Parker and Alfreda lay on the blanket talking to each other and staring at the clouds. They'd had an after-dinner smoke and the import had them both in a very pleasant mood. They laughed and argued like old friends. They'd eaten all the food in the basket and had, on two separate occasions, tried unsuccessfully to have pizza delivered to the alcove; unfortunately, 'round the corner from that fishing spot' wasn't in any of the pizza shop's delivery areas. So, they'd settled on food for the soul; old fashioned conversation as the main course with laughter and shouting as the side items. The current course included a discussion on Alfreda's relationship.

She and Parker had originally agreed not to talk about relationships or romance, but that covenant had only lasted for the first hour and a half. They had now amended their covenant to say that they wouldn't talk about a relationship with each other; that they were able to adhere to, most of the time.

"Do you love him," Parker asked in a hesitant tone.

"Yes," Alfreda replied, as she traced shapes in the clouds with her finger. "He's always been there for me plus helps provide for my child. That he would show that much concern for my loved ones is admirable. So yes, pretty sure I love him."

"You're pretty sure," Parker questioned as he inhaled the import. "What does that mean?"

"It means that I'm pretty sure I still love him."

"What, you used to love him more than you love him now?"

"No," Alfreda corrected. "I knew I loved him back in high school; now I haven't started hating him as a person, so I guess I still love him." Alfreda rolled a leaf between her fingers. The leaf tore and split but refused to break apart.

Parker took a hit off the import. He rolled the smoke over his tongue and then jettisoned it down his trachea. The import settled into his lungs for a peace occupation. Parker turned toward Alfreda and continued the conversation.

"Do you know what love is," he asked.

"Yes, I do," Alfreda replied.

"What is it?" Parker pressed.

"Huh?" asked Alfreda

"What is your definition of love?" Parker clarified.

"Love is love," Alfreda replied, a little flustered. "Caring about a person. It's when you want to make a person happy," she answered with a little more confidence. "Love is the commitment that two people make between each other. That's love."

"Ok, I can accept that," Parker commented. "That's what you do when you're in love, but what is love to you?"

"I just told you, bonehead!"

"No, you told me what you do when you're in love. You care about someone when you're in love. You want to make someone happy when you're in love with someone. But that's not what love is."

"Ok, so tell me what love is then, Dr. Phil," Alfreda said sarcastically.

"Alright. Love isn't how you feel about someone; it's how they make you feel about yourself."

"Say what?", Alfreda exclaimed.

"I said that love isn't how you feel about someone; it's how they make you feel about yourself." "Ok, explain."

"When you say you love someone, it's because of the way you feel when you're with them, and not just physically with them; when you're with them with them. When you're with that person, you feel beautiful and important and smart and sexy. They make you feel that way, and it's not that you don't already know you're all those things; it's that they appreciate those things about you so much that it boosts your awareness of them. That's love, the way that person makes you feel about yourself."

Alfreda rolled over on her stomach. Her posterior sat well above the small of her back. Parker took note of it; Alfreda took note of Parker taking note of it and smiled.

"So do you love someone," she asked. "My sister and my mother," Parker replied.

"So, you're not seeing anyone," Alfreda pressed on.

"I date, if that's what you mean. I'm not in love though," Parker said matter-of-factly. He kicked at a spot in the grass with his heel. After a few kicks, the surface began to form a trench.

"Have you ever been in love?" Alfreda asked, interrupting Parker's excavation work.

"I think I knew love once."

"You think?"

"Well, it was a while ago. I haven't known love for quite some time."

"How long?" Alfreda inquired as she plucked at the blades of grass in front of her.

"Let's just say that the last time I was in love," Parker spoke, "I had on a lettermen's jacket."

"Damn! Why was it so long ago? You haven't found anybody to love you since then?"

"It's hard to get over heartbreak."

"But that hard? And that long? That's ridiculous! You need therapy."

"Probably," Parker said as he rolled over on his back. He grabbed a hand full of grass and pulled it from the soil. "I can't help that though. I have to be me. I hope one day I will find love again. Until then though, I'll have fun and love life."

Alfreda smiled. Parker smiled. They both smiled and partook of the import.

Chapter 12

Lunch with Alfreda had been the highlight of Parker's day. Now, as he sat at downtown Macon's trendy Dessert's First Café, he fed on that energy to calm his nerves. He was meeting with Deputy Dunkin. She would be arriving soon. The thought of being in such close proximity with the police made him nervous. He would have to control that nervousness. It could definitely work to a disadvantage should his soon-to-arrive guest detect it.

An unmarked squad car pulled up to the curb and Parker's heart skipped a beat. He sipped on his cola and waited to see who would be exiting the vehicle. A well-dressed attractive female wearing a black pants suit stepped out of the car. She was carrying a black leather attaché case.

Parker stood as she entered the café. "Detective DeSha Dunkin I presume," he said with an extended hand.

"Yes, and you must be Parker Grant," the lady said as she took the hand extended her. "Your pictures don't do you justice. "The detective took her seat and promptly ordered two cherry malts. "It's my treat since I picked the location," she insisted.

The two sat in the café and discussed life for a full thirty minutes before they actually began the interview. Parker learned that the detective was single with no children and that she lived alone with a pet guinea pig named Email. She joked about the way the rodent constantly licked its own ass. Parker laughed. They went through all the pleasantries of a first date without being on a date before Parker even approached the subject of identity theft.

"So, explain what you think has caused this recent rash of identity theft cases in the area," Parker asked casually.

"I'm betting it's a cashier or a ring of cashiers at a local supermarket, maybe Super Wal-Mart. They're hitting people with low- grade scamming. They write like ten checks in stores with low-grade technology and then dump the account before the person finds out what's going on."

"Are they stealing the check books?" Parker inquired.

"No. They're using computer technology that prints the checks right off the computer. Thy download them, then go at it," the Detective answered.

"How about I.D.?" Parker questioned. "How do they get around that?"

"Most places don't even check for I.D. They just look on the front of the check, and if the driver's license number and a telephone number are listed, they're fine with it."

"They use a fake license number and phone number," Parker inquired.

"No, it's authentic. All the information is current," DeSha answered between slurps.

"So, the thief has the driver's license and phone numbers of the victims too?"

"In some case, the social too. I've got a couple of victims who had cars rented in their names and everything. Then the police show up at their house responding to a stolen car report and they don't know what the hell's going on." DeSha stirred her drink suggestively. "Are you married, Parker Grant?"

"No Deputy Dunkin," Parker replied. "I'm single like you."

"We should be single together sometime," DeSha offered.

"That would be interesting," Parker said from behind an unreadable face. "Do you think I could talk with a couple of the victims? I want to get a more personal view of the effects of identity theft. Then maybe we could meet again and compare notes."

"I thought that might be something you'd like to do so I took the liberty of contacting some of them and asking if they'd mind talking to you." Deputy Dunkin reached into her attaché and retrieved a manila folder. She placed it on the table between them and opened it to the first page. "This is Connie Jenkins," DeSha stated, referring to the case in front of them. "I think you should start with her."

DeSha went over ten cases with Parker. She was thoroughly familiar with each of the cases, as well as the similarities each case shared. They talked about the possible leads and the dead ends.

When they had finished going over the files, four milk shakes had been consumed along with a dozen chocolate chunk cookies. Parker had managed to get out of going out with DeSha and DeSha had managed to bestow her home and cell number on Parker. All parties were satisfied.

"So, I'll expect to hear from you Parker Grant," The Detective stated on her way out of the café.

"You will," Parker said holding up the folder with her information on it. "Have a nice day DeSha Dunkin."

"You too, Parker Grant."

Parker called Sheila from the car and popped the change of plans on her. She was a little taken back by the idea of going to a stranger's home for drinks, but other than that she made no complaints. Perhaps it was because she didn't have the whole story.

Parker only told Sheila that they were going to have drinks and maybe hang out by the pool with a lady friend of his; he did not mention his lady friend's desire to be their playmate. That, Parker thought, was something that you just let happen. At least that's what he planned to do. With the right talk game and an ounce of his finest import, something was going to happen.

Parker arrived at Sheila's place at ten minutes to eight. It had only been two days since his last trip there, but everything looked different now. The same oak trees stood guard on the block but now they looked menacing, almost aggressive. The electric lanterns all shined their spotlights accusingly on Parker. Could the neighborhood read his karma, he wondered? Was nature privy to the invisible colors of the soul? Was his indecision so obvious to the world? His conversation with Alfreda made him question his new commitment to Sheila. Was Sheila who he really wanted to be involved with on a long-term basis? Would it be better to just wait on Alfreda, and keep Sheila on the side? He'd been here before; these thoughts were not new to him. He was a serial monogamist. Parker shook the idea out of his head and rang Sheila's doorbell. This was not the time, he thought. He was about to embark on one of his personal fantasies. He would not let his conscience fuck it up.

Sheila answered the door in a sassy black skirt with a matching blouse. Her countenance was extraordinary. She radiated a casual beauty. Parker drank her in with thirsty eyes. She smiled at him and did a little spin. The dress clung to her hips in fear of being thrown loose.

"Hot mama," Parker declared. "I'm scared of you!"
"Stop playing," Sheila said playfully. "Let's go!"

Tamena and her husband lived in an affluent community on the fringes of Bibb County. All the houses were valued in the $400,000 and up range. The streets were set up so that the farther back into the neighborhood a person went, the more lavish and expensive the homes got. The street Tamena lived on happened to be the second to the last street in the subdivision. This meant two things: one, that she and her husband had paid a good deal for their home, and two, it was a nice home. They had a very nice house. Between her husband's salary as a military officer and her salary as a research scientist, they had done very well for themselves. Their home was among the largest in their neighborhood. It was a single-story unit, but it spread out across well over half an acre. There was a pool in the rear and a patio by a side door. There were six bedrooms and eight baths. Tamena's husband had a game room for his entertainment, and she had a personal study for hers. There was a sitting room, a den, a living room, a receiving room, a breakfast room, a dining room, a kitchen and an atrium. They had a full basement that had been remodeled into a guest suite; it had two additional bedrooms, 1.5 baths, a full kitchen, and a living room. The house was expansive. As for the architecture, it was designed in the Floridian/ Spanish style with just a hint of Tudor. Parker had taken a tour of the property when he first started seeing Tamena. He'd been nervous about the details surrounding their involvement. Sleeping with another man's wife in the man's house bothered him back then; he felt like he was destroying another man's home.

That was several years ago. It hadn't taken Parker more than three visits to Tamena's to get over that feeling. Nowadays, that feeling seemed to be returning to him. He found himself thinking about things differently. Would someone be sleeping with his wife when he was away on business?'

Parker shook his head clear as he came around to open Sheila's door. As soon as he opened it, she popped out and kissed him. When she broke the kiss Parker took a good look at her. She was glowing. Her skin was absolutely glowing.

"Shall we go?" Parker suggested, offering his hand to the lady. "Why certainly, good gentleman," she replied, taking the hand offered.

Parker put his bag over his shoulder and headed for the front door. Two columns stood to either side of it. The front door, which served as the home's main entrance, stood open, but a full glass screen door helped maintain the illusion of security from the outside world. Just inside stood Tamena, ready to welcome them in.

"Welcome to my home," she said to Sheila as they reached the door. "My name is Tamena." She extended her hand in invitation.

"Thank you," Sheila replied as she took the offered hand. "I'm Sheila. It's very nice to meet you."

"As it is to meet you. Come in please," Tamena said as she stepped away from the door to allow them access. "What's up Parker?"

***

"Nothing much girl how about you," he answered as he walked into the receiving room.

"Oh, just been doing some cooking. Can I take your coat and your bag?"

"Damn girl!" Parker commented as he took off his coat. "What are you cooking up in here? It sure smells good."

"Thank you," Tamena said as she took his coat and bag. "A sister tries her best."

"Well, if that ain't your best, it damn sure smells like it; and we haven't eaten yet? Whoa! I hope that's for us!"

"You know it is," Tamena confirmed as she led them towards the kitchen. "I don't get to entertain often. I have to make the best of it."

She led them into the kitchen. It was a very spacious area. The entire kitchen was outfitted with stainless steel fixtures. The major appliances in the space included an industrial strength dishwasher, a large refrigerator, a metallic cookware shelf/utensil rack, and two oversized island food preparation and presentation areas. The two island units located in the center of the room held the meal their host had so thoughtfully prepared.

On one island, Tamena had installed a range; it was a flat top electric unit with a shiny black surface. The range's front burners held two large steaming dishes. One dish, they discovered, held soft spicy long grain rice with thin slices of bell pepper added for zest. The other dish, prepared in a deep skillet, was a mix of beef slices and exotic vegetables. The aromas that Tamena used to draw them in came from this dish. Even before he tasted it, Parker knew that the dish represented fine cuisine at its best. The flavors, Parker imagined, would complement each other well.

On the second island, Tamena had set up a makeshift salad bar. A collection of salad condiments was spread out on the surface in clear glass bowls and plates: tomatoes, onions, scallops, cucumbers, celery and shredded cheddar and Swiss cheese were arranged in two neat columns, one on each side of the island. There was also a small contention of bacon bits and croutons in attendance. Salad dressings were gathered at the center of the unit. Several dinner plates were stacked on one of the corners.

Tamena picked two up and handed them to her guests. She then informed them of the dinner rules. "This is a buffet ya'll, so you're gonna have to fix your own plates,"

"See how people treat you when you come to their house? They treat you all common and whatnot. That ain't business," Parker protested in comedic fashion.

"Stop whining," Tamena retorted.

"Let me get that for you," Sheila offered reaching for Parker's plate.

"Oh no," Tamena said and stepped between the two. "This is a buffet in a declared feminist's home. Fix your own damn plate," she ordered pushing Parker's plate away.

"Stop hating on me," Parker exclaimed with a smirk. "A brother can't even accept a little courtesy without the 'black Janice Joplin' jumping down my back." They all giggled but Parker knew that he would be fixing his own plate this evening. He truly didn't mind. He retracted his plate and began to spoon on rice.

Tamena led them to a round glass table in the breakfast room. They sat and had dinner. Tamena turned on the television that sat on a nearby counter. She then disappeared down the hall and returned with the Queens of Comedy DVD. "Ya'll cool with watching this?" she asked, holding up the case.

Both Parker and Sheila nodded their heads in agreement. They watched it between their conversations and their eating.

Dinner was wonderful. Parker finished eating before the ladies and decided to have an after-dinner leaf. He retrieved his supplies from his bag and returned to the table.

"Do you ever get tired of smoking?" Tamena asked as she finished up the last of her rice and emptied her glass. Sheila giggled but thought better of commenting.

"Actually, I don't," Parker responded as he removed the El Producto from its glass case. "I smoke when I have an inkling. I don't say anything about the way you inhale daiquiris." Tamena put down her daiquiri glass and assumed an innocent expression. Parker went on. "I don't smoke often. I smoke when I smoke though. That's me. I'm not hurting anyone," he announced as he evacuated the contents of the cigar.

"That's not what studies say," Tamena countered as she picked her daiquiri back up.

"What studies? Do studies carry more weight than real-life evidence? I'll tell you what I know. I don't suffer from any side effects. I enjoy it and I'm going to keep on enjoying it because it smokes good!"

"You're damn right it does," Tamena saluted and took another drink

"It's the equivalent of a nice cigar," Parker concluded as he finished up his construction project and held it up for inspection.

"I'll smoke to that," Sheila said

"Hell, so will I," admitted Tamena, "but not in here though. Let's retire to my study." Tamena rose from her seat and walked over to the entertainment center. "Everybody grab their dishes and dropped them off on the way to the study. I'm not anybody's mama or maid." She recovered the DVD from the player and headed toward the kitchen. True to her word, Tamena took them through the kitchen so they could deposit their dishes into the sink.

Tamena led them through several rooms into the back of the house. When they reached the study, she told them to make themselves comfortable and stepped out of the room.

The room's furniture was more of a cross between a psychiatrist's office and a ritzy waiting room than a study. The carpet was thick and soft and cushiony. Parker's feet sank into it. The study held a long paisley couch with a recliner of the same pattern. A fifty-two-inch flat-screen television hung on a wall adjacent to the couch. A small entertainment cabinet was mounted to the wall next to the flat screen; it held a DVD player and a small high-end stereo system. The wall with the main entrance to the study served as home to Tamena's library; the floor-to-ceiling bookshelf held a great number of volumes that Parker wanted to read: New Negro Spirituals, Worldwide by D. Red, Corn Rolls by S. T. Kid and the new B. Righteous Novel Big Bad Benny Johnson. In a corner, a small mahogany roll top desk sat with scattered paperwork littering its surface. It looked to be more of a disorganized file cabinet than a workstation. Beside the desk was the entrance to the guest bedroom. The door was open, but everything beyond the door was hidden in darkness.

The study, however, was well lit. Track lighting stretched the length of the ceiling in two neat rows. They were connected to a dimmer switch, which was on high when they entered the room. Tamena dimmed the lights and then went to put the DVD in the player.

Parker sat down on the sofa; Sheila came and sat down beside him. Tamena returning from the other room, sat down in the recliner as the flat screen came to life. Parker lit the import and inhaled deeply.

"This is a very fine import," Parker commented.

"Must you constantly talk as if you're the connoisseur of award-winning wines?" Tamena teased.

"Yeah!" Sheila cosigned. "He's always acting like it's sophisticated to smoke that peculiar little leaf; like he expects Robin Leech to come and interview him as some world-renowned expert on it or something! He even buys cigars in these little glass bottles," she continued as she held up the El Producto casing.

The ladies laughed. Parker feigned anger but couldn't help laughing a little in spite of himself. "See, that just goes to show how much you two know about cigars," he retorted as he inhaled the import. "An El Producto is a very fine over-the-counter--"

"Over-the-counter?"

"Yes, it's an over-the-counter cigar. It can be bought outside of a cigar shop. Now, as I was saying, it's a very fine over-the-counter cigar." Parker closed his eyes and exhaled. "It makes for very fine smoking indeed." He passed the import to Sheila who took it with very little coaxing.

Monique, the comedian currently featured on the screen made a joke about sex that everyone thought was funny. They all laughed, including Sheila who happened to be inhaling the import at the time. She began choking which brought about more laughter from her constituents. She took another pull and passed the leaf to Tamena.

"You tell it, Monique!" Sheila exclaimed as she passed the import to her host. "Do what you gotta do!"

Tamena took a second pull of the leaf and passed it to Parker.

"So, what do ya'll really think about doing erotic stuff for your man?" Parker asked as he dumped the ashes.

"I believe that you do what you have to do to keep your lover happy," Tamena jumped in. "If my sorry-ass husband did what I needed him to do sexually, I wouldn't have to get it elsewhere. The days of a sister going without are over!"

"You tell it, girl," Sheila said and hopped up to give Tamena a high five. Parker passed her the import.

Tamena went on. "Sexuality is something that you should share with your mate. It isn't about the selfishness of being close-minded to your lover's curiosities."

"Yeah," Sheila added between puffs, "the bottom line is you give it to him like he likes it. That way he has no excuse to get it anywhere else."

"There it is sister!" Tamena yelled and raised her glass in toast. The two women toasted and began chattering about giving it to their man like their man likes it. Parker interrupted them.

"Where's this alcohol that you promised us?" he asked. "Ya'll complain about my import but ya'll steady smoking it!"

"Hold on girl," Tamena said to Sheila. "Let me get the liquor so I don't have to kill this Negro!" They all laughed as Tamena exited the room. When she was gone, Parker nuzzled up next to Sheila and asked if she was having a good time.

"I'm having a good time baby," she replied as she kissed Parker on the neck.

"Good. Now, are you going to pass the import or what?" Sheila giggled and relinquished the leaf.

Tamena returned. She had two bottles in one hand, three glasses in the other, and a bottle under each arm. "The drinks are here!" she shouted.

Tamena sat the bottles on the floor in front of the couch and handed everyone a glass. Then, instead of sitting back in the recliner, she sat on the floor next to Sheila. Parker noticed the change in sitting arrangements but made no mention of it.

"Ladies first," she offered as she held up the tequila for Sheila's approval. Sheila accepted and poured a generous portion into her glass.

"I love tequila," she said. "It gets you going. Keep pouring this stuff and I'm going to be off the chain!"

Tamena poured herself a glass and looked at Parker. "And for yourself, dear gentleman, what will it be?"

Parker surveyed the bottles that Tamena had brought with her. There was gin vodka, tequila, and orange juice. "I believe I'll have the juice please.

"Come on now Parker. We're trying to have a good time. Why do you have to be so difficult? Have a drink!"

"Naw, I know what I'm doing. I'm a smoker not a drinker."

Chapter 13

Sometime during the night, they fell into the habit of playing poker. How, they didn't know. But it provided them with uncountable amounts of fun. They sat around on the floor of the study smoking the import, drinking the tequila and playing cards. Their varied strategies and skill levels made for interesting play. It was discovered that Parker was the more knowledgeable player, making him the game's professional, but that Tamena's poker face was not to be underestimated. Sheila was neither shrewd nor very knowledgeable of the game, but she played it with reserve and thus tended to win more than she lost; she was the safe player. Since money was in short supply, at least as far as Parker was concerned, they played for favors: car washes, massages, movie tickets and the lot. They used Oreos, Vanilla Wafers, and jellybeans for money markers, but this was detrimental to Parker as the import more than once persuaded him to devour his winnings. The upper hand fluctuated between the three cardsharps for some time, but in the end, the safe player won the largest jackpot. Among the spoils of her victory were six free car washes from Parker and a foot massage from Tamena. Tamena won a back massage from Parker but opted for a rain check. She did, however, decide to go ahead and issue payment to Sheila because of the uncertainty of their seeing each other again.

Sheila rose from the floor and took up her previous position on the couch. She then removed her shoes and presented her feet to Tamena.

"Nice pedicure girl!" Tamena exclaimed as she inspected Sheila's feet. "I can appreciate a woman who takes care of her toes." Parker nodded in approval as he too relocated to the couch. Sheila's feet were well sculpted; her toes were nicely defined. Her toenails were painted to match her fingernails and other accessories. They were well-oiled and held a faint strawberry scent.

Tamena ran to an adjacent bathroom and returned with a bottle of baby oil. "Gotta do it right," she said as she opened up the bottle and squeezed a liberal amount into her palm. She took a seat on the carpet in front of Sheila. She then placed her hands on Sheila's feet and proceeded to massage her.

"Mmm," Sheila moaned as she closed her eyes and leaned back onto the couch. "That feels so good."

Tamena massaged with a purpose. She was soft but firm, straightforward but seductive. She sent the energy of her karma through her fingers and into Sheila's sole. Sheila squirmed with delight. She unconsciously arched her back and moaned to the same rhythms as the music. Tamena's movements were gentle yet intense. Each touch, pull, and grasp was suggestive. Parker noticed her technique and applauded them silently.

The atmosphere was exotic and ethereal. The combination of the music and the import had a hypnotic effect. The import made the music so much more appreciated. The music made the import so much more intense. The potent import relaxed Sheila's body and freed her mind; it seemed to make the moment much more enjoyable.

They all grooved to the music. Tamena sang softly as she massaged Sheila's feet.

Parker started to massage Sheila's neck in time with the rhythm. She leaned into him and placed her head on his chest. Parker responded by reaching over and kissing Sheila. Sheila kissed him back with an import-driven passion.

Tamena saw her opportunity and took it. She moved her massage from Sheila's feet to her calf. Sheila did not resist.

Tamena's massage intensified. She alternated her movements between a feather touch and a deep tissue. Her technique had smoothly transitioned from therapeutic to erotic.

Meanwhile, Parker nibbled playfully on Sheila's lips. They were soft and pliable to his endeavors. He held her lips, each in turn, between his own and caressed them with his tongue. Her response was to lean in closer to him. As far as Parker could tell, Sheila was no longer even conscious of Tamena, and if she was, she didn't object to her being there. Perhaps she had already guessed what his plan for the evening had been. Her discussion from earlier in the evening came to mind; she told Tamena that she'd do what it took to keep her man happy. Did she know that this was his fantasy? Did she understand how close she was to fulfilling it?

Tamena moved her hands to Sheila's knee and let her massage take on a much more sensual tone. The skilled touch of her hands gave immense pleasure; this was evident by Sheila's moans.

Parker moved his hand from Sheila's shoulder to her breast and gently squeezed. Sheila moaned into Parker's mouth in response. He pushed up her blouse and began to caress her breast through her bra.

Sheila was highly aroused. Tamena seemed to have discovered this and moved her concentration from Sheila's knee to her thighs. Sheila discovered that she had opened her legs in invitation.

Parker dropped his head to Sheila's neck and began to nibble. He softly bit and then sucked at the crook of her neck. A loud low moan escaped Sheila's throat. The sexual energy surrounding her was almost visible. It rose from her body like the heat from a desert road. Each time he nibbled, she jerked involuntarily.

He needed to feel Sheila's body. He wanted to place his flesh against her flesh. He was intoxicated by Sheila's moans, and the thumping of the music and Tamena's advances. He raced his fingers along the flesh of Sheila's stomach before diving his hand under her blouse and making contact with the flesh of her breast. He was rewarded with moans of approval.

Sheila again arched her back. Her body language spoke of desire and craving. In response, Parker dropped his head to her cleavage and engulfed her breast. She took his head in both hands and urged him on.

Tamena's hand reached Sheila's inner thighs. The flesh was warm against her fingertips. It was receptive to her touch. She looked up to see Sheila staring at her with lustful eyes. She stared back with much the same look before breaking eye contact and again giving the current task her full attention.

While his mouth paid homage to Sheila's breasts, Parker's hand found the hem of her skirt and dove under it. He explored her inner thighs but was careful not to encroach on Tamena's territory.

Finally, he found what he was looking for, what had to be the wettest spot-on Earth.

Sheila sighed and gripped Parker's head tighter. Her legs fell open to his advances. Her skin was on fire. Her body was being attended to from all directions. It felt as if a thousand hands were touching her at once and the touches were good. She shuddered at the touches.

Tamena worked her magic on Sheila's thighs. She watched as Parker pulled aside Sheila's panties and submerged his fingers inside her. Tamena's breathe shortened. Watching another woman being penetrated was extremely arousing. She reached up and traced little circles around Sheila's sacred grounds, while Parker's fingers plunged deeper and deeper into the abyss. Tamena leaned forward and teasingly blew Sheila a kiss.

Parker heard, or rather felt Sheila gasp. Her body tensed up beneath him. He began to worry that she was getting uncomfortable. Reluctantly, he detached himself from her breast and lifted his head to face her. He kissed her passionately, completely, matching the intensity of his kiss with his hand. After a moment, he broke the kiss and stared into her eyes. He saw her glace down at Tamena questioningly. Parker stared back with compassion and reassurance.

Sheila seemed to sense the strength and compassion in Parker's eyes. She appeared to have decided, at that moment to give in to the desire. She closed her eyes and let the moment take over.

Tamena's hands came to the end of their journey. She had reached her true destination. She leaned in close and inhaled the desire that had formed there. She would be the first to settle on this place, at least in this way. She leaned down to the surface and gave Sheila her very first kiss.

The ascension was majestic. Parker pulled the blanket closer as he watched the sun spill over the horizon. Golden fingers of light pierced the morning air with the promise of warmer times. The sun covered the landscape with an almond glow. Trees were temporarily set aflame, and then, with the continuous rising of the sun, put out like spent matches. Dark patches of rectangular groupings gained definition and became homes and garages and pool houses and gazebos. The remaining shadows dashed for cover leaving Parker's silhouette as the only refuge for darkness on this frosty winter dawn.

Except for the occasional bird or the whisper of a breeze, the air was still. The sounds of the industrial morning did not reach this place. Only neighbors walked on these sidewalks. Traffic jams were sooner to be caused by stickball games than rush hour. The metallic scraping of the patio door stood out against the serenity of the suburban morning. Yet Parker did not turn away from nature's most brilliant cinematic achievement. The soft sliding of eager feet failed to draw away his attention also. It was not until Tamena walked up beside him and offered him a joint that Parker acknowledged her presence. "This is a magnificent morning," Parker commented, taking the leaf from her fingers.

"Only fitting for a magnificent night," Tamena returned.

"Where's Sheila?" Parker asked as he inhaled the smooth import and passed it back to Tamena.

"She's asleep in the bed like normal people would be at this time of the morning. Why do you always wake up all early and shit?"

"I don't know. It's quiet and I can think, I guess. Did you see that sunrise?" Tamena nodded in response. "It was beautiful. The way it ran over everything like a flood. It was amazingly beautiful. It was like it washed away all the darkness."

"Yeah...sure...look, are you o.k.? I can always tell when something's bothering you 'cause you go to talking in that poetic mumbo jumbo. What's on your mind?"

"Just thinking about my life and all."

"What, you having regrets about last night?"

"Hell no! That was one of the most intense experiences I've ever had."

"Good, cause I'm gonna want to do that again sometime.' "Freak."

"Man-whore."

"Adulteress."

They laughed and decided to share a lawn chair.

"Tamena," Parker said as he reached for the joint, "do you think I'm responsible?"

"What do you mean? Like take-care-of-your business type responsible or you-did-some-bad-shit-and-now-you're-responsible type responsible?"

"Just responsible in general."

"Yeah, I'd say you were pretty straight. Why?"

"Jessica and I aren't seeing each other anymore. She said that she couldn't be with a man that didn't have any responsibilities."

"And?"

"And I was just wondering if that made me irresponsible."

"You're gonna let some bitter bitch that got herself knocked up tell you about responsibility? That bitch can't even pay her muthafuckin' bills. What can she tell anybody about responsibilities?"

"I know Tamena, I've just been thinking about it. Have I been single too long? Do I need to settle down? I mean, the majority of my friends are either married or living with someone. Even my gay cousin has a live-in boyfriend. Am I acting outta place? What's the right age to start thinking about settling down?"

"Take it from me, honey, there is no right age. I was rushed into some shit that I wasn't really ready for and look at me now; I can't get enough extracurricular dick; now pussy too. Hell!"

They both laughed.

"But seriously Parker, you can't let other people's opinions of your lifestyle stop you from being happy. As long as you're not hurting anyone, do your thing. You're not hurting me. If I weren't sleeping with you, I'd probably be sleeping with someone else. It's all a matter of point of view."

"So, you don't think I'm irresponsible."

"You're a free spirit Parker. That has its own beauty. You don't have to fit anyone else's idea of how your life should be lived. Just be you. Just be Parker. It suits you. I like Parker. You make me happy just as you are. I love the way you make me feel when I'm with you; but if you decide that you need a change in your life, I'm always gonna be here for you. If you feel like you want to change any aspect of your life, do it but don't do it because someone else feels like you should be doing something else. Do it because you feel like you want to try something else. A lot of people speak out of jealousy. They see you out there with beautiful women. You're carefree, talented and damn good-looking. They have to justify why they aren't living the life that you are living. They want to validate their sorry-ass existence by invalidating yours.

Don't let them do that to you baby. Don't let them hold you down."

Tamena reached over and gently brushed Parker's cheek, then got up and headed back for the house. "You and your little hot pepper get dressed and then get the hell out of my house before my neighbors see you and cause a scandal," she said in her most comedic voice.

"Gotcha sweet heart; I'll be in a minute." Parker took one last look at the sun and followed Tamena back through the patio doors.

Chapter 14

Parker's main goal for the day had been to work on his assignment for The Cenacle. His early rise at Tamena's had not been by accident. He planned to take full advantage of such a lovely day. The procurement of information from the identity theft victims started shortly after Parker's exodus from Tamena's home. He dropped Sheila at her apartment and immediately began a campaign to contact each of the ten case subjects. His efforts were quite successful. Either by phone or in person, he'd gathered a good deal of information in a short period of time. Before one p.m., he'd visited three of the victims and phoned another four. All but one agreed to a short, informal interview. So, when Sidney arrived at his house, slightly before seven, Parker was at home and well into analyzing the data that he'd collected.

Parker's screen door was open, which was rare. The possibility of the police coming by to relocate him to less personal quarters had quailed the habit. Nevertheless, the melancholy mood of the evening had commanded that an exception be made, and Parker had complied. Sidney entered Parker's home with less ceremony than was expected when one wishes to enter another's home and Parker made his distaste for the gross disrespect of this infringement known.

"You gonna stop just walking up in my shit. That shit ain't cool," Parker declared as he rose to greet his friend. "What's up girl?"

Sidney shared a hug with Parker and then sucked her teeth in nonchalance. "If you didn't want people to just walk in, you wouldn't have the door open. That shit is just crazy. Woo! I'm hot. You got anything to drink?"

"Yeah. It's a cola in the fridge," Parker answered as he sat back on the couch. "Hey, how about you help me go over these interviews I had today."

"What are they about?" Sidney shouted from the kitchen.

"Identity theft victims," Parker answered.

"You writing the article or trying to solve the case?" Sidney said as she took a seat on the sofa.

"I just want to write a well-researched article," Parker answered. "Ok, tell me about your folks."

"Well, the victims themselves are as different a bunch of people as you can have. They're of all races, all ages, and all income classes. They're a good cross-section of people. They're from all over the east coast. I can't figure that part out."

"What do you mean?"

"See I was thinking that the vast difference in the residence of the victims was probably the key, you know. Like maybe they all vacationed at the same place, but when I questioned them, they hadn't. Hell, most of them hadn't been on a vacation in years. So, my question is, how does Middle GA connect to this mess?"

"Well, they're all connected to Middle GA because this is where the crimes against them were committed," Sidney offered. "You have to file with the law enforcement office in the city where it happened. That's how they're connected to Middle GA on a surface level. We know that the thief is based here in Middle GA. This is where he's making all his purchases right?" Sidney inquired.

"Right," Parker confirmed as he reached for a jar of import. He took a Vega and made quick work of its gutting and reconstruction.

"So, we can assume that wherever he's getting his information from is probably here also. So, think of where that many people who are so diverse would have information stored."

"That's what I thought," Parker agreed. "I thought about the schools in the area and the major tourist attractions. Now, they'd already told me that they didn't visit this area at all. I asked if they had relatives here or kids in school. None of them did."

"Okay, so it's safe to assume that the information is coming from somewhere else. Did you ask them about the major businesses in the area? Did they have the same insurance or charity or something?"

"I thought about that," Parker stated as he passed the import to Sidney. "They all had different insurance companies if they had any at all. As for charities, no. I couldn't really think of anything else so I just asked each of them to pull a copy of their checking account statements so that I could review them for similarities. They were pretty cooperative. I'm picking them up tomorrow."

"Sounds like you got it all together," Sidney stated as she lit the import.

"I like to think so," Parker bragged.

"Here's to you, Parker Grant," Sidney saluted sarcastically. The two friends partook in the import.

"...All this because you ate some blackened fish and got to second base," the television spewed.

Parker sat and contemplated sharing the events of the previous night with Sidney. He was excited about the experience but hesitated to tell her about it for fear of her preachy attitude towards his exploits, so he decided not to mention it until she did something equally naughty with which to trade sins with him.

They'd hooked up at about eleven, just three hours after Parker arrived home from Tamena's. Sidney brought over a box of Garcia Vegas and some Cajun Steamed Shrimp. Parker brought out his import collection and an afternoon of hanging out had begun.

Parker grabbed the remote and pressed scan. "Hand me another Vega, Sidney," he asked. "Hey, what's second base?"

"Say what?" Sidney asked, remembering where she was. "Second base. What's second base, as in making out?" "You've never been to second base with a girl?"

"No. I always hit a home run." Parker laughed.

"Oh yeah, mister smooth and shit."

"Not smooth, just effective. O.k., maybe smooth and effective."

"More like mister manipulator," Sidney shot back with a little more bite than Parker was used to hearing in her voice.

"I don't manipulate anybody. I just enjoy their company. I appreciate who they are."

"You don't even know who you are! How're you gonna appreciate who somebody else is," Sidney replied with a chuckle.

"I do know who I am, and it's not about me; it's about her and how much she fascinates me."

"Parker, you don't know that woman," he exclaimed with a smirk.

"I do," He retorted. "She's amazing. She's a librarian..."

"A librarian!"

"Yes, a librarian, or rather she works in a library. Anyway, she's beautiful, smart, she smokes, and she's got this big ole ass!"

"That's all that you care about, that ass."

"No, really, I like her. She's got a great mind. We were talking about women with kids and..."

"She's got kids?"

"Yeah, just one. We were breaking down the..."

"That's foul Parker," Sidney interjected.

"What's foul," Parker replied.

"Don't do her like that Parker. She has a child."

"Do her like what? All I'm doing is talking to the girl! What's the problem with that?"

"You know how you treat women. You can't do her like that. She'll probably want you to be a father to her child and shit. That's foul."

"Hold up," Parker said in preparation for his defense. "I don't plan on doing shit to nobody. And what are you talking about, how I treat women? I don't treat anybody any kind of way." Parker felt like he had been attacked, and he responded with venom of his own. "Just because I can enjoy a person's company without nitpicking them to death doesn't make me a bad person. Besides, as I recall, the last woman I dated had a child and she abandoned me."

"But why, Parker? Why did she abandon you? She cut you loose because you weren't what was best for her, all of her. That included that badass son of hers. You don't do well with kids, you know that."

"I do like kids."

"Look, just let it go. You don't want to get started on that. You know you're sensitive and shit." Sidney accepted the import from Parker again.

"I'm not afraid of a conversation. Speak your mind."

"Alright," Sidney whispered as she endeavored to contain the vapors. "You do like kids. You just don't deal well with them in situations that you deem...threatening."

"What?"

"You know you got self-esteem issues." Sheila exhaled a mostly translucent smoke. She closed her eyes and began the journey down the road she'd rather not travel. "You feel like your position with the mother is threatened by the child when you're in relationships with women with children."

"That's not true."

"Yes, it is."

"Then why do I even get involved with women who have children?"

"Because you know that there's no real hope for the relationship so there's no reason for you to invest yourself."

"No, no, I always invest in my relationships. I give my all when I'm with a woman."

"Yeah, unfortunately, it's yourself giving away the bullshit that you imagine that they want to hear."

"I don't give nobody bullshit."

"You do Parker." Sidney accepted the import on its umpteenth rotation. "You don't want to go there with me. You know how I feel about this."

"About what?" Parker said with a chuckle. "And you're laughing at it!"

"Laughing at what?"

Sidney's demeanor changed. She'd become angry in less time than it took to snatch the import back from Parker's expectant fingers. "You have no remorse! You use these women to boost your self-esteem then discard them when they find out you ain't shit!"

"Hold up now..."

"No wait! You need to hear this! You can't play with people's emotions like that! These women have feelings. If you keep fucking around with doing this shit one of these bitches is gonna snap and fuck you up!"

"Doing what?"

"Don't act stupid. You know what I'm talking about. This sick game of musical chairs you play with women. You romance them and get them to fall in love with you. You lie to them and tell them how you love them and want to build a life with them when you really just want the attention. You want them to love you so much that then when they figure out that the love talk you fed them was bullshit, you ditch 'em and move on to the next victim."

"Hold up! I don't force anyone to do anything they don't want to do! I can't help that I'm a romantic! I like chivalry."

"No Parker! Chivalry is one thing, but you go beyond that. You offer these women hope for a better future. You hold their hands and rub their feet and play with their kids. You talk about wanting a wife and a family with them! You drive through the suburbs and play "that's our house" with them. You meet their families; you cook for them and take them on family outings. To a woman that says let's settle down. You want to fuck. You don't want to build homesteads. You want to travel and have fun. You don't want a wife. You want a freak that occasionally cuddles. And that's cool. That's fine. There's nothing wrong with that if you tell them that. But you don't. You let them believe that you're going to be their husband or their superman or a father to their children. You let them get used to having you around. You let their children get attached to you. Then you leave. You just bail when you get bored. You keep a woman in the wings so you're never alone, but they are. Parker, you leave them with their hopes and dreams crushed. They put everything into you and then you just, you just ooh! Then this poor fool you're dealing with now has a child!"

Sidney was upset. She couldn't understand his inconsiderate and reckless behavior. She walked over to the nightstand and grabbed a Garcia Vega.

"Look, I know it seems like I mistreat women, but that's not my intention. I give my all every time," Parker defended. "I have to get to know a person before I decide what place they have in my life."

Sidney split the Vega and dumped the contents in the trash pail. She looked at Parker with ire. She closed her eyes and tried to remember he was her best friend. "Look Parker, I know you don't mean to do harm. But you do. You play this role like it's all about the moment. For you it is. You're 30..."

"29," Parker corrected.

"Whatever. You don't have kids. You don't have bills. You're duty-free. You only have yourself to be concerned with. When the only responsibility you have is to yourself, you act different. Your perspectives are different. You have different values. You can afford to value pride over employment. You can afford to not work where you can't be real or honest. You're only responsible for yourself. You don't have kids to feed. You can not take a job that doesn't pay you what you think you're worth. You can leave a job because you don't like the work you're doing. You can just up and leave to another area to find the job you'd like to work. You don't have to consider school districts or finding new pediatricians or daycare issues. You don't have those kind of responsibilities Parker, so you think differently. You live for the moment and don't look at things in terms of tomorrow or even later on in the day for that matter. "

"I am concerned about the future," Parker interjected.

Sidney ignored his comment and went on. "When you do the things that you do, you see it as normal romance, because that's what you're looking for. You see your actions as common courtesies to whoever the women you're dating. But that's because of your perspective on life. These women see your actions as signs of commitment. They see you as their grand knight in ebony armor. You do husband-type shit," Sidney declared as she sat back down on the couch and grabbed the mason jar.

"Like what," challenged Parker?

"Like going to their kids' ballet recitals and taking them on picnics and introducing them to your aunts and uncles. That's husband type shit."

"True, true," Parker admitted in reflection. He'd done those things. He'd never felt any particular reservations about doing them. They had just been experiences. Things to write about. He hadn't placed any special significance on the events. Perhaps it was because they had no underlying implication in his dream life. He didn't already have a child to try to fit into his ideal fantasy. These women did so that it made sense that they would be reading his actions as signals for commitment. Parker listened on in silence.

"Man, I don't even want to talk about this," Sidney said as she rose and started gathering her things.

"What? Now you gonna get mad and leave," Parker questioned sarcastically.

"Naw, I gotta go anyway. I have a trial to prepare for. I'll catch you later," she replied as she headed for the door.

"Yeah, whatever," Parker replied nonchalantly. If she wanted to act stank than he would let her. He'd tried to listen with an open mind, but she chose to leave. He wouldn't be held accountable to anyone. Even Sidney.

The door slammed and Parker was alone.

Chapter 15

The night was a quiet one for Parker, considering the evening he'd had the night before. He decided to stay in and do some writing rather than going out or inviting anyone over. After a couple of hours of solid productivity, he turned in at about ten-thirty and had been sound asleep for about four hours when the phone brought him out of his slumber.

"Hello," Parker answered fumbling for the phone. He waited

but got no response. "Hello, are you there?" he repeated. Who the hell is this he thought as he rolled over and glanced at the flashing number. The caller identification box said Alfreda Redwind. The identification box only flashed listed residence, so he knew the call was from her home. Parker immediately grew concerned. He was unsure what to do. She usually called him from an unlisted number. "Hello! Is anyone there?!" he asked again with an implied meaning. It could be her man checking her phone for numbers, he thought.

He and Alfreda had never discussed the possibility of her boyfriend finding Parker's number and attempting to contact him. They didn't have a plan for such an event. He'd known guys who did that sort of thing to their women. He also had to entertain the idea that it might be

Alfreda in a situation where she couldn't speak. What if she was in trouble? "I don't know who this is, but I'm hanging up now," Parker baited. Parker hoped that if it was Alfreda and she couldn't talk, she'd at least push a button or something. If it were her boyfriend, maybe he'd gotten mad and screamed out. Either way, he wasn't going to continue to listen to the dead end of a receiver.

Parker wanted to hang up when he heard her whisper his name. "Parker," she breathed more than speaking. "Parker, it's me, Alfreda."

Parker eyed his clock radio. The numbers glowed a pale red in the darkness. "Hey, what's going on? What are you doing up this time of the night?"

Alfreda burst into tears. "I just had a fight with my boyfriend," she got out between sobs. "He called me all sorts of stuff and threatened to kill me. Parker, I'm scared! He was hitting me and yelling at me in front of my son. He did that shit in front of my child, Parker!" Her fear had given way to anger. "I can't have that in front of my child!"

"Whoa! Whoa! Calm down." Parker sat up and turned on the night lamp. "What happened? I thought he treated you good. Are you O.K.? Physically, I mean. How's your son?"

"He's fine. I'm gonna take him over to my sister's. She's got a son his age. He'll be okay over there."

"And what about you? Do you need to go to the hospital?" Parker was up getting dressed. He threw on a pair of fleece sweatpants and a long-sleeved tee.

"No. I'm all right. I've got some bruises on my arms but that's about it."

Parker pulled on his socks and headed to the dressing room for a pair of sneakers. "What can I do for you baby? How can I help? Do you need me to come over? I won't let him lay a hand on you."

"No. No. I don't want you getting into an altercation over me. Besides, I'm not going to stay here tonight. I don't feel safe."

"Do you want to come to my place...? I'll sleep on the sofa, and you can have my bed. Just tell me what you need." Parker grabbed his car keys and went out to warm up the Cadillac. He'd gotten it started and was idling it when Alfreda responded.

"I just need to get away from here and talk. I'm so sick of this shit! I don't want to live like this!"

"Where do you want to meet? We'll grab a cappuccino and talk. I thought you said he treated you good?"

"I didn't want you to think I was crazy for being with him. I liked how you made me feel Parker. Parker, I'm sorry for laying all this on you. I haven't known you that long, but I feel like you've always been in my life. I feel so comfortable with you. I'm sorry for even asking you to get involved with it, but I've alienated all my friends. They won't deal with me anymore because of him. If you don't want to deal with me, I understand." Alfreda broke down in a storm of sobs. She covered the phone with her hand, but her muffled cries still scratched at Parker's heart. He went back inside to gather his wallet and his cell phone. "Call me on my cell, ok?" he asked.

"Alright," Alfreda responded and a minute later their conversation continued.

"It's ok. Just tell me where to meet you. I'm leaving right now. "Parker turned off the lights and locked the front door before hurrying into his driver's seat.

"I've got to drop Benny off. By that time, you should be in Macon," she got out between sobs. "Meet me at the Waffle House on Hartley Bridge at three o'clock."

Parker looked at his dashboard clock. It was two-thirty. "I'll be there. And baby?"

"Yes, Parker?"

"Don't worry. It'll be fine. You'll be ok. We'll figure it out together."

"Parker it's not your..."

"I'm making it my problem, Alfreda. I'll see you in thirty." "Ok."

Alfreda hung up and Parker hit the road.

The Waffle House didn't sell cappuccino, but they did serve hot chocolate. Parker and Alfreda had several cups in the corner of the dingy orange-and-brown colored traveler's paradise. Parker sat beside her rather than across from her so that he could hold her when she cried. At first, she was reserved with her explanation of the evening's happenings, but as she realized that he would not judge her, the pain shot forth in a monologue of considerable significance.

"I just can't leave him. He's the backbone of my financial plan. He knows it too. He knows it and uses it against me. He tells me that no one will do for me like he does. And he does help me, Parker. He pays bills for me." Alfreda looked at Parker who nodded in recognition of her statement and rubbed her shoulder in encouragement. "But he doesn't treat me right, Parker. He doesn't treat me like I'm special. He just, he just, he just says things to me and does things to me that no man ought to do to the woman he says he loves. Then he does it in front of my son!" Parker raised his eyebrows in recognition of the statement's significance, but Alfreda offered an explanation, nevertheless. "I don't want my son thinking that that's the way to treat a woman, but that's all he sees. He sees how I'm treated," Alfreda spoke before she began to sob again.

Parker picked up the sentence and finished it. "He sees how you're treated and then he sees you, his most trusted mentor and teacher, his mother, allowing this type of behavior and he figures that it's

acceptable behavior."

"Yes," Alfreda whimpered.

Parker took her hand and rubbed it gently between his own. "But Alfreda, your son can only see it as you condone that behavior. What damage is being done to him by staying in that relationship? Is whatever bill he's paying worth your child's future?"

Alfreda didn't answer. Instead, they sat quietly. Periodically Alfreda would shake from the flood of emotions. During those moments, Parker would hold her closer, pulling her head to his shoulder and whispering soft reassurances in her ear.

When he wasn't reassuring Alfreda, he was thinking of the situation that he was quickly allowing himself to be caught up in. Parker thought of why he was here. He was touched by her pain. Her vulnerability tugged at his heart. She was a broken soul trapped between the immediacy of now and the inevitability of the future.

His yearning to comfort her seemed natural, he thought. But what drove him to want to help? Was it his natural desire to help Alfreda or, as Sidney said, his subconscious need to have Alfreda see him as some sort of hero?

Was his motivation for being here selfish as Sidney had claimed, or was he the kind soul that Alfreda claimed she saw in him?

I'm a good man, Parker said to himself. I'm here to help a friend. She's special to me. I enjoy her company. They both felt the chemistry between them; nothing could erase that. But what about the other women he'd dated? Hadn't there been chemistry with them also?

Parker brushed Alfreda's hair with the back of his hand. She wasn't like them. They could make it together. They could be the forever love that they each looked for. There was no pattern to his love interests, Parker concluded. He had no problem committing to a woman with responsibilities. If Alfreda ever gave him the opportunity, he'd prove it.

Alfreda moved and brought Parker out of his thoughts. "I've got to go get ready for work," she said straightening herself in the cramped space of the diner booth.

"Yes, of course," Parker said.

He stood and reached to retrieve the bill, but Alfreda grabbed it first. "No. Let me take it. You came for my benefit."

"I came for my benefit also," Parker admitted with an air of truth. "You know how I feel about you. I want you happy and with me. Anytime I can spend a little time with you is to my advantage."

Alfreda smiled and rose. She grabbed Parker around the neck and hugged him. She held him for a small eternity. When she finally let go, she turned and walked towards the register without a word. She handed the cashier a ten-dollar bill, well beyond their tab and headed for the door. Before she walked out, she turned and mouthed the words "thank you" with trembling lips and watery eyes. Then she was gone.

Parker walked out of the diner with a hollow feeling in his chest. He knew that she would go back to him. She had no other choice. The reality of the situation was that she and her child had to survive. Parker knew that whatever Alfreda had to do to protect and provide for her son, she would do. The only hope Parker had was if she realized that her situation was more harmful than beneficial.

And even if she did leave him, what type of assistance could Parker provide? He couldn't even pay his own bills. He was a wanted man. Was he implying some form of help that he couldn't give?

I'm reading too much into it, Parker decided. He started his car and began to back out of his parking space. I'm just being a friend, he decided. A friend...who was he kidding?

Parker dedicated the remainder of his morning to the identity theft article. He reviewed his files and went through his interviews. All his information led him to one place: The collection firm of Milton & Chase.

Milton & Chase was a low-level collection agency in the downtown area of Macon. They served a variety of clients including several national department store chains. All the victims had made payments to Milton & Chase during the last year. Odds were that the thief had gotten the information from the collection agency's files. The thief probably worked there, Parker thought. He fished out a phonebook and searched for the agency's number. He had no luck in the online yellow pages but found an entry in the white page listings. He dialed the number and waited for an answer.

"Thank you for calling Milton & Chase. This is Ms. Chambers. How may I direct your call?" came a voice.

"Yes, Good morning. Could I speak with a manager please?" Parker requested with as much politeness as he could muster.

"Sure," the lady replied. "Who shall I say is calling?"
"Mr. Grant from The Cenacle," Parker replied. "Okay. One moment please," the lady responded.

Parker sat on hold for several moments before anyone came to the phone. When the voice came on the line, it was aggressive. "This is Mr. Leavitt; how may I be of service?"

"Good morning Mr. Leavitt," Parker greeted. "My name is Mr. Grant; I'm a reporter for The Cenacle. I was wondering if you'd be able to answer some questions about your company and its policies concerning the personal information of the consumers that your company works with."

"Our company's policy on dealing with the media is that we don't. If you check our website, we have a detailed mission statement which outlines our goals, our procedures and our methods," the man who'd identified himself as Mr. Leavitt droned. "Have a nice day."

Before Parker could retort, the phone line went dead. He attempted to contact Mr. Leavitt or any manager again but was met with polite resistance. Finally, he gave up and resigned to trying the website.

Unfortunately, the website was also useless. It was a single page, mostly consisting of the company name, logo and a two-line mission statement. Parker read it to himself. Not much of a statement, he thought.

Parker signed off and contemplated his next move. He could continue to call the agency but that wouldn't get him anywhere. He needed to talk to someone from Milton

& Chase. He evidently wouldn't be able to do that by phone. That left only one other option. He would have to go down to the Milton & Chase offices and find someone to talk to in person.

Parker grabbed his keys and prepared to leave.

Chapter 16

The afternoon had become a hot one for Parker, who'd been sitting in the parking lot of the Milton & Chase office building for two hours with no contacts. His shirt was drenched in sweat, and he was sure that a heat stroke was imminent. So far, only three people had left the building: an older gentleman in a security uniform and two younger looking women in hoochie wear. Parker wanted badly to speak with the women but thought it's better if he didn't approach them while they were in the company of the security guard. No sense alerting the management that he was on the property trying to obtain the information they'd so obviously wanted to deny him. Unfortunately, the guard posted up at the women's car and sat chatting in a manner that hinted towards a lengthy conversation. Parker had just resigned to waiting him out when his phone rang. The screen read Sheila.

"Hello," Parker answered.

"What's up sexy man?" came Sheila's bubbly voice.

"Nothing much," Parker replied. "I'm working on my article for The Cenacle. How about you?"

"Oh, I'm having lunch with Rasha. Why, are you trying to see me?" Sheila asked with hope.

"I'd love to, but I've gotta find an employee over at Milton & Chase that'll talk to me today. I tried to get them to grant me an interview over the phone, but the administration declined to comment. So now I'm sitting in front of the building waiting on someone to come out so I can see if they'll answer a couple of questions for me."

"I might know someone who works there," Sheila said mischievously.

"Like who?" Parker asked, taking the bait.

"A friend of mine," Sheila dangled.

"What friend?" Parker returned.

"I don't know if I should tell you," Sheila began.

"Come on girl; this is important."

"What are you gonna do for me?" Sheila asked suggestively.

"What do you want me to do for you?" he asked.

"Use your imagination papi," Sheila shot back. "Tell me what you'd do for me if I got you your interview."

"I thought you were with someone?"

"She's gone to the restroom. You've got a little time."

Parker analyzed his situation. He's been trying to get someone to talk to him all morning, but no one was interested, even off the record. His call to the administration had probably prompted them to send out a company-wide gag order. If he didn't take Sheila's offer, he probably wouldn't get a chance to talk to anyone. "You want to know what I'm going to do for you?"

"Yes," Sheila cooed.

"You want to know what I'm going to do to you." Parker offered.

"Yes," Sheila purred.

When they first started seeing each other, Sheila was been amazed at Parker's ability to weave stories from thin air. As their relationship grew more intimate so had the stories. The erotic tales were Sheila's favorite. She often called Parker on late nights and had him make new ones up for her to masturbate to. Parker knew that this is what she wanted. He just wasn't in the position to give it to her. He'd to play the straight role for now. "Well, I'd love to tell you, but right now I've got some very important work to do. So please just hook me up with the information and I promise to make it worth your while. Will you do that for me baby? Will you get me the information?"

"Yes," Sheila whispered, a little disappointed.

Parker felt bad. He didn't want to leave Sheila hanging. "Are you alone?"

"Rasha's in the restroom."

"Are you listening?"

"Yes."

"I'm going to follow you home," Parker said, "and corner you just inside the apartment door. I won't let you turn around though. Instead, I'm going to slowly drag my fingers down your back until it arches involuntarily."

"Uh huh," Sheila cooed. "Go on."

"When I reach your ass, I'm going to change directions and let my hands travel along your sides to your midriff. Then I am going to pull you close to me so that your ass would be pressing against my dick. I'll push forward so you could feel how much I want you." Parker paused for effect and then went on. "I'm gonna bring my hand to the cleave of your breast and lightly push you into me so that you'll be leaning back into me. Then, with one arm around your waist, I'm gonna take my other arm and bring it up to your breast. I'll then take my hand and remove the loose hair from your neck. My face will hover there, in the crook of your neck. You'll be able to feel the heat from my breath, the tickle of my beard against your skin."

"What about your other hand?" Sheila whispered.

"My other hand would be moving down your body to your supple breast. I'll be able to feel the fluttering of your stomach with my hand at your waist. The hand at your breast would be massaging firmly, while the hand at your waist would disappear into your pants. You would..." Parker stopped short of finishing the sentence.

"What's next?" Sheila asked after she realized that the silence wasn't for effect.

"The rest of the story's meant to be delivered in... person. Now come on sweetie," Parker pleaded. "I need this."

Sheila was silent for a moment then asked Parker to hold on. Parker waited a moment then heard a voice on the phone that was not Sheila. "Hello," the feminine voice greeted.

"Hello," Parker answered a bit agitated. "Where's Sheila? Please tell her to stop playing and get back on the phone."

"Oh," the voice responded. "She told me you needed to talk to me about my job."

"What? Where do you work?" Parker questioned.

"I worked at Milton & Chase Collection Agency," the woman replied. "I'm Rasha, Sheila's home girl."

"So, you work for Milton & Chase, huh Rasha. You work for Milton & Chase," Parker repeated in disbelief.

"Yes, I did, Parker," Rasha returned with attitude.

"So, you don't work there anymore?" Parker asked.

"No, I work at Bryan & David now, but I worked at M.C. for a hot minute," Rasha replied. "I know pretty much everything there is to know about the place. It's a real dive."

"What do you mean?" Parker asked as he searched for his pad and a pencil.

"They're just all shady," Rasha divulged. "There was always something strange going on over there. The managers would always try to keep shit from the employees."

"Like what?"

"Like stats and numbers and shit like that. We were supposedly working for these ultra-professional companies, you know, collecting debts for them but they wouldn't let us talk to them. We never could call them or anything. We could only talk to the debtors. If we had a question about an account, we had to ask the manager. Then he'd come up with an answer. If a debtor asked us about a charge or an amount, we were charging them, we couldn't explain it. It seemed like we were hustling the people. The managers were all hustlers themselves," Rasha declared. "Every last one of them."

"Why do you say that?" Parker asked as he scribbled notes.

"They all did time together," Rasha gave. "They're all ex-cons. How in the hell can an ex-con be in charge of a financial institution? I mean, I'm for reform and all but ain't that strange? Ain't there laws against that? They've got access to people's personal information and shit! They got socials and checking account numbers and credit card codes and shit."

"So, you think they were doing dirt?" Parker asked.

"Of one type or another," Rasha replied. "Why? What do you know?"

Parker was tempted to tell Rasha all about the article he was writing and the cases that were related to it but thought better. She might be a gossip. He couldn't afford to have his story outed before he broke it. He would keep her on a need-to-know basis. "I'm doing an article on collection companies," Parker fibbed. "So, tell me about the way the place operates. How do they handle people's personal information? Is it secured against theft?"

"Hell no. They've got a basic computer system but nothing to keep it secure. If one of the employees wanted to do something with the information, they could. They claim that they use secure lines but that's just bullshit. And then, most of the information is just out there to anyone who happens to walk by."

"So, if I were an employee," Parker supposed, "I could just pull up information on anybody that I wanted to?"

"If they had a debt that was in collections you could," Rasha confirmed.

"And no one would know anything? No bells would ring? No whistles would go off?"

"Nope," Rasha replied. "No one would know shit. That's what I mean. They're shady. The system is set up that way on purpose."

"If I had some names that I wanted to run through the system to see who had contact with their accounts could you get somebody to look into it for me?"

"I could probably get somebody to look at the official entries but that won't necessarily be everyone who viewed them," Rasha answered.

"What do you mean?"

"Well, in the system they use over there, if you don't document the account when you go into it, any sign that you were in it disappears twenty-four hours after you exit the account."

"So, unless they document the account, they're invisible," Parker offered.

"Yep."

Parker started to see how the hustle could work. If the system were set up for autonomy, then it would be simple for someone to use it for an identity hustle. "So did you know anyone who was hustling up in there?" Parker inquired.

"Well, my homeboy had a little scam going but he got fired."

"For scamming?"

"No. That motherfucker wouldn't take his ass to work. He was just flagrant with it," Rasha said with a chuckle.

"Oh. What was he scamming on?" Parker asked.

"He was doing some shit with cell phones and socials," Rasha

replied. "I'm not sure exactly what it was, but he was getting paid."

"Do you still keep in contact with him?"

"Yeah, we kick it every now and then," Rasha admitted.

"You think you could have him call me?" Parker asked.

"I'll see about it. He's still mad about getting fired. He'd probably talk about it if you didn't mention his name."

"Cool. Pass on my number, will you? I'm gonna get gone," Parker said, concluding the conversation.

"You want to talk back to Sheila?" Rasha asked.

"Naw, tell her I'll get up with her later. Peace." Parker ended the call and started up his Caddy. Now it was a waiting game. Parker hated waiting games.

Parker's cell phone rang just as he pulled the Cadillac into the diagonal parking space. A quick look at the screen told him that it was Dean. He answered with his usual greeting for Dean:

"What's up bitch ass!"

"Ain't nothing asshole. What's up with you?" Dean asked.

"I'm in Macon in front of The Righteous Room," Parker replied.

"What's going on up there?"

"They're supposed to be having a poetry reading."

"You gonna read something?"

"I might. What's up with you?"

"At home with the family, player. You know how I do it."

"Must be nice to have that stability to lean on when shit gets hard."

"Yeah, it is! It's alright player!"

They talked about Dean and his family life for several minutes before Parker decided to share his dilemma with Dean.

"Man, I've gotten myself into a hell of a mess with these checks. I owe enough to where I've been thinking about getting another job."

"What? You got a job when I wasn't looking? Unless I'm confused, your black ass haven't gotten a job in years. What do you mean another?"

"Stop bullshitting. You know I work man. You don't have to work for the man to be legitimate.

"No, you have to work for the man to get paid by the man," Dean shot sarcastically.

"That's why black people can't get nowhere. I don't plan on working for someone else my entire life. I want something of my own!"

"You're gonna have something of your own alright; you're gonna have your own six-by-nine apartment in a special place for other motherfuckers who won't work and don't pay their bills."

They both laughed. They had the uncanny ability to see the humor in even the most dismal situations. Nothing was off limits to their sick satirical humor, even, Parker realized his legal crisis.

"So, what you gonna do man?" Dean asked with a more serious tone.

"I don't know man," Parker replied. "If I knew, I wouldn't be so stressed. I guess I'll pay 'em when I can pay 'em. They can't get what I don't have."

"True," Dean gave. "Just be careful man. What time are you leaving from up there?"

"Shit, I'll probably stay up here. I got a bunny up here I kick it with so, I think I'mma go over there and chill."

"Yeah, straight. Hit me up later then," Dean replied.

"Alright then. I'll holler." Parker hung up his cell phone and placed it in his glove compartment.

Parker sat in his car for several moments debating whether to enter the storefront café. Inside, people were waiting for a poetry reading to take place. He lit a black up and tried to remember why he was here. He had long ago sworn off the cultural scene in Middle Georgia. Besides the occasional gospel plays that toured the chitterling circuit, the area was devoid of any literary arts. Booty Shake and get crunk music were kings here. Social events that involved any other media outlet received no support. Still, when they did come around, he felt obligated to attend. This event had been going on for a good while now, but up until tonight, he hasn't felt the urge to attend.

Now, with so much on his mind, he needed a break from his normal routines. This would be a break from the norm. This café was a happening spot. It was called The Righteous Room.

The Righteous Room was a quaint jazz café owned by Brother Righteous, a Middle Georgia Literary Artist of note. Righteous, as he was commonly called opened the café as an alternative to the get crunk clubs that the south was so well known for. He called it his haven for the eclectic artistic soulful misfits.

Oh well, Parker thought as he snuffed out his black and opened his car door. Here goes nothing. He locked his doors and headed for the café.

Chapter 17

The Righteous Room was located on Cherry Street, between an upscale dining establishment and a Goodwill retail store. Its official address was 582 Cherry, though no tangible marker existed to show such. The unit was one of a dozen or so that occupied this end of the street. Its front was elegant. Two cinnamon-hued columns stood to either side of the entrance; spiraling Muscadine vines had been carved throughout their length in intricate detail. A well-worked veneer in a cinnamon-and-jade striped pattern covered the walls surrounding the entryway. The entrance itself was represented by two rounded oak doors in the same palette as the columns. The doors swung in both directions but were currently propped open to better accommodate the arrival of guests. Just beyond the door was a receiving area where a large leather-cushioned chair with a mated writing table was posted. The occupant of the chair was an acquaintance of Parker's; he rose from his seat and greeted Parker with much ceremony.

"The great writer has returned," he exclaimed as he shook Parker's hand and patted him on the back.

"What's up brother," Parker replied, returning the handshake with vigor. "How you been man?" he asked earnestly.

"Oh, I've been good," was the reply. "How about you? You've been ghost for a while," he went on.

"I'm cool," Parker said and cordially removed himself from the handshake. "I've been working on some personal projects," he offered casually. "I'm trying to hone my craft."

"Like you don't already have it on lock!" Parker started to reject the compliment, but the acquaintance went on. "You know your shit is tight. You know it."

Parker smiled and quietly admitted that he was 'alright'.

"Whatever, man," was the acquaintance's reply. "Just keep doing what you do and come through more often."

"Will do," Parker returned as he reached for his wallet. "How much to get in?" Parker asked, referring to the cover charge.

"Ain't nothing for you player," was the reply.

Parker thanked him and after another elaborate handshake, moved through another set of double doors that led to the main social arena.

The Righteous Room's atmosphere was that of a classic speakeasy. There were little partially hidden nooks and alcoves built into the walls. The lighting was low. A pleasant aroma filled the air. Parker thought it was ginger but wasn't sure. As for the layout of the café, it was outfitted with the standard tables and chairs, all painted black, with mosaic tile surfaces. The walls were all mirror, which made the cafe' seem crowded, even when it was sparsely populated. Soulful music played and more than a few patrons could be seen moving to the rhythms. Although the low lighting made recognition of anyone impossible from farther off than a few feet, Parker felt like he was among friends.

There was a stage set in the café's right corner that was designed to take on the appearance of the sun come to Earth. Its base made up one-third of the celestial sphere and was raised some two feet off of the ground; the other two thirds was painted on two adjoining walls. The paint was metallic gold. This gave the performer's platform the illusion of shimmering. Thin, triangular rays of light shot out from its edges; each ray held the name of some inspirational performer as well as one of that performer's quotes or signature phrases. Among these was a ray for Marley, and Giovanni, Hayes and Common, and Forever Moe as well as a ray for the café's owner, Brother Righteous. The rays all began as thin lines at the point where the stage base and the two walls met. As they moved further out towards the edge of the sphere, they gained width; once the edge was overtaken, they slowly began to reduce themselves until they were again thin and disappearing into the grain of the floor. It was quite an exhibit of expression. The stage was occupied by a set of congas on its extreme right, an upright bass on its extreme left, and a solitary microphone at its front center.

The spot was hot, Parker thought, as he found an unoccupied table in a corner and had a seat. If his money hadn't been funny, Parker would have bought a drink, probably a crown and coke or some other whisky blend.

But his money was funny, and although he'd saved whatever funds he would have devoted to the cover charge, he was still in no position to even consider any sort of financial splurge. Hell, he thought, even being here wasn't the most financially sound decision he could have made. And it wasn't just the over-charge or drink money, or even the exorbitant amounts of cash it took to fuel the Cadillac. It was the potential for greater, more substantial, monies being required that concerned him. If he was stopped by the police or pulled aside at a roadblock or otherwise engaged by the authorities, his financial situation would worsen tenfold. The warrants that had been drawn against him were such that, once served, he would not be released until those financial obligations were satisfied. Since Parker himself had no means of providing those funds, he would either have to sit in jail or turn to his parents for resolution. Neither option was acceptable. Parker reached into his coat pocket and retrieved his blacks; he extracted one from the package and returned the rest to his pocket. He patted down his pockets in search of an ignition device, but finding none, lifted the votive from the table to use instead.

For the next several minutes Parker sat and enjoyed the atmosphere. He grooved to the music and fed off the café's vibe. People laughed and chattered around him. Genuine good times were being had. Parker saw the silhouettes of a man and a woman engaged in a conversation; he couldn't make out what was being said but their body language told him that it was of a romantic nature. Two brothers appeared to be discussing business in a corner booth near the stage; they exchanged business cards and shook hands as only brothers can. A group of sisters pointed and giggled in the direction of a group of brothers that had come in just after Parker; they made gestures and hand signs that were evidently an inside joke. He was enjoying himself. Parker was in a zone. He was alone but he was comfortable. It wasn't until he got the feeling that someone was watching him that he was pulled back into the uncomfortable mode he normally found himself in when at social functions.

Parker could tell that he was being watched. His skin tingled. His hair stood on end. His eyes scanned the crowd for the culprit. In the shadows of a distant corner, huddled with a small gathering of other shadows, a singular figure stood out. The figure had wiry, shoulder-length hair partially stuffed under what appeared to be a pile cap, a denim parachute dress supported by a pathetically frail frame, a pasty pimpled complexion and the beadiest eyes Parker had ever seen. The cafés light, or lack thereof made confirmation difficult, but Parker suspected that his watcher was Adnal Waters, one of his lesser-liked contemporaries. The watcher stared daringly at him. He stared back in defiance. We can both play watcher, he thought. Parker saw malice in those eyes; they narrowed in an attempt to convey anger and hate. The feelings were mutual, Parker thought. Still, they stared. After an eternity of staring, the watcher's lips broke into a barracuda like smile that hinted at a cruelty thought up but not yet acted on. Slowly, almost unnoticeably, Adnal made a nod of an acknowledgement in Parker's direction. Parker returned the nod in kind and broke eye contact. Sloppy Dread, he mouthed silently. Why does it have to be that way?

As Parker was contemplating the bad karma between Adnal and himself, a waitress appeared and began placing a drink, a Corona, in front of him on the table.

"I'm sorry," he said, catching her attention, "but I didn't order a drink."

"Oh, I know Parker," the waitress said, more than likely recognizing him from previous readings, "It's from the young lady over there," she replied, pointing in a direction behind her.

Parker followed her gesture to a table just beyond his on the opposite side of the café. There, in all of her splendor, sat Alfreda Redwind.

He signaled for her to join him, and she complied. She walked over with her drink in hand, smiling. Parker smiled back and offered her a chair. "Well, hello there daffodil. Not that I'm complaining but what made you send me this drink?" he asked, pointing to the Corona on the table.

"I figured you needed something to cool you down. Ole girl was staring at you like she wanted to burn a hole through your ass," Alfreda commented as she took the seat Parker offered.

"Yeah, she doesn't care much for me. She caught an attitude over the way I handled a program I was in charge of. It was silly really. I tried to talk to her about it, but she was acting childish and didn't want to solve it. So, I let her stay mad. We don't talk anymore. She just looks at me mean and I stare back to piss her off. Thanks for the beer by the way." Parker lifted the Corona to Alfreda in gratitude. She did the same, and they drank to each other.

"People act funny when they think they know you," Alfreda commented as she placed her drink on the table.

"Yeah," Parker cosigned. "But it's not that they really know you. It's that they think they do."

"I agree. As a matter of fact, I've got a theory on that. You want to hear it?" she offered.

Parker expressed his desire to hear the theory and Alfreda complied. "People think they know you. They think that they've figured you out. They make judgments on your actions and speculate on what you would or wouldn't do; but unless they know you on an intimate level, unless they're exposed to who you are in more than one setting, they don't really know you."

"I feel you," Parker said. "Go on, I'm listening."

Alfreda took a moment to enjoy her drink and then continued her declaration. "People only see you in the setting they're used to seeing you in. Take your average manager for example. You only see her as an uptight dictating bully. That's who she is to you. That's all you've ever seen. You aren't privy to her as the loving mother or the devoted wife; to you she's that bitch boss lady. That's how you judge what she does or might do. You judge her as the woman who's the bossy bitch. You don't have any other frame of reference to judge her on, so you can't really know her. You've only got a snapshot of who she is. Your view of her is one-dimensional. It's incomplete. It's not rounded off. It's just a snapshot.

"When you come to truly know a person, you learn them on multiple levels. You learn them in many ways, so you begin to have a greater understanding of what they are inside. You follow me?"

Alfreda looked towards Parker seeking some form of recognition concerning her theory. Her eyes said that she expected his agreement. Her demeanor said that it was ok if he didn't.

Parker sipped on the Corona and contemplated the rationale behind her statements. He applied her theory to several of his own acquaintances and found it, for the most part, to be sound. He took another sip and then offered her a response:

"Ok, that makes sense; so, does that mean that you should discount the criticism of those outside your intimate social circle?"

"No, just remember to take it in context. Know under what assumptions people will judge you. If it's a coworker, you needn't become distraught over their criticisms of your personal life because they don't know you like that; they only know you as a professional; likewise with associates. Their exposure to you is more than likely limited to a solitary set of similar experiences.

***

Parker was about to ask Alfreda about her plans for later on in the evening when the café lights dropped away and were replaced by a spotlight focused on the center of the stage. This, Parker reasoned, signaled the beginning of the show.

A hush came over the crowd. A solitary silhouette emerged from the shadows and the lone figure took the stage. He gripped the microphone stand as a horse jockey would a whip. He looked into the crowd. The poet scanned the audience, making eye contact with each and every member.

"This is the Dialectal Derby. Hear us race these rhythms." With that, the poet leapt into a wild and wicked flow. He bounced on the rhythm, a jockey on a horse. A slim trim kid stepped onto the stage and mounted the bass. He pulled at its reigns with determined fingers and his steed took off. He guided the bass through a suave series of orchestral obstacles, leaping from scale to scale, jockeying with the poet for position. A dirty red cat climbed onto the congas and pranced his way into the lineup. The Poet sprinted syllables on the straightaway, attempting to make a play for the lead, but the kid countered with eight bars of his own. The congas trailed them, alternating positions behind one and then the other, but never quite pushing up front. As things came to a head, the poet broke out front and dashed across his finished line. The crowd applauded in appreciation. A newcomer like Parker would have thought this was the end of the set, but Righteous Room regulars know to the contrary.

Parker too soon realized this, for only the poet had dismounted; the other attendants still rode their rhythms and as the poet left the stage, another rose from the audience and proceeded to take his place. One by one, each in turn, poets rose from the audience to ride the rhythms. Poet after poet rode, the conga and the bass their companions.

The rhythm was in him. He felt the vibe. His soul was dancing a funky tango with the divinities of groove. Parker realized that this was an open mic in its truest form. The poets took the stage at their leisure. The flow of the show was flawless. Parker found himself drawn to the stage. He yearned to slam with the rhythm.

He looked over at Alfreda. She was also grooving. Parker gave her a questioning look. Alfreda could not have known what he was asking; yet she still nodded yes. It really didn't matter though. He had been underground too long. He needed this. This is why he had come. This was his element.

When he spoke, he felt like a different person. He wasn't Parker Grant anymore. He was someone entirely different.

Parker stood up and walked towards the stage. Several people noticed him as he passed them; they applauded. Others whom he knew and who knew him gave silent signs of encouragement. Those who weren't familiar with Parker and his work watched him with idle curiosity. He mounted the stage. The music's vibration ran through his feet and ricocheted throughout his body. His

spirit embraced the melody and Parker fell into the oratorical oasis that was his zone.
Parker spoke from his soul:
"I am words
I am nouns
I am verbs
Prepositions, hyperbs
I am thoughts heard
No, I am thoughts felt
A manifestation of self
Through the alphabet I get down
Ideas form round in a dichotomy of decided indecision I am oral tradition, catechisms put to rhythm Intellectual conceptual spitting
A disciple of diction
Praise her articulate name
I am a sorcerer of slang
Pontifications main bane
The force behind the dam
The flood gate and the water main
Prince's freaky little brother
Work with me now
I speak in salsa
Fly flagrant flavors fluctuating flagrantly foreword I am extreme and exorbitant
(slow down son, you're forcing it!)"
oh I dare say I am
I slam like onyx
Like comets that extinguished the dinosaurs

I write cause that's what writing's for
And I speak cause that's what speaking for
Cause I'm a writer baby
I'm a writer cat daddy
A verbal voodoo doctor

Parker dismounted and returned to his seat. As was the order of things, another poet took his place. Parker was stopped several times by people wanting to congratulate him and ask about his current projects and whereabouts. By the time he reached the table, Alfreda had ordered another round of drinks. She rose and hugged him when he arrived at his seat.

"You do it then," she exclaimed. "I didn't know that you did poetry! That was so nice!"

"Thanks," Parker replied, a bit surprised.

"So how long have you been doing it?"

"For a while."

"Well, you're good at it. Why didn't you tell me?" she said as she slapped him playfully on the shoulder.

"It's just something I do." Parker looked at his watch and rose to leave. "Look, I'm getting ready to get out of here. You want to get something to eat?"

"Maybe next time. I'm with some girlfriends of mine so I can't just leave." Alfreda nodded towards a nearby table. Two women were looking in the direction of her and Parker. "Maybe I'll take a rain check," she inquired with a smirk.

"Cool," Parker replied. "So, I guess I'll see you around?" "Most definitely," she exclaimed.

Parker smiled and headed towards the door.

Parker's Cadillac came to a stop in the fifth position in a line of cars being corralled through the police roadblock. It was well beyond 12 a.m. As was a custom in small southern cities and towns, a checkpoint had been set up to catch drunk drivers and other unlucky miscreants who happened upon it. They used the fisherman's theory: if you throw out a wide enough net, you're bound to catch something.

This night appeared to be proving the theory true. On the roadside to the left and right of the roadblock were parked several 'things or rather 'people' who'd been unlucky enough to be over the limit or without licenses or so fragrantly high that their continued operation of a motor vehicle was dangerous to the public. They would not be going home this evening. They were, for the moment, wards of the state.

Parker stared at them with mild horror. He would soon be one of them. It was his worst nightmare come true: being stopped by the police while he still had warrants out. He'd lost his cool. What would he do? What did the law say? He was in a bad place. Before he moved another inch, he was on the phone with the only legal aid he had: Sidney.

"What's up, Parker," Sidney answered in a sleepy voice. "Do you see what time it is?"

"Girl wake up! I'm in trouble," Parker replied in a nervous tone.

"What's wrong?"

"I'm stuck at a roadblock. If they run my license, I'm fucked," Parker said confused.

"Shit," Sidney exclaimed.

"Yeah."

"Do you at least have a license to show them, Parker?" Sidney asked.

"Yes, but it's dirty. If they run it, I'm done in."

"Do you have insurance?" Sidney asked, ignoring Parker's desperation.

"Yes."

"Is your registration up to date?"

"Yes, but it's not in my name."

"Irrelevant. Just calm down and you'll be fine. It's just a checkpoint. They rarely run your identification at those things. Just don't give them cause to want to."

"Why does shit like this happen to me?" Parker exclaimed. "Parker, I think you're the devil," Sidney answered seriously. "What the hell..."

"No. I mean your actions. Nothing good can come to you until you do right. You think this type shit would be happening if you were living right?"

"You ain't no angel yourself, Sidney."

"You're right! But I'm not the one wanted by the police, pulling up to a group of police, scared that I'm gonna have to go with the police. You've got to let go of all that bullshit. God doesn't like that. He wants his children to be within him."

"Here you go preaching," Parker gave defensively.

"Just watch what you do when times get hard," Sidney declared. "Now how many cars are in front of you?"

"One," Parker answered.

"Go ahead and get your shit out so they don't have to wait on you. Don't give them any reason to spend extra time looking at your busted ass picture."

"Fuck you, Sidney," Parker spat. "I'm 'bout to get the Akon and you're playing around!"

"For real, dumb ass. Get your license, your registration, and your insurance in hard so all you have to do is hand it to them when you roll your window down. That way, they can glance at them and send you on your way."

"Cool," Parker conceded as he reached into his glove box. "Got'em," he answered after picking the necessary documents from the pile.

"Now put the phone down, but don't turn it off," Sidney instructed. "I want to know how the conversation went so that if you get locked up, I can defend you."

"Stop bullshitting, Sidney," Parker shot.

"Just do it."

Parker placed the phone face down on the seat and sat nervously in the car. He silently cursed himself for smoking the extra import; it had made him paranoid. Now, he had to deal with its effects on top of the genuine need for concern. Be cool, he told himself. Don't look nervous.

The patrolman returned the requested items to the driver in the car ahead of Parker. Then he stepped back while the driver pulled off. "Here it goes," Parker said to a silent Sidney. He pressed the lever and lowered his window.

"License and registration, please," the patrolman barked.

Parker handed the patrolman his documents and waited for doom to fall. The officer shuffled through the papers, then settled on the license. What's he doing? Parker wondered nervously. Was there some conspiracy theory secret code on driver's licenses that alerted the police to problematic people? Of course not, he thought. That's the import talking.

But Parker was concerned about his identity being randomly run through the system and it being discovered that he had warrants. He couldn't afford to be in jail. He wasn't the criminal type. *I just need time to get some funds together*, he thought.

"Where you headed, Mr. Grant?" the patrolman asked.

"Oh, I'm headed in for the night," Parker replied.

The officer hesitated.

Please Lord, Parker prayed silently. *I'm gonna get it together. Just give me another chance.*

The patrolman handed Parker his documents. "Be safe, Mr. Grant," he said as he directed Parker on his way.

"Thank you, God," Parker breathed as he pulled away from the checkpoint.

"You through?" Sidney screamed through the cell phone.

"Yeah," Parker shouted. He picked up the phone and continued. "Whoo! I was blowed girl!"

"You should have been," Sidney scolded. "Parker, grow up and take care of your shit. Be careful on your way home. You got lucky this time. Don't get caught slipping again."

"Shit, I'm about to get off this road right now," he declared as he turned his car towards North Macon. He would not be tempting fate again this night. "Thanks girl. Sorry for waking you up."

"It's cool. I'm gonna holla at you tomorrow."

"Peace," Parker answered as he turned onto the interstate and headed for Sheila's apartment. He'd been blessed. God had showed him mercy. It was necessary to take advantage of that blessing. He had to make changes, and he would start tonight.

Chapter 18

Parker rose early, which was his custom. As usual, it was hunger that called him from slumber. Since he'd had a particularly active evening, the hunger was more prevalent. Despite this, Parker denied his initial urge to go directly into the kitchen and instead stood in the entryway of the hall contemplating his evening.

It had turned out well. Sheila had been more than pleased to have him over on such short notice. His arrival at her home, a mere four- and-a-half hours earlier, had been met with much ado. He called ahead to make her aware of his imminent arrival. He had no desire to come upon Sheila unexpectedly. He'd done that before with Jessica and been met with disastrous results. The thought of that evening brought a dull pain to his heart. He remembered.

No scene had ever been so graphic, none so vivid. It was reality in high definition, images in Dolby Digital Surround Sound. Theater seating without all the strangers. The colors were fluid. Sound was alive. Life was its own personification. And Parker was its sole observer there on that night. There, etched in 3D, frozen in a single, infinite chronological unit. Life was at its most visceral. It basest; it's most common. Life was there. There, in his bed, on his sheets, there in the warmest part of his home, in his inner sanctum, in his resting place, there, where he laid down the woes of the day and rested peacefully without the anxiety of life, there where his seed's greatest hope lay, there in his bed. Life lay there with his woman, his heart, his soul mate and another man.

Parker never stopped by a woman's house without calling again. Anytime he considered it, those images flooded his mind and brought him back to reality. Experience was truly the best teacher, and, on this issue, Parker had been an A student.

The apartment was blanketed in dark. The only break in the darkness came from slices of moonlight that crept through the patio blinds and marked the living room floor with uneven stripes. The light switch was on the wall next to the front door, but Parker opted to leave the night undisturbed. He liked the dark. It was cool and comforting.

A Lazy Boy recliner sat in a corner of the room the moonlight did not reach. It was encased in compacted darkness. Hours earlier, Parker and Sheila made love there. The soft leather held them securely during a more physical period of their session; the friction of the material against their flesh heightened the experience. The sensations of the event were still fresh on Parker's mind. He turned his attention in the chair's general direction. It was his recollection, not his vision that told Parker it was there. He chose that chair to sit in.

Night vision had not yet come to him, so he used his memory and the adjacent wall to guide himself to his destination. He moved slowly to avoid upsetting an end table that he was sure had been there hours earlier. Having found the Lazy Boy just where his memory had left it, Parker plopped down, pulled his legs up under himself for warmth and began to concentrate on the objects in the room around him. After a time, his eyes became accustomed to the darkness and a shadowy version of Sheila's home came into view.

It was a nice apartment, Parker thought; well-decorated and spacious; I could do this.

A blinking green light in the kitchen caught Parker's attention. He focused on it and determined that it was the microwave. The culinary reference reminded Parker of his hunger. Just can't fight the cravings, he thought as he hopped up from the chair and descended on the kitchen.

Parker turned on the light and scanned Sheila's kitchen. It was nice. Parker appreciates a good kitchen. He had spent quite a few mornings in one fixing breakfast for his various overnight houseguests. It was one of his favorite things to do in the morning. He liked to think that he was practicing for a time when he would have a family and he'd be able to fix breakfast for them. I want a wife, Parker admitted as he scavenged through the cabinets for the pots and pans necessary to cook Sheila an A-plus morning meal. I just want the right wife, my wife.

The possibility of having a family or a house to cook for them in was looking quite bleak though. All the women in his life were wrought with drama. None of them fit his image of what his wife would be like.

Parker put the first skillet on the stove and turned the temperature to medium. What to do, he thought. I've got Jessica playing with my emotions. I've got Sheila trying to be my main lady and the one chick that I really want ain't even really available. He placed the other skillet on a side counter and looked in the cabinets for a pan for the bacon. He found one under the counter and proceeded to prepare the bacon.

Jessica was bad for him. He knew that. She brought nothing to the table. She didn't work. She wasn't in school. She wasn't working on anything that showed any sort of ambition. How could they have ever built together; she had no dreams. True, she was fine as a mutha fucka, but that was the extent of her attraction. It was just that I hate to lose, Parker admitted. And not necessarily hated to lose her, just hated to lose in general and he had lost in that particular situation. That shit had to go, he decided. No more Jessica.

Alfreda was another issue altogether. He really dug her. They had a connection that could not be denied. She was the most beautiful woman Parker had ever met. She wasn't just beautiful on the outside either; she was beautiful on the inside too. Her conversation kisses were off the hook. He really wanted her. She had everything that he'd ever wanted in a woman. She also had a man though. That shit made it unacceptable. I can't be investing myself in some shit that ain't really mine, Parker declared. Better to enjoy it for what it was and no more.

The danger was in the fact that he really liked her though. He really, really liked Alfreda.

Parker took bacon from the meat drawer and the onions from the vegetable drawer and placed them on the counter. And Sheila, Parker decided, that shit is over too. I'm not gonna be accused of leading anybody on. He would not allow this situation to get out of control. He'd talk to Sheila and make sure she understood that he just needed somewhere to stay until he could get his warrant shit taken care of. As soon as I get on my feet, I'm getting the fuck up outta Dodge, he reflected between greasing the pan and preheating the oven. Sheila was cool, though. She looked out for him. They had a good time when they went out. He just wasn't attracted to her the way that he was to Alfreda. He didn't have passion for her but was passion something that grew with the relationship or was it something that was either there or was not? Sidney said that passion came from desire and that if he didn't desire to feel passion for Sheila, then he wouldn't. Perhaps he hadn't given Sheila that opportunity. Had he ever really given her his undivided attention? Was he shortchanging his blessing?

No, he knew what he wanted. He knew what was good for him. He would follow his own path. Wherever it led him was where he would be.

He would need money to get there though, and his income was scarce at best. He had some funds coming to him from a freelance piece he'd written. He probably could get a temporary gig to come up with another couple of hundred dollars and Dean would probably lend him a small grip. He'd stopped asking Sidney for money because her loans came with the third degree.

Parker took the bacon from the pack and spread it out across the oven dish. Contraction gave it the appearance of slithering towards the middle of the pan. Did Sheila like bacon? All the time that they'd spent dining together and he didn't know what she liked to eat for breakfast. Why was that? She'd brought him countless sandwiches, yet he'd never bothered to notice what she had on her sandwich. Am I that self-absorbed? He wondered.

The pan made a soft scraping sound when Parker slid it onto the oven's bottom rack. He closed the oven door and turned his attention to the biscuits.

He'd opted for the Pillsbury frozen biscuits as opposed to the "from scratch" recipe. The entire preparation process took less than 5 minutes. Truth be told three–and-a-half of those minutes were spent figuring out how to open the resealable bag. After putting them in the oven, Parker retrieved his cell phone from the bedroom and returned to the kitchen. He found some country ham that would be just right for the omelet and put it in motion.

Parker dialed Dean's number and then began his omelet preparation. He pulled out both red and green peppers for the omelets. He liked the way the two colors looked against the yellow of the egg. Personally, he hated the taste of peppers, but he liked for his food to be visually pleasing. After several rings, a sleepy Dean answered his phone.

"What the fuck do you want?"

"Shit. What's up," Parker replied after he put a thick slice of country ham in a hot skillet.

"I'm sleeping, shit for brains, what the hell are you doing? Oh, I forgot, your ass likes the morning time. Well, normal folks don't damn it."

"Whatever," Parker answered with a dismissive tone. "Look here, I think I'm getting ready to get up outta Dodge. This shit is for the birds."

"What the fuck are you telling me for? I ain't going with your crazy ass."

"Man, I ain't trying to take your sorry ass anywhere anyway. I just call to hit your ass up for some cash. You know I'm a broke mutha fucka." Both men laughed at the comedy that only they could find. To each other, they were the two men in the balcony at the Muppets show; it was the nature of their friendship. It worked for them.

"What you need man," Dean said with a voice that barely contained his laughter.

"I'm thinking about four hundred. I've got four coming from this thesis I wrote for this guy at Mercer. I'm gonna find a quick come up for another three hundred and I'll be set."

"You good for it fuck boy, but you'll have to wait three weeks to get it. I have to plan for that kind of shit."

"Thanks, bro. Hey man, did I tell you that Sheila broke into my house man?"

"You bullshitting me!"

"Nope. I'm dead serious. Jessica left me a message telling me she saw her coming out of my house the other day and I know I wasn't there. You know that my paranoid ass don't never leave the door open so how else did she get in? She broke the fuck in, that's how!"

"Damn! What the fuck did she say about it?"

"I haven't asked her about it yet. I'll probably do it when she wakes up."

"You got her ass in your house and she busting up in your shit all Ocean's Eleven style? What kind of shit are you on?"

Parker put out two plates and two breakfast glasses on the back counter. He returned to the refrigerator and pulled out a carton of Tropicana. "She's not at my house, tittie breath, I'm at hers."

"Oh, and that makes it better! Both yawl asses' crazy! I told her stupid ass the same thing. Both of yawls are dumb as hell. And you! You like drama."

"Please! I hate that shit."

"You shitting me."

"Dean, I'm so sick of drama"

"Shit, buster you breed drama! That's all that your ass knows!"

"Man, fuck that. I'm tired of not being able to enjoy whatever chick I'm with cause I gotta wonder about who's gonna pop up unexpectedly. I need peace, bro. That's what up!"

"Peace," Dean mocked. "A piece of what? Ass? That's the only piece your ass like. You ain't trying to do no different than you're already doing."

"Naw, man, for real; I'm gonna get my shit together. I'm just trying to get enough money together to get the hell outta Dodge."

"For what? That ain't gonna change shit. You'll just go somewhere else and do the same shit."

"Fuck you Dean,"

"For real Parker. You can't run from your problems, bro. You'll just end up going through the same thing again with different people; if you get different people," Dean added with a snort.

"I just got bad karma 'round here man. This place just steals life from me. It's so fucking hard to do anything."

"Well, if you need to leave, then leave, but don't expect for shit to be different wherever you go to, cause it won't be. It'll be a different setting, but the scene will be the same. Parker being a hoe cause hoeing is all Parker knows!"

Dean's declaration echoed in a booming silence. Parker chopped red and green bell pepper and contemplated the comment. "Man, I just want some shit like what you've got. I'm tired of playing around bro. I need some stability. I think I deserve that."

"Yeah, well you've gotta straighten your shit up first bro. It ain't gonna be easy either. You got a lot of shit to be accountable for. Like dragging that damn woman behind you like you do."

"What woman?"

"Sheila."

"I don't drag her anywhere." "Negro, you're leading her on." "You shitting me, I am."

"Whatever, you know she's caught up on you and you won't let her go cause she does all that shit for you. You ain't slick mutha fucka. I see you. And what's fucked up is that she's a good person. She really looks out for you. She's crazy as fuck, but she always got your back. You need to either get it together or let her go so somebody else can appreciate her. Sheila's a good woman bro. All bullshit aside. You're gonna have a world of hurt coming if you don't get right."

"Yeah, well, I can take it," Parker responded. The ham he'd put on the stovetop started to sear so Parker moved the skillet to a cool burner. "I can take whatever it takes to get me out of this rut I'm in." Parker removed the hot ham from the skillet and placed it on the chopping board. "Be honest with me Dean, why do I keep going through all this shit?"

"Because you allow it."

"What do you mean?"

"I mean you put yourself in these fucked up situations and then expect them to turn out well. Like now, you're over there fucking with Sheila, and you probably just left from fucking with ole other girl."

"Hey man, I ain't got no ties to anyone. I'm single," Parker declared as he diced up the ham for the omelets.

"That's what your mouth says, but you don't act like it. Man, all I'm saying is get your shit together and stop fucking around. Look, I gotta go. I've told your black ass about calling me at the fucking crack of dawn anyway. Take your ass back to bed!"

"I can't. I'm cooking breakfast for me and Sheila."

"See. That's the shit I'm talking about. Your fucking Cliff Huxtable routine," Dean said, resigned. "By ass wipe."

"Later dick boy." Parker hung up the phone. Dean had said a mouthful. He did seem to bring drama upon himself. Not on a conscious level, but subconsciously, he was perpetuating a cycle of something. He just had to figure out what it was.

The grits began to bubble and pop. Parker adjusted their temperature and continued to cut up the ham. What was his cycle? What was it that he did? I spend time with women whom I find attractive, and I just get to know them. That's not a negative thing. That's normal. I don't lead them on. I don't really promise them anything. I just am myself. But that's not how Dean and Sidney saw it. Sidney said that women were playthings to him. They were courted, wooed, romanced, lead on and then, once they'd grown much too attached for his comfort, they get discarded like last year's fashion.

Chapter 19

Parker pulled two eggs from the carton and cracked them open over a deep round Tupperware bowl. What is it that brings the drama? Parker posed to himself as he mixed the contents of the bowl with a fork. He stirred the eggs with the same vigor with which the question cycloned in his thoughts. I'm polite. I give conversation. I compliment them. I listen to the things that they share with me, and I give honest and thoughtful answers. What the fuck is wrong with that?

Parker placed a fresh skillet on the burner where the grits had been and started to gather all the ingredients for the omelets on the side counter. Green and red peppers, fresh cheese, country ham chunks, ripe onions; all the ingredients for the perfect omelet, Parker thought. It'll be beautiful and satisfying. But not to me, Parker sighed.

Such a beautiful thing the omelet would be, but it wasn't meant for him. He would never be able to enjoy it. According to most, it was perfect in every way. It had all the right ingredients. It was prepared to perfection. It would be warm and fresh and smell so good, but it wouldn't be for Parker. It didn't satiate him.

Part II

Parker rose before the sun. He rolled out of bed and began to prepare for the tasks he'd set forth for the day. The night before, he'd pressed his blue suit and hung it in Sheila's closet. He retrieved it and entered the bathroom for a hot shower. Normally, his showers were quick. He would get in, wash himself and get out. This morning, however, he lingered beneath the spray of the near-scalding water. He let the shower head's intense stream massage his body. The water cascaded down his shoulders and did a good job of alleviating the tension that gathered there. By the time he stepped out of the water, he felt ready to take on whatever the world had to offer.

Parker made quick work of toweling dry and prepared to leave the bathroom. He put on a white terry cloth robe that hung on the back of the door. Sheila had bought it before he moved in. She said it was for the nights he stayed over. Now that he was living in her home, he'd make use of it; it fit him well, he thought. He exited the bathroom to the smell of breakfast, Sheila-style.

"Good morning handsome," Sheila called from the kitchen. "I see you found that robe I got for you. How was your shower?"

"Good morning. It was just fine," Parker answered as he adjusted the knot on the robe's belt. "Yeah, I found this robe. It's a good fit. Hey, aren't you up early?"

Sheila smiled and blew Parker a kiss. "Yeah. I figured I'd hook my man up with a little breakfast before he went out to get a job!" She lifted several slices of bacon from a pan with her cooking fork and placed them on a plate line with a paper towel. "Besides, you need a good breakfast if you're planning on putting in applications at all those places," she said referring to the hefty stack of employment packets that Parker had prepared the previous evening. "Do you know where you're headed first?"

"Yeah," Parker replied as he headed down the hall towards the bedroom. "I've got them lined up according to location. The first one is in East Macon and then the rest just migrate back this way. I'm trying to drop off at least fifteen packets today," Parker announced as he shed the robe and began to get dressed.

"Isn't that a bit ambitious?" Sheila called from the kitchen. "What if you have an on-the-spot interview?"

"I've thought of that also," Parker responded between pulling on a tee shirt and pulling up his socks. "I've got fifteen destinations. Of that fifteen, six of them are preferred employers."

"What do you mean preferred?"

Parker pulled on his shirt and began fastening the buttons. "That means that of all the other companies that I'm applying to; I would rather work at one of those six. They're the only ones that I'm planning on giving the opportunity to interview me on the spot."

"Oh! Aren't we cocky!"

"No, I'm not cocky. I just plan my moves," Parker countered.

"Orange juice or apple juice?" Sheila inquired.

"Orange," Parker called back. "What are your plans for the day?"

"I'm not sure," Sheila shouted over the humming of the microwave. "I don't get a lot of days off, so I'm going to make the best of this one. Then again, I'll probably just relax. You know, sit around and enjoy doing nothing."

"I don't blame you. I'd do the same thing." Parker finished buttoning his shirt and tucked its tails into his slacks. He slipped his tie over his head and pulled the knot taut around his neck. "Hey, have you seen my ankle boots? I thought I put them in the closet?"

"Yeah," Sheila called from the dining area. "They're on my side of the bed. How many slices of bacon do you want?"

"Three is cool," Parker said as he grabbed his shoes and headed for the kitchen. "Now, haven't you been the busy bee?"

The dining room table was filled with all manner of breakfast foods. There were biscuits, pancakes, eggs, fresh fruit, sausages, ham, hash browns and toast. "Oh, I can burn now," Sheila returned with a bit of attitude.

"Now, who's being cocky," Parker returned as he slapped Sheila from behind and reached up to open the cabinet nearest him.

"What are you looking for?" Sheila asked as she slapped his hand away from the cabinet knob. "Everything you need is at the table. Your plate is fixed and everything. All you have to do is sit down. So, sit down and enjoy it."

Parker raised his eyebrows and gave Sheila a nod of appreciation. An old-school woman, he thought to himself. He sat in the chair that Sheila had indicated was his and waited for her to sit. He could get used to this, he thought. He could get used to this indeed.

Sheila stood in her apartment window and watched Parker walk away. He had confidence in his stride, she thought. He moved like he was somebody. Sheila felt the tingle that came when she thought of Parker Grant. He was one sexy brother. And now he was here, living under her roof, at least temporarily.

She watched him enter his car and pull away from the curb. Parker looked very nice, she thought. He'd spent a good amount of time putting together his ensemble. It had been almost perfect. Sheila returned to the kitchen, thinking about the spot on Parker's shirt. Parker needed a new white shirt. He'd changed the subject when she brought it up. That was probably because he didn't have the money to buy it, she thought. He was too proud to ask her for money though. He'd rather wear the one with the spot on it. That was simply unacceptable; she decided as she went into the kitchen to put away the breakfast dishes.

Sheila was thinking of who had a sale on men's dress shirts when the telephone rang. She dried her hands and picked up the cordless handset from its base on the counter. "Hello," she answered.

Rasha's vibrant voice came booming through the telephone. She was happy to speak with her friend. "What's up girl," she asked.

"It ain't nothing. I'm up in here washing dishes and preparing to do nothing all day," Sheila proclaimed.

"That's right! You're off today. Let's do brunch at Desserts First," Rasha offered.

Sheila thought about her recently set shopping expedition. She could get Parker a new shirt and still make it to Desserts First in time for brunch with Rasha if she made her purchases at the mall. There was a Macy's, a Parisians, and a Dillard's, as well as some other specialty shops there; she should be able to find something he would like, she thought. "That's cool. How about eleven?"

"Good. I've been wanting one of those dangerously Delicious Double Dark Chocolate Sundaes anyway."

"Uhh, I had one last night," Sheila answered.

"You went to Desserts First last night?" Rasha asked. "No, playgirl. I went to bed with Parker."

"You so nasty."

"Don't hate!"

Rasha had been waiting for over twenty minutes at the Desserts First café' when her friend finally arrived for their late brunch. Sheila entered the café loaded down with shopping bags and apologizing profusely.

"I'm sorry girl," she said as she deposited the bags on the far end of their table and took a seat across from Rasha. "I got caught in line at Dillard's. Those cashiers do like to take their time."

"I hear you, girl. I hear you. You could have called though. And what's in all these bags?" Rasha asked as she fumbled through the bags on the table. "Oh, hell naw," she exclaimed as she rummaged through a bag of men's dress shirts. "I know you ain't gone out and spent a bunch of money on this man!'

"I sure did," Sheila proclaimed as she crossed her legs and signaled for the waitress. "Among other things. Yes, I bought my man some shirts. What's wrong with that?"

"Nothing," Rasha answered. "If it's for your man. But that ain't the nature of yawls relationship. He just lives with you and y'all occasionally fuck," Rasha said matter-of-factly. "But go ahead girl. You're grown. I can't make you understand how crazy it is for him to be staying at your house rent-free, so how can I expect you to understand the danger of buying clothes for a man that ain't officially yours?" The waitress came over and took their order. Rasha waited for her to leave and then continued. "I just don't want you to get hurt, girl. You're my friend and I care about you."

"I know girl, but he just looks so good in his suits and I'm always seeing something that'll look good on him that I want to get it for him. I like buying him things," she admitted. "Should I not be me just because he's unsure about who he is?"

"No, but you don't have to go overboard with it. Look at all these shirts," Rasha said, pushing the bag of shirts back to the other end of the table. "He's gonna think you're trying to buy him."

"Well, I'm not," Sheila concluded.

"I know that! I'm just doing what friends do."

"And I appreciate that," Sheila admitted, "but I've got it under control. I just... hey! What's going on with you?" Sheila stared at her friend closely. Rasha's left breast was on the verge of spilling out of her brassiere while her right breast hung low on her chest.

"I know, right," Rasha said as she attempted to adjust her breast. "I think the elastic in the straps broke. I look deformed!"

They both laughed hysterically. Rasha's breast shook like the unbalanced side of a weighted scale. "It looks like it's trying to escape," Sheila put in between laughs.

"Whatever," Rasha retorted in spite of her own hysteria. "What are we doing today?" she added once she regained her composure.

"Well, I need to go to the grocery store before it gets too late, but I guess Parker and I can do that this evening. What do you want to do?"

"Let's go see a movie or something. My treat."

"Didn't we just go to the movies? There isn't really anything worth watching out there," Sheila commented between each forkful of her recently arrived chocolate delicacy.

"Yeah, well, how about we go shopping?" Rasha offered as an alternative. "I know that I could use a new pair of sandals."

"What are your toes looking like, girl? You don't want to be out there with the stank foot."

"You went with me to the nail shop the other day! You know how they look! Your ass is just trying to be funny." Sheila just laughed and enjoyed her dish.

"Right now, I'm gonna eat this cake," Rasha answered. "After that, let's just ride girl."

"Home girls on the stroll," Sheila announced. "Home girls on the stroll," Rasha seconded.

After crumbling up his fifth application, Parker stopped filling them out. He simply flipped to the back of the employment packet, and if there was a background check authorization form, he'd give the clerk, manager, receptionist or whoever was in charge of dispensing the application back their paperwork and leave. He had no desire to embarrass himself or waste anyone's time. He had a warrant out for his arrest. It would surely come up on any background check that was run against him. He could have the warrant lifted if he could just get a job to earn the money he owed, but he couldn't get a decent job because he had a warrant. It was a catch-22. He was in a no-win situation. Parker smelled defeat and it had only taken a day. It was not quite a full day at that.

Financially, he could not afford to have many more days like today. He'd spent nine hours driving around looking for employment. Driving around took gas. Gas cost money. Money was a luxury that was in short supply for Parker. At the current rate, his funds would run out in a week-and–a-half. Then he'd be screwed. The Cadillac would not run on air. That much was certain. He would have to find something.

Chapter 20

The clock read six-thirty when he pulled into a parking space next to Sheila's car. She was home, he thought; probably waiting for him to tell her about the new job he didn't have at the new building he didn't work in with the salary he wouldn't be receiving. How pitiful was that?

Parker exited his vehicle and started the short trek to Sheila's apartment. He held his attaché case in one hand and a bag with two #3 value meals in the other. He'd wanted to take Sheila out to show his gratitude for looking out for him during his rough time, but he couldn't afford it. If today were any indication, he'd never be able to afford it. At least he'd tried, he thought as he clutched the bag a bit tighter. When he reached the stairs, the aroma of home-cooked fried chicken filled the breezeway where Sheila resided. Somebody's eating good tonight, Parker thought.

The smells of somebody else's supper brought Parker's thoughts back to his dilemma. Someone had a good meal waiting for them when they came home from work. They had provided the finances necessary to prepare a meal like that, a home-cooked meal. He had burgers and fries.

When he reached the apartment door, Parker was all but salivating. The food smelled marvelous. What was worse, he was sure that Sheila probably smelled it too. She'd think him a fool for bringing home a couple of greasy burgers when it was obvious that she wanted more.

Parker was turning to leave when he heard the lock to the apartment door turn. Sheila had heard him.

"Hey, baby," she said with a start. "How was your day? Oh, you brought dinner," she continued, reaching for the bag. "Can we eat these later? I kind of cooked for you. Come on in," she said as she took his hand and led him into the apartment. "I cooked some chicken, sweet peas and made some potato salad and butter biscuits. Sit down and rest, sweetie. I went and got you some shirts and a tie or two. Here's your plate." Sheila placed two trays in front of the television. "So, what's your strategy?" she asked as Parker made his way to his seat. Parker looked at Sheila with mild confusion.

She had read his look and came to her own conclusion. "I'm sorry, baby," Sheila said. "I assumed you would take at least a week or so to pick a job. I know I did. Did you find something you like today?"

Parker was shocked. Sheila thought just the opposite of what he'd assumed she would. She knew it would take more than a day when he hadn't. Parker sat down. His soul felt lighter. The pressures of the day fell away. "No, no. I didn't choose anything today. This smells great. I can't believe you cooked all this."

"You like it?" Sheila asked with a smile.

"I sure do. I could smell it coming up the sidewalk." Parker picked up the biscuit and bit into it. "This is divine.

You know, I was outside jealous of whoever had food that smelled so good. I didn't think of it being me."

"Oh, I got you a special surprise," she said with a start. Her hand disappeared beneath the sofa and reappeared with a magnificently prepared two-fingered import. It was beautifully wrapped and smoothly covered in a Cuban-cultivated Double Corona. The tip exposed a bright green botanical that was aromatically potent. "You like?" Sheila asked, offering her creation.

"Indeed I do," Parker answered, taking the import in hand. "I'll save this for later." Parker placed the import next to his beverage on the tray. He looked over at Sheila and said a silent prayer of thanks for having such a wonderful friend.

Two days into his job search and Parker hadn't gotten one good offer. He'd gone to all the major white-collar companies as well as all the manufacturers in the area with no results. Several restaurants had shown interest in hiring him as a shift or assistant manager, but he wanted to save those offers for a last resort; coming home every evening smelling like fry grease and burnt meat was not his preference. The City of Macon had several positions available that he was most definitely qualified for, but he couldn't pass the background check.

How ironic, Parker thought. I can't get a job because I've got warrants but I can't pay the warrants off because I don't have a job. Overall, it had been a pitiful week. The only positive news he'd received had been from Rasha's hustler friend from Milton & Chase.

The guy, who went by the name 'Oink,' had been very willing to talk about the corruption going on at his former place of employment. Apparently, he and a manager at Milton & Chase had been involved in some low-level scams together. They'd made a good deal of money in those scams but when Oink was put on the chopping block for his tardiness, the manager left him out to dry. Oink felt betrayed by his former partner. He wasn't bitter enough to go to the police over it, but he was bitter enough to talk to Parker. He spent about 15 minutes explaining the way the manager's ID scam worked and then gave Parker the guy's private cell phone number.

Parker called it but only got his voicemail. He left a message asking the manager to return his call. He left enough information so that it would be obvious that he knew what was going on and that he wasn't the police. Hopefully, he'd call and at least make contact.

It was late in the afternoon and Parker hadn't eaten. He decided to grab a burger and head back over to Sheila's. He wasn't going to get a job at 4 o'clock. Most managers were closing out their books for the day and heading home. He planned to do the same. He was pulling into a local burger joint when his phone rang. The caller ID said Alfreda.

"What's up beautiful?" Parker answered with a smile.

"Hi, Parker," Alfreda answered with the sweetness of a July peach. "What's going on?"

It had been almost a whole week since he'd seen her at The Righteous Room. Since he didn't officially have a number, he could call her at, he had to wait for her to initiate contact. He was happy to hear from her. "Nothing as important as hearing from you. How have you been?"

"Same ole, same ole," Alfreda replied with a bit of sorrow. "Look. I'm actually in the middle of something, so I can't talk long but I wanted to ask you if you'd like to get together this evening?"

"Oh, that would be nice," Parker answered with a lot less excitement than he was feeling. "Where would you like to meet me?"

"Why don't you pick the spot," she offered.

"Okay. How about Bennie Johnson's out on 247?"

"Yeah, that's cool. Alright. How about 8:30 p.m.?"

"That works for me," Parker replied. "I'll see you then."

"Later then," Alfreda said as she hung up the phone.

Great, Parker thought. My day is looking up. He pulled up to the menu board and placed his order.

When Parker arrived at Sheila's apartment, it was almost five-thirty p.m. Sheila hadn't returned from work yet, but she was due in by six. That gave him precious few minutes to take a shower and get out before she arrived. Parker didn't want to have to explain to her where he was going. It would be better if he could just leave her a note. He wasn't even sure he owed her that. They had no official ties, but he was living at her home. He didn't want to make her feel uncomfortable, so he decided to grab some clothes and head over to a friend's house to shower and change. That way, there would be no discussion about where he was getting dressed up to go or when he would be returning.

He went into the closet and grabbed a pair of jeans and a nice shirt. He switched out his dress shoes for boots and hung his suit jacket in the closet. Socks and underwear, he rolled in a ball and stuffed it in his jean pockets. Lastly, he grabbed his saddlebag from the hall closet and

extracted a pen and a tablet on which to jot down a note for Sheila. He placed it on the kitchen counter and then hurried out the door.

It only took him a minute and a half to get down the stairs and into his car. If he'd gone left instead of right going out of the parking lot, Sheila would never have seen him. He had gone right, however, and that took him directly in Sheila's path. She was in the southbound line waiting to cross traffic and turn into the apartment complex. Had she seen him? Probably not. She hadn't called his cell phone.

Damn, Parker thought. What to do, what to do? His destination was south but turning south would require him to wait in the same traffic that held Sheila up. She would surely stop as she pulled into the complex to ask him about his day.

Parker pulled into traffic and headed north. He would go up to the next intersection and turn over a street, then double back. He looked into his rearview mirror and saw Sheila's hand waving from her window.

"That muthafucka's riding out, girl," Rasha exclaimed from Sheila's passenger seat. "I know he saw us."

"Shut up," Sheila pouted. "He probably was messing with the radio or something. Hand me my cell phone so I can call him."

"You don't think he saw you waving your arm out the window like a fool," Rasha returned. "You've got to be kidding me!"

Sheila accepted the phone from her friend and speed-dialed Parker. "We'll see," she said as she waited on Parker to answer. "Hello. What's up, baby? You didn't just see us waving at you?"

"No, baby," Parker replied. "I wasn't paying attention. I've been trying to get my radio to act right. Where were you?"

"Across from the complex," Sheila returned.

"Sorry, sweetie. I was working on my radio."

"Oh, okay. That's what I thought, but Rasha said you were trying to be funny," Sheila said as she pinched her friend. "Where are you going?"

"I've got a meeting to go to. I'll be back later."

"Oh. Well, I was going to cook and Rasha and her friend were gonna come over and play cards."

"I'm sorry baby. I didn't know. Do you want me to try to reschedule my meeting?"

"No. That's all right. You go ahead. We'll just chill then," Sheila said, with disappointment in her voice.

"Thanks for understanding baby. I'll talk to you later, okay," Parker finished.

"Okay, but how did your job search go today," Sheila interjected before Parker could end the call.

"No luck."

"Well, don't give up, baby. It'll come. Just be patient," Sheila said.

"See. That shit is shady," Rasha said as soon as Sheila ended the call.

"What? He's got a meeting," Sheila defended.

"Yeah, but he couldn't stop to tell you that? He was trying to get out of here before you got back," Rasha said.

"That's not what happened. He didn't see us!"

"That's what he said but I know bullshit and that was bullshit," Rasha declared.

Sheila pulled into her parking spot and turned off her ignition. "Anyway. Just because you deal with trifling asses doesn't mean everybody is trifling."

"Whatever," Rasha gave as she exited the vehicle. "Shit stinks no matter where it rests. That bastard probably ain't got no meeting to go to and if he does, it's not a business meeting."

"Alright. Thanks. I'll call you later, okay?"

"Okay. See you," Sheila ended the call.

"So, what do you want to do now?" Sheila asked, ignoring Rasha's accusation.

"Well, since we ain't playing cards, we might as well go out. Let's call some home girls and have a ladies' night out," Rasha decided as she headed up the stairs to Sheila's apartment.

"Let's do that," Sheila agreed. "I don't know if I've got anything to wear."

"Please," Rasha exclaimed as she pushed passed Sheila and rushed into the apartment. "You got more clothes than any bitch I know. Let me in that closet. I'll find you something to wear."

"Stay out my closet, bitch," Sheila called. Rasha rushed for the bedroom and Sheila was about to follow but the note on the counter caught her attention. "See," she said to Rasha. "He left me a note. I told you."

"Whatever," Rasha said. "He's just covering his tracks. Let's get dressed bitch."

"I hope you wash your ass first," Sheila called back to Rasha. "I hope you wash yours too."

They reached Fabulous Nails just before the shop closed. It was exactly six p.m., and the policy of the shop was no treatments would be started after five-thirty. Being regular customers allowed them to slip in for service despite this policy. It was a testament to the frequency with which Rasha and Sheila visited the establishment. The rows of colored vinyl chairs were now empty. Only one other patron remained in the shop. The customer was an elderly lady who was being serviced by Mrs. Nong.

Rasha and Sheila sat on the far end of the shop. They had dispensed the pleasantries and were well into their nail treatments. Normally, they received service exclusively from Mr. And Mrs. Nong, the shop owners. On such short notice, however, the only techs available were Kiki and Lili, the Nong's two daughters. The girls attended the

University during the mornings and worked for their parents in the afternoons. Since Sheila and Rasha usually had Friday morning appointments, they rarely got an opportunity to observe the girls at work. Sheila assumed that the girls were probably very good students but doubted their proficiency in nail application and design. Subsequently, she'd spent a good deal of time observing the techniques Kiki, her surrogate nail tech, applied and had been unable to participate in the conversation Rasha had chosen to carry on, with or without her input. "You know that was shady, Sheila," Rasha insisted. "He saw us. He knew you were trying to stop him. He just didn't want to stop."

"That ain't what happened," Sheila answered, finally surrendering to Kiki's professionalism. "And why you gotta be all negative anyway. Can't you be happy for a sister?"

"I am happy for you. I just don't want you to be so happy that you miss the things going on around you. What do you think about me getting a hundred-dollar bill sign on my middle finger? You think it's ghetto?" Rasha asked.

"Your ass is ghetto," Lili mumbled in Vietnamese. She added, "Hundred-dollar design is very stylish," in English for good measure.

"Are you wearing it for a special occasion or on a daily basis?" Sheila asked as she eyed the electric file in Kiki's hand.

"Well, I'm getting it for tonight, but you know I'm not going to take it off until I come back," Rasha admitted. "How much is the hundred-dollar bill design?"

"This one?" Lili asked, pointing to the numeric design.

"Yes, that one," Rasha confirmed. "The one with the number."

"Can you believe this cheap bitch," "Lili chimed to Kiki in her native tongue. "She wants the baller signs but don't have the baller dimes. If she was balling, then she wouldn't need to ask."

"Be quiet, Lili," her sister scolded with a stifled laugh. "It is ten dollars extra ma'am."

"Okay," Rasha said with suspicion. "What did you say to her?"

As did most nail shop patrons, Sheila and Rasha had gotten into the habit of carrying on conversations of a personal nature in the presence of their nail techs. It wasn't that they trusted their confidence in keeping all things heard unspoken. It was more of a subconscious reaction to the nail techs habit of speaking primarily in foreign languages in the shop. They assumed that their language barrier was not mutually exclusive. They knew that the nail techs talked about them and discussed their business in their native tongues. As long as the nail techs never translated it or confirmed those suspicions, it was overlooked. "I was asking about the price of the hundred-dollar sign," Lili interjected.

"Oh, that's what I thought," Rasha accented with hostility.

"Eat the moon, bitch," Lili said with a smile in her native tongue. "Sisterhood is universal," she translated for Rasha's entertainment.

"It is indeed," Mr. Nong said as he stepped up behind his daughter. The conversation had brought him into the fray. "Lili, there is no charge for the dollar sign today. For Ms. Rasha, it is free." Mr. Nong walked around and placed his hand on Rasha's shoulder. "You are a loyal customer. I appreciate your business."

"Thank you, Mr. Nong," Rasha said with a smile. Mr. Nong was always very nice to her, she thought.

"Don't piss me off," Mr. Nong cooed to his daughter in Vietnamese. He added a smile that was more decipherable than his dialect. "Ms. Rasha, Ms. Sheila," he said and returned to his office.

"Yes, child. Parker Grant is good to me. I ain't gonna lie," Sheila exclaimed after a brief minute. "I think I love him."

***

"Who doesn't know that," Rasha responded as she looked at the nail polish sample board. "I like this one," she decided pointing to a neon green florescent. "Do what you do, but I told you that man is not the settling down type."

"Isn't that the same guy the library lady was in here talking about yesterday?" Kiki asked Lili in their native tongue. "Nice color," she directed towards Rasha in a language more amicable to her deciphering.

"Sure is," Lili answered with dual meaning.

"Why do you say that, Rasha? Because he isn't looking to settle down at this point in his life? I understand him," Sheila defended. "He wants to have his life together before he steps into a relationship. He wants to be able to give any relationship a fair shot. He just doesn't feel he's there yet. I can respect that." Sheila accepted the color board that Kiki handed her and studied the hues with earnest effort. "Do you have any metallics?" she asked.

"Lili, hand me that metallic board over there on that station," Kiki requested. "Sister don't have a clue," she added for good measure.

Lili grabbed the board from the adjacent station and passed it to Sheila. After a moment of deliberation, she chose a color. "I think I'll take this one," Sheila decided.

"Excellent choice," Kiki complimented. "My library friend picked the same one." They all laughed but only Kiki and Lili truly got the joke.

Chapter 21

Big Bad Bennie Johnson's Billiard Parlor was housed inside a renovated warehouse in the industrial district of Macon, GA. Outwardly, it had the appearance of an I-shaped storage facility with high ceilings. Inwardly, however, it was nothing short of a designer's paradise. The concept behind the interior was that of a southern colonial era establishment that had been built with soul. It was classy; it was tasteful, and it was quickly becoming a happening nightspot for African- Americans in the Middle Georgia area.

The property was divided into three sections: a bar area that held the parlor's entrance, a billiards chamber that served as the sporting area for those who indulged, and a lounge area that served as the epicenter for the parlor's socializing.

At the forefront of the parlor was a full-length wrap-around bar. It was housed in a large nook that spread out to the right of the main chamber. The bar was fully stocked and crafted in the manner of an English pub. Everything was built from fine wood and accented with polished steel. The bartenders wore pinstriped trousers and vests with white shirts and ties. The remaining area was covered with bar tables and freestanding floor sculptures.

The majority of the parlor was dedicated to the sport of billiards. It held fourteen billiard tables, each a magnificent AMF Renaissance Signature Series Goeblin®. They were adequately spaced along the length of the center of the parlor. All met the WCBS regulations for height and length. As for their appearance, they were elegant and well-made. Their felt surfaces alternated between burgundy and hunter green respectively. They were kept in immaculate condition. No gashes marred their manicured facings. No blemish defaced their polished surfaces. They were the most beautiful tables money could buy. Embossed steel corners joined sculpted mahogany guardrails to produce an exquisite show of craftsmanship and character. Constituted leather lined the pockets, concluding in fringe at their bases. The side panels were also made of the finest mahogany; three small glass ports holding liquid levels were located at measured intervals along each side. A wide spherical joint sprang out where each leg joined the table's base. The legs formed out in the impression of large hairy paws.

Large high-back leather recliners stood sentinel around four large wooden columns that ran down the center of the billiards area. Some of the chairs held waylaid players who were waiting on an opportunity to redeem their reputations with the cue. Others provided seating for ladies who did not actually play pool but had accompanied gentlemen to the parlor.

Elaborately framed portraits of Donald Goines, Langston Hughes, Nikki Giovanni, Richard Pryor, Ruby

D., James Weldon Johnston and Eldridge Cleaver hung high in the billiards area.

The likenesses were painted with great distinction. The gentlemen were dressed in fine suits with stiff collared shirts and ties, while the ladies were outfitted in Victorian-styled dresses and Sunday going-to-church hats. Antiquated electric lanterns were mounted on the wall next to each side of the portraits. Their soft light along with that of three crystal chandeliers suspended from the ceiling brightened the windowless parlor.

Between the personalized artwork and the wall-mounted light fixtures hung several intricately designed cue racks. Their bases were much like any other cue rack, having a small indention for each of its would-be residents. The upper portion of the rack, however, was different. Normally a bar with vertical holes drilled from its base to its zenith served to stabilize the cues from above. In the case of these specialized racks, however, ten outstretched arms carved from fine white oak had replaced that bar; the arms ended in a closed fist with openings that held the cue stick as a player waiting his turn might hold it.

At the rear of the parlor was a lounge. It was set up to allow patrons not involved in the sporting of billiards to socialize comfortably. Several small, round tables with simplistic wooden chairs where patrons could sit and drink with friends were scattered across the hardwood floor. A crowd stood around a smaller bar that served the customers in the rear of the parlor.

None of these interior design marvels held Parker's attention, however. For the majority of the time that Parker had spent in Big Bad Bennie Johnson's Billiard Parlor, he had been thinking of his situation with Alfreda. She had become so much to him so fast. She'd made herself a staple in his life. He liked that. He enjoyed being into her. It didn't happen to him often. He wasn't the type to find someone to make him happy. She did it for him. He decided he was cool with that.

Being cool with that and a rather hefty intake of the import allowed him to concentrate on other things. At that moment, Parker contemplated the contents in his glass. Little icebergs floating in a captive sea, he thought. Gigantic miniatures caught in a finite, fantastically frigid float towards death by rapid decomposition. Shivering silently, sliding towards extinction. Melting to your beginning. In your ending is life.

It was because of this contemplation that he did not see Alfreda until she was right in front of him. "Hi Parker," she said with a smile.

"Alfreda! Nice to see that you keep your promises," Parker said as he stood to greet her. "Here, let me take your coat. "

"Thank you, Parker. How are you doing?" Alfreda responded as she turned and dropped her coat from her shoulders.

"Oh, I'm cool. How about you, ladybug," Parker asked as he stepped up to take her coat. Aromas of sensuality permeated from Alfreda's body; they summoned Parker's attention and further elevated her in Parker's regard. He leaned in close and gently pulled at the lapels of the overcoat. The soft leather material fell easily from Alfreda's body. Parker stepped back and discovered what God would look like if God is a woman. She was there, God, in all God's glory: 36C, trim waist, the most perfect thighs and ass that anyone could ever conceive, and delicate shoulders that most assuredly could hold your whole world up if God so chose. She had skin that paled the sun and reflected a new moon, a poise that personified deity, a being that, if any did, certainly deserved worship. Yes, Parker thought, if God is a woman, this is most definitely God.

Alfreda carried an untamed ebony mane as her crown. During their previous encounters, she had always worn her hair straightened and pressed. This look was more exotic, Parker thought. He liked it a lot. In the light of the pool hall, her Afro sparkled as if it had been sprinkled with jewels. Golden hoops hung from her delicate ear lobes. A necklace of a similar design lay around her neck.

Alfreda wore a backless, sleeveless caramel blouse that tied at the neck and hung low on her bosom. The sequined silk garment fell flawlessly over her breast and expired at her hips. Sleek black slacks with caramel pinstripes adorned her lower extremities; the lines traced the contours of her ample thighs and generous backside. She floated on liquid black Kenneth Cole sling-back sandals with three-inch heels; Alfreda's magnificent feet sported a French pedicure that had to have been a pleasure to administer.

Parker placed the jacket on a nearby coat rack and made the only customary statement that he could muster. "May I offer you a drink?" he asked as he broke the spell of Alfreda's magnificent body, only to fall victim to her hypnotic eyes.

"Sure, I'll have a Smirnoff Twisted Apple," Alfreda replied as she sat in the chair next to Parker.

If it were not for the import, speech would have failed Parker. As it was, the wittiest statement he could manage was, "What's that?" as an inquiry about Alfreda's drink.

"It's a refreshing blend of crisp green apples and Smirnoff Vodka," Alfreda replied in her best commercial announcer's voice.

"My, aren't we the walking Smirnoff spokesperson," Parker shot back after regaining some of his charisma.

"Hey, I just know what I drink. You can't fault a sister for that."

"True. True. Excuse me, madam," Parker called to a nearby waitress. "Can I have a Smirnoff Twisted Apple in a high ball glass, please? Oh, and can you refresh my drink also, please?"

Alfreda waited until the waitress was out of earshot and then inquired about Parker's drink. "So, what's your sauce?"

"Hydrogen Oxide on the rocks with a twist of Citrus Limonium," Parker replied in his best college professor voice.

"Huh?" Alfreda replied with the appropriate bewilderment.

"Water with lime, girl," Parker admitted with a chuckle.

"Well, why didn't you just say water with lime?" Alfreda protested with a charm that only a southern colored girl could produce. "And what kind of drink is that anyway; water with lime!" You're out on the town, at a very nice establishment, with a drop-dead gorgeous woman, and you're drinking water?"

"Yes," Parker answered with and overcompensated confidence. "And I like it that way." The waitress returned with their drinks and Parker paid and tipped her. After she left, he continued with his declaration. "I don't drink that often and when I do, I prefer it to be in more intimate surroundings."

"So, you don't drink when you go out," Alfreda asked between sips.

"I rarely do."

"So, you don't drink anything to get you going up in the club?"

"No."

"And nothing to get you and your special someone in the mood?"

"Not anything to drink, no."

"Oh, I get you," Alfreda exclaimed as Parker's point finally sunk in. "The import."

"Yep!" Parker said with a smile. "That's all I need." Two gentlemen approached the bar with pool balls in a triangular tray. "Looks like a table's opened up. Would you like to play?"

"Sure," Alfreda answered as she gathered her things to follow Parker.

The attendant took Parker's identification and gave him the tray of balls for table #4. Because of its location, table #4 was a prime social location. Those who engaged in sport at table #4 were privy to the best view in the bar. They had an unobstructed view of everyone entering the parlor and everyone socializing in the lounge. In addition to this, you were the first thing that anyone entering the parlor would see. It was an appointment of honor. Parker knew this and so did Alfreda. "Nice placement. We can see everything from this table," she said as she relocated her purse and jacket to a nearby countertop. "I'm glad I'm not looking like a mess."

"Like you could ever look a mess," Parker said with a smirk. He was getting his mojo back. Alfreda was in trouble.

"Please, Parker," she retorted as she worked her way through a hysterical outburst. "If a sister could believe all that shit you keep going in her ear, it would be cool, but no, I gotta watch out cause you're one of these artist motherfuckers. You could be gassing me up with the same lines you use on the next bitch; know what I'm saying?"

Parker burst into laughter. She was right. He had a way with words. He knew that. But he knew what made her different. "Baby, their getting second-hand compliments," Parker shot back innocently.

"What do you mean?" Alfreda asked between giggles.

"Cause every compliment I ever gave originated with you, baby," Parker said in his best Billie D Williams voice.

Alfreda stopped laughing and looked into Parker's eyes. A brief flicker of radiant energy seemed to cross her eyes. "You're good. Oh, yes motherfucker, you're good," Alfreda said as she broke eye contact with Parker and took a sip of her drink. "I'm breaking," she called defiantly.

"I know," Parker replied coolly. "I wouldn't have it any other way.

***

The cat-like stance that Alfreda assumed when she took her shots may not have been textbook correct, but it was effective enough to have allowed her to arrive on the 8-ball a full three shots ahead of Parker. So far, she had made it her business to rub this fact in Parker's face thoroughly. She'd cat-called and loud-talked him for a full ten minutes while they'd traversed the length of the table. Now she was quiet but not for lack of appropriate material. She was trying to concentrate on sinking her final shot. Parker was trying to distract her.

"She's poised for the final shot, ladies and gentlemen," Parker said in his best sports announcers' voice. "She's fought ball for ball throughout this match up and now her efforts have brought her to this last all-encompassing shot. The 8-ball rests just outside of the side pocket. Can she sink the 8 without scratching?"

"Shut up," Alfreda shouted at Parker between giggles. "Who're you supposed to be?"

Parker ignored her and went on. "Alfreda Redwind, champion billiards diva, takes her patented kitty cat stance. She lines up with her target."

Alfreda gave up trying to deter Parker and concentrated on her shot. She lined up the ball and was about to take her shot when her phone rang. It startled her and she forgot to put English on the ball. The result was a scratched shot; the cue ball went into the pocket behind the 8-ball.

"And she chokes ladies and gentlemen!" Parker announced, pretending not to hear Alfreda's phone going off. He could not pretend that he didn't see the worried look on her face, however.

"Parker, can you excuse me for a second?" Alfreda asked with a hint of nervousness in her voice.

"Sure, sure. Is everything alright?"

"Yes, it's fine," Alfreda assured him as she put down her cue stick and gathered her purse. "Which way is the restroom?"

Parker nodded towards the rear of the lounge. "It's around that corner over there."

Alfreda mumbled a thank you and darted in the direction Parker had indicated.

It was obvious to Parker that Alfreda had been startled by the phone call she'd received. Yet, she hadn't answered the ring or even looked at the display screen; how did she know who the caller was? Perhaps it was the ringtone. It was different from the standard optional tones.

Parker racked the balls and set the table for a rematch. If she wanted to pretend, she wasn't bothered, then he would play along. Besides, he thought, I'm not going to allow anything to disrupt my evening.

"Parker baby, I've gotta run," Alfreda announced as she made it back to table #4.

"Oh. Okay," Parker answered. "Is everything alright?"

"Yeah, I've just got drama, that is all." Alfreda took a long sip of her drink and then turned to face Parker. "Baby, I had to lie to get him to baby-sit for me."

Him, Parker thought. He knew who "him" was.

Alfreda continued. "That's how I was able to get out of the house but now he's gotten frustrated with the baby and wants me to come home. He says he's gonna just leave my baby there by himself. Sorry, but I've gotta go, Parker," she said as she put down her drink and slipped into her jacket.

"I understand ladybug. Let me walk you out," Parker offered.

"No, baby. I'll be alright," Alfreda responded. She placed a hand on Parker's shoulder and squeezed it. "Just stay and enjoy yourself. I knew this might happen. He just doesn't want me to go out anywhere."

Parker pulled Alfreda to him and held her tight. He buried his face in her hair and inhaled deeply. "Be easy, ladybug," he cosigned.

"I will," Alfreda said as she broke the embrace and headed for the exit. "See ya, baby."

Alfreda paused at the parlor exit. Should I look back, she contemplated. I should just leave. He's probably not even watching me. Maybe he is, she thought. Maybe he's watching me walk away, dreaming of the next time he'll get to see me. If he's not, then I can take that too. I've read the book. Maybe he's just not into me.

Alfreda held the door and looked back right into Parker's eyes. He was watching her. Unfortunately, at the same moment that she chose to look back, a group of nightlife divas chose to enter the parlor. What was worse was that they were heavily engaged in a conversation and did not notice her either. Before Alfreda could turn back around and discover she was headed for a collision, the collision had already occurred.

She stumbled but rebounded nicely, thanks to some assistance from one of the divas with whom she'd collided. Alfreda's purse fell from her shoulder, but she was able to catch the strap and prevent a nasty spillage. It wasn't until after she'd caught the purse that Alfreda saw the divas that collided with and subsequently rescued her. If she'd seen them prior to the catch, she probably would have been too shocked to make the save.

There, in front of Alfreda, stood three young women; one of them was Rasha, her boyfriend's sister. Alfreda momentarily froze. Time stretched out to an unbelievable length. A long stream of profanity shot through Alfreda's mind.

If Rasha tells her brother that she saw me here instead of at work, there's gonna be trouble, Alfreda realized. She didn't need that kind of stress. If Rasha had seen her with Parker and started asking questions, there would be more trouble. I damn sure don't need that, Alfreda screamed inside her skull.

"Hey girl," Rasha said with a start. "What are you doing out? I ain't seen you since the baby was born. My brother must not know you're out?"

Alfreda hugged her pseudo sister-in-law and then carefully chose her next words. She didn't need this nosy bitch on her trail. "Hell no, he don't know, and don't you tell him. A bitch can't even grab a beer after work without him whining. Let a bitch breathe, okay!" she exclaimed. Better to be upfront with her, Alfreda thought.

"Damn girl, it's good to see you," Rasha replied. "Don't worry; I got you. Look, these are my home girls Comeka and Sheila," she announced, presenting her two girlfriends. "Y'all, this is Alfreda."

Alfreda exchanged greetings with a polite swiftness. She knew better than to give Rasha an opportunity to ask her anything. It would only take one question to set the ball rolling in the wrong direction. She tucked her purse and then said her goodbyes. "I'll see you later girl. It was nice to see you again, but you know that crazy brother of yours. He's already blowing my phone up looking for me."

"Half-brother," Rasha corrected. "I understand. He's my brother but that mutherfucka ain't shit. I know what the deal is. I'll see you later girl."

"Bye girl," Sheila and Comeka said in unison. "They're all crazy, girl. Just be strong."

Alfreda smiled and then ducked out of the parlor. In less than two minutes, she was in her car and leaving the parking lot. If she'd stayed another minute, she'd have heard Rasha ask Sheila if that was her man on table #4; she'd have heard her say that Parker Grant wasn't shit either.

Parker burst a series of coronaries as he observed his very own personalized horror scene unfold. Here, in the same location, less than thirty feet away, engaged in casual conversation stood Alfreda, his current sweetheart, and Sheila, his soon to be ex-girlfriend. And they were talking; more specifically, it was Sheila's nosy friend Rasha who was engaging Alfreda in conversation.

He watched them. They were discussing something. He was sure that he saw Rasha's mouth the words 'ain't shit'. She was sure to be speaking of him.

So, this is how it was going to go down, Parker thought; out here in the open. This would be ugly. Obviously, Sheila had seen him hugging Alfreda. Why else would they have stopped her? And now they were involved in a conversation.

Chapter 22

The previous evening, which had started so nicely, had almost ended in disaster for Parker. A freak meeting had brought all the key players in his sick and twisted game into the same arena much sooner than he'd ever expected them to be. Luckily, it had worked itself out with no one any the wiser. It wasn't a common occurrence; Parker counted his blessings.

The cell phone rang but Parker did not answer it. He could see the phone's electric green LCD screen. He could read the caller's name. He knew it was Sheila. He knew she was calling to check on his job-hunting progress. He knew that when he told her that no one had shown any real interest in hiring him, she would say they were missing out on a great employee. He knew that she would have something uplifting to say. Parker knew that Sheila would find a way to put a positive spin on the day's dismal outcome. He knew all these things, but he wasn't in the mood to hear her optimism. He couldn't take another pep talk. Not today. He'd listened to it the first few days of his search and had been very appreciative. At first, it had been reassuring. He'd felt energized and rejuvenated when she called with her positive outlook and unwavering faith in his ability to obtain gainful employment; she had been his personal cheerleader. She held his corner down with a dedication that was almost cultic. And he liked it. It was nice having someone who believed in him.

Now though, after almost a full week in the muck and mire of the job market, his spirits were down. Sheila's words were taking on the form of daggers that stabbed away at his soul. He felt as if he was becoming a disappointment. He couldn't live up to her high expectations. He hadn't realized any of the dreams that she'd so beautifully painted for his future. He had dived head-first into the foray and hit a stonewall. Now he was starting to feel desperate. It wasn't as simple as he'd thought it would be. The shadow of wasted potential loomed overhead and Parker was not one to take such pragmatic situations well.

Originally, he thought himself extremely marketable. He was intelligent. He had a very professional demeanor. He spoke the language of corporate America. He walked the walk of a confident man. Although he's yet to finish his course of study at the University, but he was learned enough to promote himself in that aspect. Overall, he felt he was a good hire. On paper, he was a good hire. He was visually attractive. He was audibly attractive. He was educated and well-rounded. There wasn't any task required in any position that he'd applied for that he couldn't perform. Most he was over-qualified for. If he'd lived anywhere else, Parker would have been hired at every company he'd applied at on merit alone.

Unfortunately, he didn't live in an area that hired on the basis of merit. He lived in the South. Not just in the sense of geographic location. He lived in the sociopolitical South; the South that was still run by wealthy unyielding Southern-minded white aristocrats. Parker lived in a South that would not hire a black man that was too together or too confident. A black man in this South could be too educated to be employed. In the South that Parker lived in, creativity in a black man was seen as uppity, as bucking against the system. If he's white, they would have seen him as an innovator. He would have been groomed as a catalyst for change, but he wasn't white. He was black. That meant instead of confident, he was uppity. That meant instead of an innovator, he was a troublemaker. That meant that Parker was unemployable.

The phone finally stopped ringing and registered one missed call. Parker cleared the message and went back to preparing his import. This day had been lost to him, he thought. He'd been to three interviews and had been given the soft boot three times. It was either you're too qualified for the position or we're looking to promote from inside. How the hell can you be too qualified for a position, he screamed silently. Why wouldn't they want someone who could go above and beyond what was customary? And if you're going to hire from within, why post the position in the paper anyway? It was all bullshit, he decided as he finalized his construction project.

Parker pulled out his Bic® and put flames to import. It pulled evenly and immediately brought about a calm that he desperately needed. He closed his eyes and savored the taste of the high-end product. The smoke traveled to his lungs with a smoothness that was uncommon among most imports. That damn Casper, Parker thought as he exhaled the residuals.

His phone rang again but Parker ignored it. Instead, he opened his eyes and took in the scenery. The day was a gray one. The sun hid between the clouds and projected a pale reflection. He was seated on an old railroad crossing behind the NBC studio building. The overpass was constructed during the early part of the twentieth century. The walls were concrete and cobblestone. Underneath, there were old wooden beams that had originally been used for support but now only served aesthetic value. From the distance, it appeared to be a massive cave. The upward slope of the street that penetrated its center made it seem deep and foreboding. He admired the place for its character. It was dark and shadowy. It fit his mood. His phone ceased ringing and instead began to chime the chime of text message alert. Sheila was forever the trooper, he thought.

Parker picked up his phone and scrolled through the message. It was Sidney that had called. The message requested that he return her call as soon as possible. What could she want, he thought. As he pondered the question, his phone began to ring again. The screen read Sidney. Parker answered it with the enthusiasm of a dead man walking. "What's up chick?"

"Nothing," Sidney replied. "What's up with you?"

"Nothing. I'm sitting on the old overpass downtown enjoying an import," Parker replied without emotion. "The old train overpass," she inquired. "That's the one."

"How's the job thing going?"

"It isn't."

"What do you mean?" Sidney inquired.

Parker inhaled the import and held the fumes. They tickled the muscles of his larynx. "Nobody's hiring Negroes this week," Parker said as he exhaled.

"Come on now. Don't be like that. It's only been a couple of days, Parker. You gotta give it some time," Sidney offered.

"I'm frustrated, Sid. I've been out here for over a week, and I haven't gotten so much as a lukewarm reception."

"Just be patient, Parker. It'll come," Sidney consoled. "You've gotta keep at it."

Parker inhaled and went on, "Naw, Sidney. This shit is for the birds. You have no idea how it feels not to have a job. You're an attorney; you'll always have a job."

***

"True," Sidney admitted. "But that doesn't mean I don't understand what you're going through. I see you trying bro. I know you're out there every day beating the pavement. It's not easy. You've just got to keep at it."

"Yeah, I know. I just feel the pressure is all."

"Well, how about we grab something to eat and go chill with Casper? He called and told me he just got in some Indonesian import that's flagrant," Sidney offered to her discouraged friend.

"Yeah, that's cool. Where are you?"

"I'm headed for you now," Sidney replied. "You can park your car downtown and ride with me. There's no need in you taking any unnecessary risks driving. You're over by the bus station, right?"

"Yeah, behind the television station," Parker confirmed. "I'm gonna park my car at the terminal and meet you out front. How long until you get here?"

"I'm about five minutes out."

"Good. I'm leaving now," Parker said as he took a final hit of his import. "I've got a half we can share on the way." "See you there partner."

"Word," Parker replied. "Word indeed." He extinguished his import and headed for his Cadillac.

Parker almost missed the call. His phone was on vibrate and he hadn't been paying attention to it at all. Sidney had an early appointment though and wanted to know the time. Since none of Parker's friends wore watches, it was common practice to rely on cell phones as timepieces. Parker was looking for his when he felt it vibrating in his pocket.

"Hello?" he answered with hesitation. The number had come up 'unknown' and he wasn't normally in the practice of answering unidentified calls.

"Hey, Parker," came Alfreda's voice. "What are you up to?"

"Oh, nothing," Parker answered as he gathered his black and headed outside for privacy. Casper and Sidney verbally assaulted him for his choice of discretion. Parker smiled but continued to search for a suitable location to engage in his conversation. "What are you up to?" he said as he settled in on the last rocking chair on the porch.

"I think I'm coming over to see you," Alfreda replied.

"Oh really," Parker said with mild surprise. "When did this decision come about? Why was I not informed?"

"I'm telling you now," she replied with defiance. "Unless you don't want me to. I mean, it is about to rain and all. I could just stay home and sleep, but I thought it might be nice to enjoy and import and appreciate God's glory."

"Word," Parker commented as he stared up at the dark clouds rolling in. "Hey, it's about to storm. We need to be rolling out," he yelled to Sidney. "I'm in Macon right now. You want me to come scoop you from somewhere, so you don't have to drive in the rain?"

"Yeah. I'll meet you at the Waffle House on Hartley Bridge in about twenty minutes."

"Cool," Parker said as he looked toward the screen door. "I'll see you there." Parker ended his call and went to get Sidney. Before he made it into the house, his phone began vibrating again. He looked at the LCD screen. It read Sheila. Parker pressed the end button until his phone powered off and went inside to get Sidney.

Sheila got up and checked the thermostat for the umpteenth time. The dial read 68 degrees, but she felt like it was one hundred. She'd taken a shower before going to bed but the heat she was feeling would not be quailed by it.

She thought of the last time she and Parker had made love. It had been extremely intense. He'd ravaged her with the determination of a driven man. His strokes had been deep; penetrating, strong and unyielding. Each time he entered her, she felt as if his dick was in the back of her throat. Hell, it had been for a while, she admitted with a chuckle. Sheila wasn't ashamed. She loved to suck Parker's dick and what a dick he had. It was long, thick and extremely dedicated to the pleasuring of her pussy. When he was inside of her, every nerve ending in her body tingled uncontrollably; he filled her completely. Sheila placed her hand on the spot in her stomach were Parker's stroke most often landed. Her pussy jumped at the idea of it. Sometimes, days after they'd had an intense sexual excursion, she could still feel him inside her. Her body loved him and did not easily adjust to him being gone. On nights like tonight, it ached for their reunion.

It had been quite a while since she'd been with Parker, but she could still feel the spirit of him inside her. He alternated spending his nights between her home and his own. On this night, she wished he was here. During their last coupling, he introduced her to the erotic art of shaving. Her hand crept down to the place where her bush had been before Parker last shaved it off. The skin was smooth now: he'd done an excellent job. Sheila replayed the memory in her mind. She remembered how erotic the experience was. Parker turned something so mundane into an orgasmic event. He'd used a Lady Bic® razor, a bowl of water, some warm shaving cream and a very vibrant electric Remington® to blow her mind; he started with the Remington®. The vibrations from the electric shaver were so intense that she'd come twice before he even switched to the disposable. Sheila recalled feeling the warm water trickling down into her most intimate crevices; she thought of the slow pull of the razor against her skin. Parker's thick capable fingers performed their task with a sultry precision. He completed his task by running his thick talented tongue over every shaved inch of her pussy. Her entire body turned to fire. Her skin felt electric, hypersensitive. She'd lost count of the times she'd climaxed on the tip of his tongue. It was no wonder sleep evaded her, she thought. She needed her man.

Sheila massaged her fingers into the places that Parker had shaved clean. She imagined that her hands were his hands and that he was there with her, just beyond her reach. The familiar tingling that came with her arousal began to take hold. Her fingers inched down from the firm flesh below her belly button to the delicate folds between her thighs. Moisture had begun to gather there. She spread her legs to allow herself better access and inadvertently pulled the scratchy blanket across her hardening nipples. The friction of the fabric on her flesh sent electric shocks across her breast. Sheila shuddered involuntarily.

Sheila's fingers sank between the moist folds of her labia. She imagined that her index finger was Parker's tongue and that he was slowly dragging it across her clitoris. She let her other fingers caress and explore the wet slick walls of her canal in the manner that Parker's oral efforts often did. She imagined Parker's lips suckling on her folds and his tongue gliding across her flesh.

***

Sheila ground her palm into the wetness that was hers at a quickening pace. She imagined that her hand was Parker's pelvis, and her fingers were his thick delicious dick pounding into her. She took hold of her right breast and squeezed it firmly. She took the nipple between her thumb and forefinger and pinched it sharply; the pain of it increased her desire.

Her hand now moved at a rapid pace, its index digit planted on Sheila's clitoris, its other digits churning away in her canal. At that moment, Sheila exploded. A fever overtook her. Her movements were no longer her own. It was not her hand that was pleasuring her; it was Parker's tongue. It was not her fingers that were plunging tirelessly into her; it was Parker's dick. As the orgasm overtook her, Sheila held one thought in her mind: She was no longer alone. Sheila was with her man.

Chapter 23

A drizzling rain fell. On this morning, the sun had risen but did not shine. Gray clouds moved lazily across the sky. Sudden winds raced through trees and rustled leaves from their resting places on high. Windowpanes suffered the cadence of persistent precipitation as the sky watered the world. Flowing rivers ran through gutters, cascaded down waterfalls and formed expansive deltas across the lawn. Silence sang uninterrupted save the sound of the rain. A serene stillness endured. The world was painted in pigments of pale blues and ghostly grays. Second-hand light slipped through the clouds and blanketed the earth with an eerie iridescence. A chill was about.

The coolness that often accompanied these types of days was very good sleeping weather; the climate produced was significant enough to require those exposed to it to seek some sort of covering but not so much to require that covering to be of any real bulk. Consequently, Parker and Alfreda, who'd spent the previous night sprawled out on a mattress in the living room, had only covered themselves with a silk sheet and even that had been hastily applied during one of the night's brief respites. All the windows had been raised to allow the breeze to permeate the house. The smell of fresh rain was in the air.

Parker sat on the sofa and enjoyed the moment. He loved rainy days. The melancholy mood they triggered in him was extremely conducive to writing. What Parker appreciated most about rainy days, however, was the magnificent lovemaking they seemed to promote. All night the rain had fallen; and all night, they made love. It had been effortless; every movement came naturally; every craving had been satiated. Their consummation had been an excellent performance. It played like a scene from life's most pleasurable production. It had been a rare meeting of souls in the physical realm. Few people could achieve such an intense feat. Parker had been with a few people, so he felt sure of this. Yet, he and Alfreda had done so over and over and over again. It was as if their lovemaking was some sort of ancient ritual of soul stirring. They had opened the doors to their souls and allowed each other to enter. Now he felt a bond with her.

Parker admired her shapeliness as she slept. Alfreda lay peacefully across the mattress. The pale light that penetrated the clouds and crept through the blinds bathed her body in a heavenly glow. A sheet partially covered her stomach and pelvis but left the rest of her body exposed. Her hair framed her face in an angelic silhouette. The delicate skin of her neck reminded him of the petals of a flower. He watched her torso rise and fall with her breathing. Her breasts were full and ripe like fresh peaches. The curve of her hip met the bow of her thigh in perfect symmetry. Her legs were well-formed; they ended in the most delectable feet Parker had ever had the pleasure of touching. Alfreda's body was as beautiful as he'd imagined it to be. He was drawn to her.

Parker crept closer and brushed the hair from her neck. He traced the crook of her shoulder with his finger and then retraced his path until he reached the cleave of her breast. His hand lingered there for a moment, then journeyed across each of her silky mounds. Parker teased the dark flesh of Alfreda's nipples with feathery touches. She moaned softly in her sleep. Parker used the back of his hands to brush against the side of Alfreda's torso. She moaned again and shifted her body in response. She was so damn lovely, he thought.

Parker gently pulled the sheet away from Alfreda's body. He placed an outstretched hand on her taut belly and allowed his fingers to traverse the short distance to the dark thick patch of pleasure between her thighs. Alfreda inhaled sharply but did not awaken. Parker smiled inwardly. How much pleasure would it take to steal the sleeping goddess from the clutches of slumber, he wondered and determined to discover the answer.

He lowered his head to Alfreda's honeywell and inhaled deeply. Faint whiffs of strawberries tickled his nose and awakened his desire. He felt himself hardening with anticipation. His tongue darted out and grazed the folds of her womanhood. The flavor of arousal coated her lips. Parker let his tongue delve deeper and caused Alfreda to moan once again. The power of arousal was starting to overcome that of slumber. Her body stretched, signaling her imminent awakening.

Parker squarely repositioned himself between Alfreda's outstretched legs and began to feast upon her delicacy earnestly. He parted her creases to provide him access to her hidden treasures; he took her lips between his and nibbled them gently. His hands found her breasts and caressed them. Alfreda released moans from deep low places. Parker took this as a good sign and intensified his efforts.

Alfreda announced her awakening by taking Parker's head between her hands and pulling him even deeper between her thighs. Her hips ground against his face. Her wetness dripped down her legs and saturated the mattress beneath them. Alfreda scooted up in an attempt to curtail her building orgasm, but Parker would not be undone. He removed his hands from her breast and secured them around her legs. Now she was trapped. Now she was caught, Parker thought. She would be forced to ride the oncoming orgasm to its end.

Parker zeroed in on the zenith of Alfreda's erogenous zone. His tongue swirled in ridiculously complex patterns of movements. A barely audible humming came from his throat; the vibrations it caused intensified his lover's pleasure. Alfreda clamped her thighs around his skull in response. Parker closed his lips around his target and began a slow, encompassing suckling. He gradually increased the intensity in tone with the volume of the muffled moaning that penetrated the vise grips that Alfreda's thighs had become. The final blow was dealt with the rapid-fire flickering of his tongue across the swollen surface of the most secret place.

Alfreda's breathing became ragged; her muscles revolted; her body began to convulse uncontrollably. Her vision left her and was replaced by a sky of colors and prismatic movements. Sound stopped; time stopped; life stopped, and Alfreda felt Parker's promise fulfilled.

Parker heard music coming from the direction of The Cenacle's offices when he pulled into the parking area. What's this pimp doing, he wondered. It was not unusual for the guys at the body shop to have a CD blasting but they were the country music type and the sounds floating in the air weren't the country music type. They were the Frankie Beverly and Maze-type music. He exited his vehicle and was met with the smell of good cooking. He followed it to the area of The Cenacle's offices.

Parker turned the corner and saw his boss and friend dancing in front of a picnic table that had been converted into a makeshift kitchen. An orange power cord lead from the office to a circuit breaker that supplied power to three hot plates set upon it. Theodore stood over a large copper pot stirring a very aromatic mix. He wore a green apron over a pair of khaki cargo shorts and a crisp white tee shirt. When he saw Parker approaching, he laid the spoon aside and came to greet him. "What's up Parker Grant, roving reporter?" Theodore accentuated with a hearty hug.

"What's up, Theodore?" Parker returned with a solid pat on the back.

"Oh, I'm on some gourmet hot plate shit today, partner," Theodore proclaimed as he disengaged from the manly greeting and returned to his culinary endeavors. "I got my Frankie Beverly and Maze playing, my New Orleans style gumbo simmering, my Michelob in hand, and my woman at my side," Theodore declared as he slapped his wife, who'd come out to bring him a fresh beer, on the behind. She playfully swatted his hand away and after saying hi to Parker, disappeared back inside the office.

"I love that woman," Theodore admitted. "This is what I do it for man." He took a swig of his beer and continued. "I feel good man. I'm happy to be able to do simple things like this," he said, referring to his impromptu gumbo cookout. "You need to get you a woman, Parker, someone to share the spoils of your labors with."

"Well, I'm not at the point where I have spoils yet," Parker admitted as he surveyed the contents of the pot. "You got some serious-sized shrimp in there."

"Yep! And fresh sausage, and chunks of chicken and pineapple and all sorts of other good shit. This gumbo is the bomb, player." Theodore spooned out a particularly saucy-looking shrimp and presented it for Parker's sampling.

Parker plucked it from the spoon and popped it into his mouth. "Divine," Parker declared. "I didn't know you could burn, brother!"

"Indeed I can!" Theodore returned the spoon to the pot and then turned his attention to Parker. "So, what's up? How's that article coming?"

"I'm actually done. I came over to bring you the final draft." Parker handed over the folder he'd been holding onto. Theodore took it and opened it to the first page. "Be careful. You've got sauce on your fingers."

"Whatever," Theodore said, licking his fingers. "This is great Parker. I knew there was greatness in you." He turned through the pages and stopped on the pictures. "She's quite the looker."

"Yeah, but give it up player. You can't fade her."

"I don't shop anymore, partner," Theodore said with a nod towards the direction of his wife, "but I still like to look in the window!"

Parker knew what Theodore meant. He saw the love he had for his wife. He saw how well they worked together. They were a team. On top of that, they had genuine love for each other and passion. Theodore would never cheat on his wife because he knew there couldn't possibly be anything better. "Like I don't know you love that woman in there," Parker verbalized. "You ain't gotta tell me. Anyway, I've got a disc in the back pocket of the folder if you want to make any changes."

"Thanks. Look, this is good writing. I want you to continue to look into this thing though. Push a little deeper and see if there's a back- story in it. Let's play big news for a while."

"Cool," Parker answered.

Theodore stirred his gumbo. The aroma of seafood well-seasoned drifted through the afternoon breeze. The music was calming. Soft singing came from the direction of the office. Parker saw the beauty in the scene that was Theodore's marriage and was saddened by his own lack of love.

"Alright, pimp, I gotta get outta here," Parker said as he readied himself to leave.

"Hey, that's a good article you got over there," Theodore said, nodding towards the folder on the table. "You're a good writer, Parker."

"Thanks man. I'll holler." Parker turned and walked away.

Chapter 24

In celebration of Parker's first week of job-hunting, Sheila organized a surprise card party. She invited Dean and Paula, who brought Little Dean along for good measure, Sidney and Casper, who brought import of a considerable measure, and Rasha, who discussed everything in short measure. The gang was all there. Parker arrived at seven-thirty after stopping at his Fort Valley residence to grab clothing for the following week. The activities were well underway when he arrived. His inability to obtain even the possibility of employment notwithstanding, Parker's evening was looking up. All his close friends had gathered in one place to hang out.

Sidney and Casper were paired up against Dean and Paula. As for the intensity of the competition, it was a mismatch at best. As a whole, the players were an excellent group of cardsharps. Dean and Sidney had been brought up at card tables and Casper and Paula lived similar experiences. All four players knew the game; it was intrinsic to their social development. Spades was a game of partners. Though Dean and Paula were married, they didn't have the experience of playing as a team that Sidney and Casper had. They hadn't learned to read their partner's plays. They understood the general signs of fishing for spades and playing off and bid stacking, but it was the subtle unconscious signs that they lacked experience with. On the contrary, Sidney and Casper had been partners for almost a decade. They worked a table with delicate destruction that was legendary. They were always the team to beat.

What Dean lacked in cohesiveness, he more than recouped in shit-talking. No one but Parker talked shit like Dean. "Get that shit off the table," Dean exclaimed as he made short work of a deuce that Sidney had fished with. The game was intense. Casper had cut diamonds off the bat and usurped two books that Dean had counted on. Since Dean's hand had only held those two diamonds and he'd counted on at least one cut book from the suit, he was forced to sacrifice his king. It was an expensive casualty but Dean's positioning to Casper's immediate left made it a worthy risk. Casper pushed clubs in an effort to find his partner. Sidney responded by playing the queen against the odds that Dean didn't have the king and was rewarded with an excellent split; she followed up with the ace, which caught Paula's king and cost her team another book. Paula rebounded, however, by capturing the initial book in hearts and then slicing all those that subsequently followed. By the hand's end, Dean and Paula had regained their lost books and given Sidney and Casper a run for theirs.

Parker reappeared in a burgundy signature Guayabera that Sheila purchased for him during an earlier shopping trip. He rounded out the ensemble with Khaki-colored linen trousers and Johnston & Murphy soft leather sandals. He stood in the doorway and observed the card play for a moment before joining in the foray.

"So how long do I have to wait before some professionals get on the table," Dean asked with sarcasm.

"Well, if you get the hell out of my seat, a professional will get on the table," Parker interjected from the doorway.

"You just shut up. You ain't even on the table," Dean shot back.

"That's because I'm the main attraction and you guys are just the opening act. I don't even show up until its main event time," Parker proclaimed as he relinquished his position by the door and swaggered into the living room area.

"Nice of you to join us," Sidney said. "Do you think that you and Dean could hold off with the shit-talking at least until you all are actually playing each other?"

"I'll try," Dean responded, "but there's just so much shit to talk about Parker."

"Fuck you, Dean," Parker responded with a smile.

"Fuck you too, Parker," Dean answered with a corresponding hand gesture.

They both laughed. This was the nature of their friendship. Parker walked into the kitchen and poured himself a drink. The kitchen counter was covered with all manner of party foods. There was a dish of honey barbeque wings sitting on top of the toaster. A pot of meatballs was simmering on the stove. At least a half dozen bags of potato chips along with a generous selection of dip sat on another counter. There were plates of ribs, hamburgers, grilled hot dogs and cheese spread across all the available surfaces. Sheila had truly outdone herself.

Parker grabbed a paper plate and piled as many meatballs and chicken legs on it as would fit. Sheila came into the kitchen and took it from him. "Go chill out. I got it, baby," she said with a grin. "Relax. Enjoy your friends."

Parker stepped back and gave her room to operate. "Go ahead then, superstar. Do your thing."

"Thank you," Sheila replied. "Go sit down in the other room and wait for our turn to play."

Parker stepped up behind Sheila and pressed his body against hers. His hand found her waist and pulled her to him. "I appreciate you," he said earnestly. He kissed her neck before leaving the kitchen for the living room.

Dean had offered up an import and Casper was preparing a second. Their discussion was typical. "Hey Casper, what do you think was on Noah's mind when he packed the import on the Ark?" Dean asked between puffs.

"Stuck on a boat, with one woman, and all those kids, for forty days and forty nights," Casper commented as he constructed a Havana sport, "what the hell do you think he was thinking? This is 'bout to be a rough ride!" Both men burst into laughter; Parker and Paula joined them.

"Noah was gonna get his freak on," announced Rasha, who until just that moment had chosen to remain silent for much of the night. Rasha was the kind of person who used silence to her favor. It became her. It used mystery to project the very strong possibility of greatness.

It gave imagination a wide berth. Rasha, in her silent moments, had the look of a scholar in deep thought. She was looked upon during these moments as having some great wisdom to impart to any who would be privileged enough to experience it. Then she spoke and all the wonder and mystery and awe that, a fraction of a second earlier had engulfed her simply disappeared. The sudden and immediate revocation of her dignified persona was quite the sight to behold. As with most observations of this event, this one was met with laughter.

Sidney managed to maintain some semblance of a straight face while she defended the morality of Noah and the social reputation of women everywhere. "How messed up is that! Noah didn't even have import on the Ark and if he did, he wasn't thinking about enhancing his sex life."

"Who's talking about sex," Parker interjected. "He was smoking for the stress. Can't you hear all that whining, complaining and screaming? Clean up the boat, walk the wolves, take out the trash, and a brother couldn't even leave! I'd have been stressed the hell out," Casper commented with a laugh.

***

"Shut up," Sidney shouted over the laughter. "He didn't even take the import."

"He took some of everything," Dean interjected.

"That means import too."

"No, it doesn't. He took seven of every animal, not plants,"

Sidney retorted.

"If he didn't take plants, then what did all those animals eat?" Casper countered as he finished up his constructive efforts.

"Touché'," Parker interjected.

Sidney snatched the import from Casper's hand and scrunched up her face at him. She put fire to the import and inhaled deeply. She rolled the smoke around in her mouth and then ejected it through her nose. "So, your contention is that God had Noah bring import into the new world?"

"Yes," Casper replied with a smirk.

"Alright, Casper. Then you're saying that smoking is okay with God," Sidney posed.

"I'm saying that God says all things in moderation," Casper clarified. "As long as it's not indulgent, God doesn't mind us smoking. It's when it interrupts his plans for us then he has issue."

Sidney pulled the import. A long tubular column of ashes hung from its tip. She flicked them in the ashtray and then handed it to Parker, who'd taken up a seat to her left. "So, God is pro import," Sidney presented.

"Who's to say?" Parker interrupted. "I think his point is that God doesn't bother with the action as much as he does with the motive behind the action."

"You're agreeing with Casper," Dean exclaimed. "I gotta hear this." Dean leaned in closer for effect before adding, "Please continue."

"Well," Parker began, "It's really quite simple. You have to look at the spiritual significance of an event. Take killing for example. Killing, at its base level is not against God's law." Sidney began to raise her voice in protest, but Parker did not allow for interruptions. "Murder, a form of killing, is against God's law, but killing itself, is not. God commanded Abraham to kill his son as a sacrifice. He had David kill Goliath. God himself killed every living soul in Sodom and Gomorrah. So, killing itself is not necessarily wrong in God's eyes. It's the context in which the killing is done, that dictates whether it's acceptable in the eyes of the Lord.

"Now you have to apply that same standard to smoking or drinking or any other action or activity. Under what context are you smoking? Is it for enjoyment? Merriment? Jubilation? That is, in my opinion, okay with God. Now if you're blowing off your rent payment or calling off of work in order to smoke, then I think God has a problem."

"It's like Jesus at the wedding party," Casper added. "He made wine. He probably drank wine, but he did it in moderation."

"Okay, so crack is all right if you do it in moderation," Paula posed, coming to Sidney's support.

"Hell naw," Parker answered. "Crack is dangerous to your health. There is no moderation with crack. That's different from the import."

"They're both drugs," Paula offered.

"Not really. Imports are natural. Crack is a perversion that man made," Parker commented. "Crack defiles the temple of God. The import doesn't do that."

Sheila came and stood behind Parker. She handed him a plate of food and then put in her two cents. "We really don't have any conclusive proof of what the effects of the import are on people. The studies they supposedly conducted turned out to be propaganda and lies."

"Yeah," Casper added. "The government just wants it outlawed cause they can't tax it."

"But what does that have to do with God's preference for the import?" Paula countered. "Let's keep focused on the issue at hand. I think God isn't opposed to it. I think he's opposed to the over-indulgence. I think he's opposed to anything that takes away from his mission, be it import, drinking, gambling or even whoring. Yes, even whoring. Anything that you do should be in his will."

"How is whoring in his will?" Dean asked suspiciously.

"Well, I call it whoring," Paula clarified, "but in the Bible, it's when these men have multiple wives." The room erupted into chaos. Paula brought up an often debated but completely unsettled question: Did God condone or condemn men with multiple women?

"Please don't start these fools arguing," Sheila pleaded. "You know how they get about that," she continued, "We don't even have time for that type of argument.

For once, everyone was in agreement. Parker was the first to say it. "Okay, just let it go then."

"How about we play some cards," Dean suggested. "Parker ain't doing nothing but avoiding an ass-whooping," he added.

"You ain't even on the table," Parker retorted. "How about you sit on the sideline and wait for this ass-whooping to come your way!"

Dean smiled. It was on!

Sheila liked to watch Parker work. She liked the way he lined his pencils up on the desk. She admired how methodical his movements were.

She stared at Parker longingly. She searched his face for some sign that his moving in had not been a mistake. Presently he was searching through a small stack of checking statements that he'd collected from fraud victims. Sheila placed the sandwich she'd prepared for Parker next to the stack of papers. "I fixed you a tuna salad sandwich, baby. Do you mind eggs in your tuna? Is that alright?" Parker nodded in agreement, smiled briefly and went back to work.

He had been working non-stop on his latest writing assignment. Sheila admired his work ethic but was in sore need of attention. Each evening he came home, ate dinner and then poured himself into his work. He often fell asleep at the computer or collapsed on the couch. They never talked anymore. Sheila missed that interaction. Now that she had taken a day off from work to spend some time with Parker, he still wasn't available. Sheila stood by in indecision. Finally, she took a seat next to Parker and began a conversation. "So, how's it going?"

"You'd be surprised how many people shop at the same chain of department stores," Parker replied as he put down the paperwork he'd been reviewing. "What have you been up to today?"

"Nothing. Just typical Saturday girl stuff," Sheila answered. She hesitated momentarily and then went on with her conversation. "Would you like to go see a movie or maybe go for a ride or something?"

"I'd love to," Parker said as he stepped away from his work and pulled Sheila to him, "but I need to finish reviewing these files. Can I take a rain check?"

Sheila looked quite disappointed, but her voice carried none of it. "That's cool, baby. Do your thing. I'll just go hang out with Rasha."

"Are you sure, baby? I don't want you to feel neglected. It's just that I've got all this stuff to go through and I'm not even half done. "Parker massaged the back of Sheila's neck. She closed her eyes and enjoyed the sensation. The stress left her face and was replaced with a much calmer expression. "Go out and have a good time with our home girl. I'll be here when you get back."

Sheila looked up into Parker's eyes. She smiled and kissed him gently. "Okay, baby. I'm gonna go hang with Rasha. If you need me, call, okay?"

"Okay," Parker replied. He kissed her once more before releasing her. "Hey, do you have a couple of dollars I can borrow for gas? I'm kind of low on cash, and the Cadillac is coughing fumes."

Sheila went to the counter to retrieve her purse. "I think I've got a twenty. Is that enough?"

"Yeah, baby. That's fine. I appreciate it." Parker accepted the bill that Sheila handed him. He placed the money in his pocket and returned to his workstation. "Tell Rasha I said hello."

"I will," Sheila answered as she gathered her things. "It's a couple of subs in the fridge if you get hungry.'

"Thanks." With that, Parker returned to his work and Sheila went out the door.

Chapter 25

Parker happened upon the article by accident. He'd run a google search on collection agencies in the middle GA area and found nine. He'd glanced at each one and discovered the name Pat Purroscoe listed on the administration page of one of the smaller seeder companies.

Pat Purroscoe had been fired from Milton and Chase. It was a name that both Rasha and her coworker had mentioned during their interviews. Parker had tried to contact him, but the agency had been unwilling to divulge information about former employees to a journalist. They'd been unwilling to divulge any information for that matter. Parker had followed up as best he could, checking for phone and property listings but had come up with nothing. A google search had yielded several references to underhanded dealings Purroscoe had had with other corporations. He'd also discovered that Purroscoe was allegedly connected, at least indirectly, with the Mafia. The guy was filthy but not so filthy as to not be able to hide among the anonymous population of the small towns of Middle GA.

Parker had initially seen him as the main lead in the investigation. Tracking him had proved too time consuming however, and no one really connected him to any criminal activity. Parker had given up looking for him. That hadn't changed the fact that Purroscoe just seemed shiesty.

Parker hadn't thought about the fact that a career collection manager like Pat would probably just move to another agency. He'd assumed that he'd gone back to whatever gutter he'd crawled from.

And now, there he was. Listed as the vice president of operations for McDonald & King. Here he was. The one person that Parker felt knew the answer to all his questions.

Parker dialed the number and listened online in hopes that there was someone in the office. It was a collection agency after all. He'd had collectors call him on the weekend, so there was a chance that this agency was also open. An extremely unprofessional operator answered. The phone. "McDonald & King," she gave, in a nonchalant greeting.

"Yes," Parker answered in his most official voice. "This is Mr. King, Pat Purroscoe, please."

"Oh, yes sir," the young lady said in a more professional tone. "One second."

Parker waited. He hoped that his hustle would work. Odds were that the workers that answered the phone had never heard Mr. King's voice. They were more likely to transfer him directly in.

After an unbearably long moment, an irritated middle-aged nasal voice slithered onto the line. "Pat Purroscoe."

"Pat," Parker greeted with a calmness that he did not feel. "How are you?"

"I'm fine. This isn't Mr. King," Purroscoe proclaimed.

"No, it's not. This is the guy that knows all about Milton & Chase," Parker replied on a hunch.

"Who is this," Purroscoe demanded.

"This is Mr. Grant. I'd like to talk to you about some things."

"Why would I want to talk to you?" Purroscoe asked suspiciously.

"Better me than a detective," Parker replied.

Purroscoe was quiet for a moment, most likely contemplating the surprise of Parker's statement. Then he said the words that told Parker that he had guessed right.

"Not on this phone. Give me a number and I'll call you shortly. We can meet somewhere then."

Parker smiled.

He scanned over the rack of discs as he waited on a call from the identity theft informant. The guy had left a message for Parker that requested that he be available for a call back at around three p.m. It was his intention to convince the guy to meet him somewhere in Macon that afternoon, so he'd come to the mall to be nearer to his eventual destination.

Parker read the producers notes on the back of the Jazzyphatttnasties CD with admiration. Okay players, he said to himself. Quality material. He was debating whether to purchase their newest offering when his cell rang: caller unknown.

"Girl this mutha fucka done tried me," Sheila exclaimed as she pulled into the parking lot of her complex. "I'm so damn mad now that I don't know what to do."

"Well, calm down girl! Give me a second to get off the floor and we can talk. Rasha worked at a low-end collection agency in downtown Macon. The office was an open room with rows and rows of snap-lock style stations. Approximately one hundred fifty people occupied the space in close proximity. Rasha had a cubicle, a computer, a desk and a phone. There was no privacy, so when discretion was needed, it had to be sought in the break room or in the restroom or outside. It was called "off the floor."

By the time Rasha returned to the phone, Sheila was heading up the stairs to her apartment. "What happened?" Rasha asked after she'd gotten comfortable in a corner of the break room.

"Girl, I was at the mall and looked in the music store and saw Parker, right. He was leaning over a rack reading the back of some CD. Now the nigga told me he had some writing to do, so he couldn't hang out with me, but he up in the mall! So, I went in there to ask him what was up. If he didn't want to be bothered, he could have just said that, right?"

"Right, right," Rasha cosigned.

Sheila unlocked her door and continued. "Anyway, I was walking up to him, but his back was to me, so he couldn't see me coming and then I notice that he's on the phone. So, I slow down so that I can hear his conversation without him thinking I'm eavesdropping."

"There you go, Inspector Gadget," Rasha interjected.

"Anyway," Sheila retorted with the vocal equivalent of rolling her eyes. "I'm behind this nigga and he don't know it and he just rapping to some chick on the phone. I mean, this nigga is in serious mack daddy mode; the smooth voice, the sweet words, the pimp stance you know the whole shebang." Sheila plopped down on her sofa and kicked off her shoes. She pulled her feet under her and then continued her conversation. "So, I'm standing there right, and he must have been finished talking cause he was like, 'well, I'll see you later baby' and hung up. So, I'm like 'so who are you talking to?' right. Girl, that nigga 'bout jumped out of his skin! He looked so caught! He went to lying and shit, talking 'bout how he was writing and needed some CD to write to and how he was talking to his home girl!"

"That nigga was caught, girl," Rasha concluded.

"Hell yeah, he was caught! But the nigga wouldn't admit to it. Like I don't know that nigga. I can tell when he's lying. He knew he was lying. "

"So, what did you do?"

"Nothing. I couldn't prove shit and you know with that nigga, you got to be able to prove it 100% before he admits to anything."

"Bitch, fuck that. Cut that nigga loose. He lives with you. You don't need him. He needs you."

"I just wish I knew beyond a shadow of a doubt, you know," Sheila admitted.

Rasha evidently did know. "Fuck that, I said! You don't need shit. You ain't married to that nigga. He ain't all that anyway. Put his ass out bitch!"

Rasha was right, Sheila thought. She didn't need proof to act on what she already knew. It was her heart that told her she needed the proof, not her mind. Her mind told her to abandon this bullshit before it blew up in her face. It was confirmation of what she already suspected. There was definitely another woman involved.

"I just wish I had some proof," Sheila said more so to herself than to Rasha.

"Damn. You just gotta do shit the hard way, huh? I guess we all do," Rasha resigned. "Well, why don't you call the other bitch, or better yet, go over there and see if the nigga's there."

"I ain't got that bitches phone number and I damn sure don't know where she stays."

"Bitch I'm a bill collector. All I do all day is track people down! You still got that phone bill from the time you broke in his house?"

"Hold on, let me see." Sheila went to her closet and pulled out an old purse that she used to hold loose papers. After several seconds of searching, she came across the phone bill. "I got it."

"Is there an online billing access code on there?" Rasha asked.

Sheila scanned the first and second pages of the bill before she came across the code that Rasha had asked about. "Yeah, I got it," She answered as she headed for her computer.

"Good. You can go online and look at the detailed billing statement. Go on there and find out what the number was he was talking to earlier."

Sheila tapped the website listed in her destination bar. The cellular company's logo popped up in big blue letters. After entering the code and several other pieces of sensitive information that Sheila had happened upon, the personal account information for Parker Grant popped up. Sheila selected the detailed billing option and then scrolled down to the time area where the call would have been located.

"Hurry up, bitch I'm at work," Rasha requested.

"I'm almost there. What are you gonna do with the number anyway? I'm damn sure not calling some other bitch looking for a man. I ain't never been that desperate."

"Bitch, let me handle this. I'm a bill collector and everybody got a bill somewhere. I'm gonna plug that number into this database I got at my desk and find that bitch's address. You gonna go over there.

Fuck a phone call. Catch that nigga in the act. Maybe then you'll wake the fuck up and move on!"

"Hi there Parker Grant," came the sultry voice he knew to be Deputy Dunkin. "How's my favorite roving reporter doing?"

"I'm doing just fine, DeSha," Parker replied. "How's Bibb County's most beautiful Detective doing?"

"She's doing just fine," DeSha answered. "Speaking of fine, what are you doing this evening, good looking?"

"Well, I'm actually working on our little group project this evening, gorgeous. I'm meeting with a guy who may be able to crack the mystery of the stolen identity," Parker offered. "We're meeting in a few minutes."

"Excellent," the Detective exclaimed. "What if I meet you there, then afterwards, we can discuss our...body of evidence."

Parker knew what body DeSha wanted to discuss; it had nothing to do with the case. "How about we connect afterwards. I don't want my source to be spooked by my beautiful but highly duty-bound lady friend."

"Aw," DeSha pouted. "When can we hang out then, Mr. Grant?"

"Call me afterwards. I plan to be available," Parker offered. "Okay. You be careful then, Parker," DeSha added. "Even white-collar criminals can be dangerous."

"I will. I'm meeting him in a public place with plenty of lighting. You know The Righteous Room downtown? I'm meeting him there. "Parker pulled into a parking space and continued. "The guy is supposed to meet me here now. I'll call you right after he leaves, okay?"

"Okay," DeSha consigned. "I guess I can wait. When you get done though, you make sure you call me handsome."

"Will do pretty lady," Parker concluded and hung up the phone. Here we go, he thought as he turned off the ignition and gathered his things. He exited his vehicle and headed for his meeting.

Parker made it about two minutes before he started to have second thoughts about coming to the meeting alone. Perhaps there was some validity to Deputy Dunkin's concerns. A criminal was a criminal. He wasn't the type of guy that was accustomed to regular bouts of violence. He contemplated calling Deputy Dunkin back and getting her to meet him there, but she might spook his informant; he didn't need to lose the source this close to the finish line.

Parker picked up his phone and dialed Dean's number. He waited for an answer but instead got the voicemail. Damn, he thought. No Dean. But it was just as well. Dean couldn't really leave his family on such short notice anyway. Plus, he was over forty minutes away. He couldn't make it here before the informant arrived. He dialed his boss, Theodore, but got the same response. What to do, what to do, Parker thought. As he contemplated his situation, his cell phone went off. It was Sidney. Parker answered it with moderate relief. "What's up girl? Where are you?"

"I'm on 75 south coming through Macon," Sidney replied. "What's going on?"

"Nothing. Well, I'm at The Righteous Room waiting on this guy to show up and talk to me about this article I'm researching. I'm a little uncomfortable talking to him alone. Could you meet me and hang out at the bar while I talk to him? I'll pay for your drinks," Parker offered with a mix of sincerity and desperation.

"With what money, broke ass," Sidney cracked as she exited the interstate and headed toward her friend. "You know that. What do you need me there for anyway? You want more free legal advice?"

"No silly," Parker replied with a nervous giggle. "I'm just a little nervous meeting someone who I know is crooked."

"So, you want me to come up there and get my head cracked open with yours, huh?" Sidney asked in mock anger. She pulled her car into the space next to Parker's Cadillac and turned off her ignition. "Where's your chivalry? I'm a lady! You shouldn't want me in harm's way."

"Fuck that," Parker exclaimed. "I want somebody to watch my back in case shit got wild. Are you gonna look out or what? You don't even have to sit with me."

"You're gonna pay for my drinks, right?" Sidney asked as she exited her vehicle and headed into The Righteous Room.

"Yes, you lush! Now, are you coming or not?"

"I'm right behind you," Sidney confessed as she entered the main sanctuary. "Where do you want me to sit?"

"Over there in the corner and stay on the phone. I might need a witness if it goes bad."

"Alright scaredy cat. Excuse me, can I get a martini please?" Sidney requested a nearby waitress as she made her way to a corner table.

"Don't break me, Sidney," Parker whispered. "You know I'm on a budget."

"What-ever! You weren't saying that shit when you were begging me to come save your ass!"

"I'm just saying..."

Hey, I'm just kidding. It's cool, Parker. I got you," Sidney assured Parker.

"Thanks."

The two friends sat and waited for the informant to arrive.

Chapter 26

Two hours and six drinks later, Parker and Sidney sat in the corner still waiting on the informant to arrive. They had given up on pretending not to have known each other and had instead, adopted the cover story of having discovered each other in the bar and were making small talk until their respective guest arrived.

"Parker, as much as I enjoy spending your money and drinking your liquor, I think it may be time to entertain the idea that maybe your guy isn't coming. "Sidney said between sips.

During their time at the bar, Parker made numerous calls to the informant. None of those calls was answered. Perhaps it was time to call it a night. "Let me give him one more call and then we can go," he decided.

Sidney watched Parker dial the informant's number and then watched him end the call. "Let me guess. No answer, right," she asked.

"No answer," Parker mimicked. "Check please," he called to the waitress. "Let's get out of here. I've been enough of a sucker for the day."

"Ah, don't think of it like that," Sidney said as she stood and prepared to leave. "Maybe something happened to him. He could have had an accident or gotten detained at work."

"Whatever," Parker countered. "He could've called or something." Parker left the money for the bill on the table, along with a sizable tip and escorted Sidney out of the establishment. "Are you okay to drive?" he asked Sidney?

"Yes, I'm fine," Sidney answered as she opened her car door and plopped into the seat. "You be careful. You're staying at Sheila's tonight, right?"

"I'm not sure yet," Parker replied. "I'm leaving my options open."

"Anyway," Sidney said as she started her car. "Be careful."

Parker pushed Sidney's door closed and stepped back. "I will," he called as he walked around to his Cadillac door. As he was opening his door and getting in his vehicle, his phone rang. The LCD screen read Freddy, the code for Alfreda. Parker waved to Sidney as she pulled out of her space and then answered the phone. "What's up pretty lady," he cooed.

"Nothing much, good-looking. What are you doing?" Alfreda asked with a sultry twang.

"Leaving a late-night interview; why, what's up?"

"I was wondering if I could come by and see you," Alfreda asked.

"Sure," Parker answered. "Is everything alright?"

"Yes, it's all good. I just wanted to see you, that's all," Alfreda answered. When are you headed home?"

"I'm going there now. Are you headed that way too?" Parker asked as he backed out of his parking space and headed for the Interstate.

"I am now," Alfreda answered. "See you soon."

Alfreda disconnected and Parker was about to call Sheila and make an excuse as to why he wouldn't be home when his phone began to ring again. This time the screen read Deputy Dunkin. "Hi. I was just about to call you."

"I figured as much," Deputy Dunkin gave. "How did the interview go?"

"He didn't even show," Parker said as he merged into the turning lane. "We ended up with squat!"

"Well, it happens like that sometimes, handsome," DeSha consoled. "It comes with all investigative work, both police and journalism. I tell you what though," she said with enthusiasm. "How about you and I salvage the rest of this evening with a couple of drinks down at The Righteous Room. My treat."

"Actually, I just left The Righteous Room. I'm already headed home."

"Aw, I wanted to go over the evidence with you, boo," DeSha pouted. "How about we meet somewhere closer to where you are now."

"How about giving me about thirty minutes to get settled, then give me a callback. We'll work something out then," Parker lied.

"Okay, sweetie. I'll talk to you then."

Parker ended the call and prepared to deal with Sheila. She had not been very receptive to his all nighters lately. She probably wouldn't be receptive to this one either, he thought. He was single, however, and didn't owe anyone an explanation or anything else. It was a living arrangement; nothing more.

Parker merged into traffic and headed down 75 south. He busied himself with creating an excuse to give Sheila for his absence. Had he not been so involved, perhaps he would have seen the gray Cutlass that had been trailing him since he left The Righteous Room merge into traffic as well.

Rasha pulled the car up to the curb and shut off her engine. "Are you sure you want to do this?" Rasha asked Sheila.

"How are you going to ask me that?" Sheila replied. "It was your idea to come down here, all incognito and shit; got us up in your grand mama's car two streets over from our destination. You're crazy!"

"Girl, you needed proof, so we're gonna get proof," Rasha returned. "Didn't he say he was going to his house to finish an assignment? Well, he should be here, right?"

"Yeah, but why do we have to drive your grand mama's car? It smells like Ben Gay."

"Because Parker doesn't know this car," Rasha replied as she opened the car door and stepped out onto the street. "You don't want him to see you sitting in his driveway and get spooked. So, we'll walk around the street to his house and see what the deal is. He said he was staying at home tonight, right? So, let's go see!"

"This is ghetto," Sheila proclaimed as she stepped out of the vehicle.

"Your constant complaining about not being happy and not knowing whether he's cheating or not is ghetto," Rasha hissed. "You need to get a grip. You shouldn't even be with someone you can't trust. But you are and this is the only way to get you to see the foolishness of that. So, I'm out here with you in the middle of the night because I'm your friend, but don't get it twisted. I don't believe in doing this sort of shit. It's beneath me as a woman. It's beneath you too," Rasha said, grabbing her friend by the shoulders, "But love has got you by the throat and refuses to let you go." Rasha released Sheila and stepped over to the sidewalk. "So, are you coming or what?"

"Let's go girl," Sheila said, joining her friend on the sidewalk. "Let's get this over with."

***

Parker brought his Cadillac to a halt at the furthest end of his driveway. A gray Cutlass passed by without stopping. He turned off his ignition and was about to step out of his vehicle when a pair of headlights pulled in behind him. The driver brought the car's passenger window even with Parker's driver side window and stopped. After a brief moment, the window receded, and Parker saw Alfreda's face silhouetted against the driver's side window.

"I'm gonna park on the side," Alfreda shouted across to Parker.

"That's cool," Parker replied. "Just pull up on the backside by the window." Alfreda nodded in acknowledgement and drove her car down the driveway, across the back lawn and disappeared behind the house. Thirty seconds later, she reappeared and joined Parker, who'd exited his vehicle and was waiting at the door. "Welcome back, butterfly." Parker greeted Alfreda with a hug. "I'm so glad to see you," He continued as he unlocked the door and held it ajar.

Alfreda walked through the door and placed her purse on the table. "I'm glad to be here. You have no idea how hectic a day I've had," she exclaimed. "I just need a breather."

"I feel you," Parker agreed. "It's been a long one for me too. "Alfreda scooted over and made room on the couch for Parker. He plopped down next to her and pulled her close to him. "Now my day is getting better," he said with a honey-dipped tongue.

"Mine too," Alfreda answered. She leaned into Parker and kissed him passionately. Her arms found their way around his body and clamped together at his back. She pushed down on his body with her body until Parker was lying against the armrest. She climbed atop him and straddled his waist.

"You got a problem with it?" Alfreda asked as she unbuckled Parker's belt and unbuttoned his slacks.

"Not at all little lady; not at all." Parker reached for Alfreda's belt and made quick work of it. He unbuttoned her pants and was about to push them down when his car alarm went off. "Shit," he exclaimed. "Always at the most inopportune moment."

Parker's car alarm blared through the night. He grabbed his keys from the table and hit the reset button. The alarm went silent. Parker breathed a sigh of relief. "Now, where were we?" he asked, pulling Alfreda back down on top of him.

"I think we were here," she replied, placing her hand on Parker's crotch.

"Oh yeah, we were." Parker rose up from the couch and took Alfreda with him. He was about to lead her to his bedroom when the car alarm began blaring again. He reached for his keys and hit the reset button on his alarm remote. The blaring stopped for a split second before beginning anew. "Damn," Parker exclaimed. "Look," he said, turning to Alfreda. "I need to go out and manually disarm this thing. Otherwise, it'll bother us all night. Why don't you get comfortable while I handle it."

"That's fine, baby," Alfreda answered. "Hurry okay," she added. She squeezed Parker's crotch again for good measure and then disappeared into the bedroom.

Parker just smiled and rebuttoned his pants. What a woman, he thought as he hurried out of his house. Parker opened his front door and looked out into the night. The yard was dark. The streetlights had long ago burnt out and the moon was strangely absent. A solitary porch light on a neighboring home provided the only illumination; it cast a dim light across the yard and bathed the Cadillac in a grayish hue.

The thicket served as excellent cover for Sheila and Rasha. Rasha recognized the sedan as they scrambled to avoid being spotted by the oncoming sedan as it sped past their hiding place. It belonged to Alfreda, her half-brother's girlfriend.

"What the hell is she doing down here?" Rasha asked. "Probably creeping," Sheila answered as she climbed from behind the thicket and brushed herself off.

"Damn, everybody's on the creep," Rasha exclaimed. "Hey, isn't she turning into Parker's driveway?" She stepped to the center of the street and watched as the sedan disappeared into one of the driveways at its other end. The distance between Parker's place and her position was about a third of a mile and it was dark. She could be wrong but there were only three houses on that end of the street with driveways. Two were homes that were occupied by families. Why would Alfreda be going there? She had no family in Fort Valley, Rasha concluded. "Hell naw," She whispered in disbelief. "She better not be at Parker's house. Hell naw."

"Who the fuck is Alfreda?" Sheila asked after joining her friend in the street.

"You remember the girl who ran into us at Bennie Johnson's," Rasha offered.

"The one who was acting all jittery?"

"Yeah," Rasha confirmed as the memory of the event came to her. "Yeah, you remember how much of a rush she was in to get out of there?"

"Yeah girl? That bitch was up in there with my man! She probably saw us come in and tried to rush out," Sheila decided.

"And remember how shook Parker was when we walked up on him?" Rasha added. "He tried to tell me he was drinking that twisted apple! Ain't this some bullshit! Let's get down there and bust his muthafuckin' bubble! And I'm gonna call my brother and tell his ass right now," Rasha declared as she headed down the street.

Sheila walked hurriedly beside her friend praying silently that they were wrong.

Just as Parker was about to step out into the night, his cell phone began to vibrate. The LCD screen read: Detective Duncan. "Hello," he answered once he was out of Alfreda's earshot.

"Hi sweetie. What's with all the racket?" DeSha asked, referring to the car alarm.

"It's my car alarm going crazy. Hold on while I fix it." Parker placed his phone on the roof of the car and opened up his car door. He popped the latch and then proceeded to raise the hood.

Parker never made it beyond raising the hood of his car. Before he could secure the latch and begin the process of deactivating the alarm, he was struck by a moving shadow and grappled to the ground. He opened his mouth as if to scream or shout in protest but was barred from doing so by a swift blow to the neck followed by a knee to the stomach. His assailant delivered several severe blows to Parker's chest and skull with some unrecognizable object being brandished as a Billy club.

The alarm blared away, covering the sounds of the struggle as well as any sounds of alarm he could raise himself. The only sound that Parker could hear was that of his attacker's vice; it was as clear as it was deep and foreboding. As he struck Parker, he accentuated each cluster of blows with the same statement. "Don't write this article. It's bad for your health."

Parker found himself in a bad gangster movie playing on the wrong side of a "hush party." He threw his hands up to protect his head and face, but his assailant was exacting; every blow that he launched landed true. A swift knee whizzed through Parker's field of vision and landed with excruciating accuracy on his arm. Parker attempted to strike his attacker but found his arm no longer worked correctly. It was bent at an irregular angle just below the elbow.

"Don't write the article," the assailant repeated viciously. Pain racked his chest and limbs. His skull felt like it had been used as a battering ram. Blood ran down Parker's forehead and impaired his vision. From the corner of his eye, Parker saw two crimson forms join the fray. The new forms joined with the original assailant and became one mass of wanton violence. All of a sudden, Parker was aware of an interruption in the assault on his body. Just before he lost consciousness, a new war cry rose in his ears: "Get the fuck off my man!"

Chapter 27

They had come upon the attacker unexpectantly. Sheila and Rasha had taken their time maneuvering up the street to Parker's home. They ducked into the shadows when they saw Parker come out of his home to silence his car alarm. They had been almost fifty yards away and out of his line of sight, but they didn't wanted to take any chances, so they hid in the shadow of a neighboring house.

They hadn't figured on spotting the stranger who had also been sneaking up on the residence. They'd watched the unknown interloper with mild fascination until he sprang from his hiding place and attacked Parker. Sheila didn't hesitate to react. She'd run the distance between her distressed lover and herself without thinking; Rasha also covered the distance with amazing speed.

Now they were upon him, striking him with their fists, attacking him with sticks and anything else that they happened upon during their rapid race to Parker's aid. Sheila clawed at the attacker's eyes. "Get the fuck off him," she screamed with the viciousness of a cornered tigress.

The attacker had been caught unprepared. They had stunned him. He attempted to rise from the ground, but the force of Sheila's assault propelled him backwards instead. Rasha chose that moment to make her move. She brought the full weight of her thick solid frame down on the assailant's knee. It bent at an angle that was wholly unnatural. A snapping sound was followed by an expression of excruciating pain that made Rasha flinch but not relent.

Between the war wails of the three combatants, Parker's moans and the sirens of the car alarm, the gentle evening had become a mad house. The assailant busied himself with alternating attempts to fend off Sheila and Rasha and escape before the entirety of the neighborhood was alerted. His success at both endeavors was minimal. Porch lights began to come on up and down the street; Alfreda peeked her head through the screen door to see what the matter was.

Only then did Sheila and Rasha relinquish their hold on the assailant and set their eyes on a new invader: Alfreda.

Between the car alarm blaring, the scuffle in the yard and the screaming of the injured combatants, the police were bound to show up. A total of three squad cars arrived rather quickly; two of them responding to concerned neighbors and one at the behest of a frantic Detective DeSha Duncan, who thanks to the excellent reception of Parker's cell phone had been privy in an auditory capacity to the entire incident. Having arrived and discovered an adverse reaction to his assailant's assault, the officers summoned an ambulance to attend to his injuries. Meanwhile, one set of officers made it their business to attend to a wounded Parker. They gave him water to fight the shock and placed a pillow beneath his swollen head to provide him with some level of comfort.

Another set of officers had to be wholly devoted to containing Sheila, who upon discovering Alfreda in Parker's home partially clothed, had preceded to visit upon her a most vicious welcome. Rasha, though vocally malicious refrained from entering the foray and instead stood by taking note of all that took place for the purpose of reporting to her half-brother.

The remaining officers after receiving reports from several observant neighbors, promptly placed the stranger under arrest and transferred him and his broken knee into the back of a squad car. The neighbors were, after all, the only uninvolved witnesses available.

One neighbor, Ms. Taimeka Brooks, with whom Parker had in the past shared several passionate evening was extremely helpful. According to Ms. Brooks, she 'happened' to be watering her lawn when she noticed several suspicious characters converging on Mr. Grant's home. According to Ms. Brooks, late-night visitors were commonplace at the residence but most persons arriving did not go to such great lengths to conceal their presence. She also added that the two female combatants one of whom she'd observed entering the Grant residence through a window on a separate occasion, had also trespassed on numerous other properties on the street. Scouting out the area for future criminal activities, Ms. Brooks speculated. When questioned as to the rationale behind her late night landscaping activities, Ms. Brooks simply replied that her floral clusters were of a nocturnal variety; therefore, her labors concerning them reflected such. As to her opinion on the violent stranger who'd initiated the aggression on Mr. Grant, Ms. Brooks' testimony helped further convince the authorities that detainment was indeed the best policy for the scoundrel.

That action was excellent policing that led the officers to detain him, not long after entering his name into their database, it was discovered that he had several felony warrants for his arrest. Unfortunately, the same search brought up Parker's warrants as well. The news found him partially conscious and entirely unprepared.

"Mr. Grant," the tall slim officer said, leaning down where Parker could hear him, "I'm afraid I'm going to have to place you under arrest. We've got a bench warrant in the system for you."

Parker just moaned. Sheila, however, wasn't quite as soft-spoken. "What in the hell? He needs medical attention."

"We'll make sure that he's attended to," a large officer said with a firm voice. "Just let us handle this," he continued as he stepped between Sheila and his detainee.

"Oh, I know how you all take care of a person," Sheila exclaimed; she remembered how she had been handled and grew even more agitated.

"Girl, you must be slap crazy," Rasha interjected with more than her usual degree of pessimism. "You caught this man, with another woman, a half-naked woman, in the middle of the night and you give a fuck whether he goes to jail or not? Fuck Him! Fuck Parker Grant," Rasha exclaimed as she crossed her arms and turned her head away. "He wasn't thinking about going to jail when he brought his ass down here to fuck that hoe," she continued, pointing directly at Alfreda so there would be no misunderstandings as toward whom her comments were directed.

"I ain't no hoe," Alfreda shot back through the screen door.

"You're out here fucking my man! That makes you a hoe," Sheila shot back, showing that her anger was not quite as quailed as she'd let on. "Bitch!" she screamed as she started towards Alfreda with malicious determination. Only Rasha's quickness stopped her from reaching her target.

"I didn't know he was seeing anybody else," Alfreda answered, determined not to be cowed by Sheila's escalating signs of aggression. "He never mentioned he had a girlfriend."

"Bitch, they live together," Rasha yelled over her shoulder, "just like you live with a man, bitch! And just as soon as I get a chance, I'm calling my brother and telling him that while he's up there babysitting, you down here laying up. Then we'll see how you like it, bitch!"

Sheila pushed against Rasha, but her friend would not release her. Finally, Sheila gave up the struggle and just collapsed in her friend's arms. Then Sheila cried. She cried a long, desperate, defeated cry. Sheila's usually strong and proud frame crumpled in on itself. She collapsed, relying on the strength of her friend to support her crushed spirit. Rasha gathered her friend up and cradled her close. She led her to the rear of the vehicle and helped her take a seat on the edge of the trunk.

A hush came over the yard. Police officers, neighbors, and the like all felt a tinge of sorrow for Sheila. Even Ms. Brooks, who had until that moment, been informing all who would listen of the numerous nighttime visitors that frequented the Grant residence, fell silent. It was obvious that Sheila was in pain. They all heard it in her cries, saw it in her face, felt it in her wails.

Rasha took a napkin offered by a nearby officer and held it out for her friend. Sheila accepted it, wiped her eyes, looked around, and started to cry again. It was too much for her to absorb at once.

The car alarm finally disarmed itself and completed the eerie silence that had engulfed the yard-turned-crime-scene. It had done its job. It had sounded the warning: someone is fucking with your shit. Sheila just wished she'd heard it sooner.

His legal woes had also been righted by the unfortunate events. As for Parker's liberation from the hands of the authorities, it was Parker, or at least Theodore representing Parker, who would be credited with his release. According to the clerk's office, it would require exactly $1500 in a certified check or money order to satisfy the judicial system's question as to whether Parker was fit to exist among the citizens of Middle Georgia again. A bail of $150 would give him a brief reprise from the county's guest quarters but would commit him to a query with a local municipal at a later date, at which time, he would most surely be persuaded to part with a much greater sum than the first two combined.

Therefore, the most logical option would be for Parker to pay the initial fee and be done with it altogether. Unfortunately, Parker was unaware that he had access to either amount. It was Theodore who had petitioned and acquired funds on Parker's behalf.

At an earlier time, while in another frame of mind and wholly unaware of even the possibility of needing said funds for the purpose that they would eventually serve, Theodore submitted several of Parker's articles, including the one which had caused his assault, to the press pool for let.

A day or so later, Parker's assault took place. Being a small town, Fort Valley found the scuffle to be of great interest and let it be known that they were the center of a grand nation-wide theft ring. Several regional media outlets, having no other pertinent news to report, ran Parker's assault along with a piece about a cow that got struck by lightning at a county fair as lead stories. Some intern at CNN did a google search and discovered that, for the most part, the town of Fort Valley was right; the burglary of over eight thousand individuals was indeed a grand thing. CNN ran the story at the top of the hour and every thirty minutes thereafter. The public was outraged. The media scrambled to get the first, best, most exclusive story. Newsweekly pulled Parker's article from the pool and ran it; then compensated him handsomely. Normally these funds would be held in escrow, but Theodore pulled some strings and made them available at a more rapid rate. He then deposited those funds into his account and used them to extract Parker.

As it turned out, the silent muscle that had been sent to deal with Parker wasn't so silent after all; and as for the constitution of the muscle, when the unpleasant pressure of confinement was set upon his shoulders, the gentleman's strength shriveled and all but withered away. It was said that the weight of the assault charges, terroristic threat charges, concealed weapon charge, assault with a deadly weapon charge, and violation of probation charge was more than he could bear. No one outside of City Hall really knew what his disposition was at the time of his arraignment. It was a generally accepted fact, however, that he took an offer from the local D.A. to 'take some of the load off' in exchange for the dropping of several 'dimes' and a lengthy conversation about his financial benefactors, the primary contributor being Purroscoe. The information gleaned led the police department to expand Deputy Dunkin's investigation from a one-woman operation to a company-wide directive. Almost overnight, a very small number of collectors and managers were discovered to have been defrauding a very large number of their customers. The chief of police called it an identity theft ring, but it was more of a pyramid with Purroscoe at its zenith. It just as quickly became a headline news story with Parker Grant's revised article leading the media release. This was due in part to Parker's excellent writing techniques and part to the faith of a friend. As he'd promised, Theodore submitted Parker's article to the Associated Press article pool on the day before the assault. That guaranteed Parker dibs on the byline. Newsweekly ran it as a cover story. The eight thousand-plus counts of identity theft that Macon PD uncovered made it national news. The FBI's taking over of the case made it global news. Parker had broken the story. He was, for the moment, the golden boy of the journalistic society. For the moment, all eyes were on his accomplishment. He should have been enjoying the celebration of the single greatest accomplishment of his professional life. His voicemail was overflowing with requests for follow-up articles and in-depth interview requests.

The article had gotten him work, gotten him out of debt and gotten him out of jail. Not a bad outcome for a couple of days' work. Parker was released on a brisk Tuesday morning. Sidney picked him up and deposited him in front of his drive. She offered to walk him in, but he declined. He needed a moment alone and she knew it. She promised to come by later and check on him. He watched her drive down the street and disappear into the morning traffic, then made the short trek from the road to his front door.

Chapter 28

Two trash bags, three boxes, and paper sac; that was what it took Sheila to extract Parker from her life. Those two trash bags, the boxes, and the paper sack sat neatly stacked under the awning of Parker's front door. The wind had knocked over the paper sack, but the other items lay undisturbed until Parker was released from the hospital. A stack of notes rested atop the boxes with a rock serving as paperweight. A letter from Sheila was taped to the largest box. Parker waited until he'd moved his things into the house and rolled a Vega to read it. Before he read the first words, he knew what it would say. Sheila hadn't returned any of his calls. Other than seeing him at the hospital and through his surgery, she had not been there to see him at all. She'd sent Rasha to retrieve his key to her apartment. His mother had been there, so Rasha was respectful, but there was no question as to her disposition towards him.

He lit the import and set about reading the letter. It wasn't long or harsh or preachy. She said she loved him and that she wished him well. She said it was over and that she hoped he'd stay out of trouble.

And that was it. That's how she ended it. No long goodbyes. No arguing. Parker was perplexed. How had it been so simple for her? Where was the love that she claimed that she had? How could she just leave? But wasn't that his plan? he thought. He'd put her aside for Alfreda. He thought that Alfreda was the one. Where was Alfreda now? She had virtually disappeared. She hadn't called or answered his messages. Bumble wouldn't talk about her. He wanted to broach the subject with Rasha but thought better. He'd invested all that time and energy into her, and she was gone. And now he was alone. No one. He had no one. He was free though. He didn't have to play the game anymore. He didn't have to be constantly on the lookout. He had a job that he liked and that paid. He had no bills. He could travel if he wanted to. He could find a better life.

Parker hit the random play button on his remote and Marvin Gaye's Trouble Man came on. Fitting, he thought. He puffed his Vega and lost himself in his thoughts until he heard a car coming up the driveway. His first impulse was to run to the window and see who it was. He fought the urge. He was grown. There was no need to hide who he was or what he was doing to anyone. His warrants were lifted. His affair exposed. Let whoever come. He was an adult, at home, grown.

Headlights shone through the blinds. After a moment, a car door slammed, and someone crunched through the gravel to the door. The door handle turned, and Parker's father walked in. It was then that Parker remembered that he held the import. His father had never seen him with the import. It was not that his father didn't know, it was that they never acknowledged it. He partook.

That's how he knew Parker partook. Parker had pilfered import from his stash. His father never mentioned it because that would mean he would have to admit his own fondness for the import. And that could mean admitting that they had something in common. Neither wanted that, the elder wanting his son to be better than him, the junior wanting to be better than the father.

And now it was out. How ironic, Parker thought. He rose from his seat and offered his father the import.

Made in the USA
Columbia, SC
27 April 2025